BOOSTED

THE LUCIE RIZZO MYSTERY SERIES

ADRIENNE GIORDANO

THE LUCIE RIZZO MYSTERY SERIES

Dog Collar Crime

Knocked Off

Limbo (novella)

Boosted

Whacked

Cooked

Romantic suspense books available by Adrienne Giordano

PRIVATE PROTECTOR SERIES

Risking Trust

Man Law

A Just Deception

Negotiating Point

Relentless Pursuit

Opposing Forces

HARLEQUIN INTRIGUES

The Prosecutor

The Defender

The Marshal

The Detective

The Rebel

JUSTIFIABLE CAUSE SERIES

The Chase

The Evasion

The Capture

CASINO FORTUNA SERIES

Deadly Odds

JUSTICE SERIES w/MISTY EVANS

Stealing Justice

Cheating Justice

Holiday Justice

Exposing Justice

Undercover Justice

Protecting Justice

Missing Justice

STEELE RIDGE SERIES w/KELSEY BROWNING

& TRACEY DEVLYN

Steele Ridge: The Beginning

Going Hard (Kelsey Browning)

Living Fast (Adrienne Giordano)

Loving Deep (Tracey Devlyn)

Breaking Free (Adrienne Giordano)

Roaming Wild (Tracey Devlyn)

Stripping Bare (Kelsey Browning)

BOOSTED

A Lucie Rizzo Mystery
by
Adrienne Giordano

1

————

Lucie stood on the sidewalk under a soothing stream of October sunshine while Fin, an eight-month-old Australian shepherd with more energy than a horny frat boy, sniffed at a giant maple tree on Chicago's West Side. After this stop, she'd call it a day. As soon as she got horny frat boy off the tree.

Not always an easy task.

Time to break out some Alpha Lucie. "Okay, Fin. Finish up. No more stalling."

Fin swung his head around, stared at her with his one blue and one green eye, and Alpha Lucie crumbled. Just completely melted. *I'm useless to the Alpha population.*

In her own defense, Fin's eyes—shades of tropical seas—could take down an entire army. She simply could not get mad at this dog.

Even when he hurled himself at her, blasting her in the chest with both front paws and knocking her on her butt. Or when he decided to stop, plop his furry bottom on the sidewalk and bark—*woof, woof, woof.*

Three rapid-fire barks meant, at least in Fin's mind,

playing fetch. Which he could do for 90 percent of his waking hours.

But she'd been working on him. Giving him a treat every time he kept pace with her. He might be fifty pounds overweight by the time she finished with him, but he'd be a dog walker's dream. A graduate of Coco Barknell.

On the street, a car rolled by, slowing as it went. Probably someone looking for a parking space. They wouldn't find one on this block. Every parked car was squeezed bumper to bumper.

Fin's ear went up, and he barked at the car. Her hero. She bent low, gave him a nuzzle. "You make me crazy, but I love you."

A wet tongue slapped across her cheek. The bonus of working for dogs.

"Aw, you two are the cutest." A middle-aged woman hoofed down the sidewalk wearing a flowy skirt, an equally flowy blouse and a long cardigan against the late afternoon wind. She carried a briefcase in one hand.

Lucie scratched Fin's snout before standing tall. "He's a good boy and deserved some love."

The woman stopped just a few feet away. "Can I pet him?"

Something in Lucie's spine fused. After the dognapping of the Ninja Bitches last spring, she didn't take to strangers wanting to come near her clients. The woman must have sensed Lucie's sudden-onset Terminator and gestured to the auction house behind her.

"I'm Estelle. I manage Bendorf Auctions. I've seen you out here with this cutie."

Lucie let out a long, silent breath. "Fin."

"Sorry?"

"His name is Fin. You can pet him. Sorry. I'm protective."

Estelle glanced at Lucie's messenger bag with the screen print of a winking poodle wearing a diamond collar. The Coco Barknell logo created by the fabulous Ro, aka Lucie's best bud. And currently the squeeze of Joey, Lucie's ape of a brother. *Blech.*

"You're a dog walker?"

"Yes. I'm Lucie from Coco Barknell. We also have a line of dog accessories." Lucie slipped one of her business cards from the easy-access front pocket of her bag. There'd been a time when she'd been too shy to even tell people about her fledgling business. Now she was a pro and whipped out her card to anyone with even a passing interest. Her growing bank account helped inspire this newfound aggressiveness.

Estelle took the card. "Thank you. I have a little guy at home myself. A mutt, but the cutest darned thing. Maybe I'll buy him a collar or something."

"Sure. Check out our website. If there's something you see, let me know, and I'll drop it by next time I walk Fin."

"Oh, that'd be great. Thank you."

Finally, Estelle bent over and gave Fin a good rub.

"Stay, Fin," Lucie warned.

Please don't let him launch. With Fin, she never knew. One second he'd be calm and the next—airborne.

But, lookie here, he stayed put. He'd definitely get a treat for that.

"Good boy, Finnie!"

Lucie pulled out another treat. Peanut butter this time. Although the carob seemed to be his favorite.

He made a move to jump, but Lucie tightened her hold on the leash. "Stay."

"Well, now I've made a new friend." Estelle gave him one last pat. "I'll be sure to look out for you now, Fin."

"He loves people," Lucie said. *A little too much.*

"I see that. It was lovely meeting you, Lucie." She held up the card. "I'll check out your website."

Estelle wandered up the walkway to the entrance of the auction house, an old, brick building with a door the color of the purest blue sky. Such an interesting choice. Eclectic, yet elegant.

Fin finished his treat and stretched out on the sidewalk for one of his siestas. "Oh, no you don't, mister. Let's get this walk finished."

Lucie took two steps, but Fin—as usual—didn't move. "Come on, boy." She clicked her tongue—the treat sound—and he popped right up. Lucie sighed and tossed him another peanut butter nib.

In order to fix one bad habit, she'd created a treat monster. She'd deal with that later. After saving her precious schedule.

At the corner, they turned right and looped around the front of the auction house. Fin spotted something on the ground and charged, dragging Lucie with him.

As they approached she recognized the telltale eye—the blue in the middle—of a peacock feather. Actually, this one had two eyes. How cool was that? The sun glinted off the iridescent green and turquoise, and images of Fannie and Josie—the Ninja Bitches, a couple of shih tzus long on attitude and short on stature—wearing those colors flashed in Lucie's mind.

Gripping the leash so Fin couldn't snag the feather, Lucie bent low and scooped it up. She'd take it back to the office so Ro could create some sketches of peacock doggie coats.

"That, Fin," Lucie said, "would be a best seller. I just know it."

With the walk complete, Lucie gave Fin a good-bye smooch, hopped on her scooter and zipped off. Her day had run half an hour over schedule, and she needed to get home and get cleaned up for dinner.

It had been an interesting couple of months in the Rizzo household, what with Dad home from prison.

Early release for good behavior.

He'd done two years on a tax-evasion conviction, and in that time Lucie had been downsized out of her investment banking job and moved home with Joey and Mom.

Joey drove her insane with his big mouth and constant teasing, but he'd taken care of their mother while Dad was gone. Now, at 29 years old, he'd finally moved out. Which left Lucie and her mom in the minefield known as living with Joe Rizzo, Mob Boss.

But they were adjusting. All of them. Dad might have been having the hardest time. While he'd been gone, his wife had learned a little thing called independence. She'd also learned to tell him to "make his own damned dinner" once in a while.

By five fifteen Lucie walked in the front door of Chateau Rizzo. "Helloooo?" she called in her usual greeting. "I'm home."

She stopped just inside the door and enjoyed the sensory overload of cooking meat and rich spices. Her mother made the best roast beef ever. And that was no exaggeration. Whatever the secret spice was, it gave the meat just enough of a kick. Lucie often threatened to sign her up for one of those cooking-show battles. Mom versus a famous chef. Mom and the roast would win. No doubt.

"Lucie!" Dad hollered.

"Hi, Dad."

He appeared in the doorway that led from the small dining room to the kitchen. He wore flat-front slacks and a crisp, baby-blue dress shirt. "You're late. You said you'd be home by five."

Welcome to living at home with a protective father. "I know, but the walks ran long."

"You should call if you'll be late."

Sigh. "Okay, Dad. Sure."

The door behind her opened and whacked her hard enough to send her spiraling forward. *Whoopsie.* To keep from falling, she hooked her hand on one of the staircase spindles, gripped it hard enough to pop a knuckle and fought a battle with momentum. She hung on for a second —whew—and pulled herself back to her feet.

Joey stood in the doorway holding the door open for Ro.

Ro rushed in, her arms out. "Luce, are you all right?"

"Luce," Joey said, "what the hell are you doing behind the door? I could have killed you."

"Thanks for your concern, Mr. Sensitivity."

"Hey, next time, don't stand there."

"Joey," Ro said, "zip it."

He scrunched his face and stabbed his hands in the air. "What? Now it's my fault?"

"Joey," Dad warned in that low, scary voice that always made his son snap to, "shut that mouth."

"Sorry, Dad. Where's Mom?"

Her father circled his hand. "Ran to the store for bread. She'll be back."

Ro, working a tight, black skirt, stilettos and a light-pink cashmere sweater sauntered by; and, pig that he was, Joey cocked his head sideways to watch as she gave Dad a hug.

In a lot of ways, Ro was the female version of Dad.

Tough, but with a tender side that popped out when least expected. And, of course, if someone messed with her loved ones, she took them out.

"Hi, Mr. R.," she said. "It's so great having you home again."

Dad grinned and released her. "My wife is fattening me up."

"Oh, pee-shaw. You were too thin when you first got home."

Lucie couldn't argue with that. "She's right, Dad. You look like your old self now."

"Luce," Ro said, "I worked up sketches for some new couture coats. I'll show them to you tomorrow."

Wackiest thing ever, but Ro was convinced the market for couture dog clothes was untapped. As crazy as it was, Ro might not be too far off. Some of the high-end clientele usually went for ostentatious when it came to the samples Lucie brought them. Between the two of them, Lucie and Ro had developed an affinity for knowing which client would go for what.

"Speaking of, I found a peacock feather today. I left it on my desk at the office, but the colors are amazing. I was thinking we could do something with them."

"Feathers! I love that idea."

"Well, I was thinking more the *colors* of the feather, but if you want to play, go for it."

"Oh, I'll play. I can totally see those Ninja Bitches running around with feathers on their backs."

"That's what I thought! I swear we think with the same brain."

At that Joey grunted and Lucie smacked him on the head.

"Hey!"

"Knock it off," Ro said. "Both of you."

Whatever.

Leaving Ro to entertain Dad and Joey, Lucie headed upstairs for a quick shower before dinner and to call Tim. Detective O'Hottie, as Ro called him. Six feet one of muscle with the strawberry-blond hair and blue eyes inherent to Irish boys, Tim O'Brien had it going on.

And currently, he had it going on with Lucie. Just thinking of him, that big hand wrapped around her waist, sliding across her back or down her neck when he kissed her, sent a liquid flutter streaming right to her privates.

Privates that hadn't seen any activity in months, because O'Hottie was giving her space. They'd been not-so-casually dating. In truth they were in a lovely place. All exploration and newness. That exquisite time before the relationship moved to sexual intimacy, but the buildup was flat-out killing her. They'd had some pretty heavy make-out sessions —eh-hem, third base!—but each time, he'd hit the pause button, telling her he wanted to make sure she was over Frankie, her former boyfriend-slash-fiancé who'd moved to New York two-and-a-half months ago for a job.

Tim had no interest in a turf war with Frankie.

He wanted Lucie all to himself.

Her phone buzzed, and she slipped it from her pocket to check the screen. Tim. He must have sensed the pheromones releasing.

Lucie closed the door to her bedroom and flopped on her bed. "Hello, Detective O'Hottie. How's your day?"

Tim snorted. He'd never once complained about the nickname. He was just cocky enough to privately enjoy it.

"My day would get better if I could take you for ice cream later. Maybe that place you like down by the lake."

Oh, the man was a master. "The custard place?"

"Whatever you want, Lucie."

You. That's what she wanted.

"I'd like that," she said. "I'm having dinner with the 'rents but should be done by seven thirty. Shall I meet you there?"

"Or, here's an idea, I could pick you up."

Pick her up. Noooo. Her father, the mob boss who dreamed of a son-in-law with an Italian last name, wasn't ready for an Irish cop.

"That's okay. You don't have to drive out here. I'll just meet you."

"When are you going to let me meet your parents?"

"I'm afraid they'll scare you off. You have no idea the level of insanity that exists within these walls."

Again, Tim laughed. He wasn't stupid, though. He knew she was terrified her father wouldn't like him. "I get it, Lucie, but sooner or later, we need to get it over with. I don't like the sneaking around."

Who could blame him? She didn't like it either. Secrets could be fun, but this one wasn't. Not when she had to hide an amazing man from her family. That seemed wrong on so many levels. Tim O'Brien made her feel, for the first time in a very long time . . . beautiful. Funny.

Protected.

Yes. That was it. Frankie had been good to her in so many ways. For years she couldn't imagine her life without him, but there had been that one overlying issue. The one where he always took his family's side over hers.

Always.

After a while, she'd simply given up. Had gotten used to being in second place. To bending to satisfy everyone else's needs.

Bending and bending and bending.

It made Frankie a loyal son, which she admired. And there was the rub. She loved him for his loyalty, for his unwavering devotion to his parents.

She also resented him for it.

Enter Tim O'Brien, a man who'd figured out how to love his family, but not be ruled by them.

And she'd been hiding him.

What is wrong with me?

"Tim?"

"I'm here."

"I don't like sneaking around either. Let me talk to my mom. See when might be a good night to have you come over for dinner. How's that?"

"Tell me where and when, and I'll be there."

"I know you will."

For that, she adored him. "So, custard tonight?"

"Yep. I'll meet you there."

She hung up with Tim and hopped in the shower to rinse the scent of dogs off and just generally wipe away the fatigue of the day. She stepped out of the tub feeling at least a little more perky. While managing her business, she'd hired and trained two new dog walkers in the last eight weeks and opened their new Coco Barknell headquarters in the old Carlucci shoe store.

Throw in the emotional roller coaster of Frankie leaving for New York and Tim O'Brien coming on scene, and it had been a wild ride.

"Lucie!" her father yelled from downstairs just as she finished toweling off.

"What?" she yelled back through the door.

"Dinner! Ten minutes!"

"Okay!"

Couldn't even shower in peace around here. She

wrapped herself in her fluffy bathrobe and padded across the hall to her room, where she picked out a pair of trendy cargo pants and a light sweater she'd bought on a shopping trip with Ro. Suddenly, she'd figured out that she could be comfortable in things other than jeans and T-shirts.

She'd always be a jeans-and-T-shirt girl, but once in a while it was nice to do a little more. Particularly when seeing O'Hottie.

The Irish cop she was about to unleash on her father.

Or vice versa.

———

AFTER DINNER, MOM UNWRAPPED A FRESHLY BAKED COFFEE cake—Dad's favorite—and set it on the dining room table. The table that had been Grandma's and a mainstay in the Rizzo household since her maternal grandmother had passed. In truth, it was a little too large for the twelve-by-twelve room—particularly with the breakfront shoved against the far wall—but none of that mattered.

All that mattered was having Grandma's furniture, things she'd lovingly cared for and placed thousands of family meals on. For Lucie, no matter how dated the furniture might have been, as long as it was there, so was Grandma.

A lot of things had been inherited from Gram. Including dinner not being complete unless it was followed by home-made dessert.

Lucie sat back. Cake and then custard with Tim. It would be a three-day sugar buzz. From the living room, the familiar *dun-dun-dun* from the nightly newscast began. Seven o'clock. She'd texted Tim that she'd meet him at eight. If she left by seven forty, she'd make it in time.

"Oh, my God," Ro said from her spot across from Joey, "more cake. I've gained five pounds since I dumped that rat-bastard husband and started eating here more."

Wasn't that always the way? Lucie could eat an entire side of beef and not gain an ounce. Ro, the one with the curvy body that hospitalized men? She gained weight at the drop of a coffee cake.

How was that fair?

Dad reached across and patted Ro's hand. "That dumb-ass. All the strip joints around here, he goes to the one in town?"

"I know!" Ro cried. "I should have killed him for being stupid."

Lucie stared straight ahead, meeting Mom's gaze, instinctively knowing they were both thinking the same thing. Ro had busted her husband banging a stripper, and all she and Dad were offended by was his choice to not take his bad behavior out of town.

"They're twisted," Lucie said to Mom, "but they're our twisted."

The room grew quiet as everyone, including Ro, took their first sampling of Mom's cake. The minute it hit Lucie's mouth, the sweet, buttery flavor melted over her tongue, and she slouched back, let her eyes roll.

Mom giggled.

"It's so good," Ro said. "I have to stop. After the next bite. I have to stop."

From the living room, the perky, perky, perky Maureen Gibbons from the local Chicago station delivered her newscast to her legions of fans. "An armed robbery occurred today at the Bendorf Auction House. Let's go to our on-scene reporter for the latest."

Lucie's head snapped toward the living room. "Wait. What?" She hopped out of her chair, ran to the television.

"What happened?" Mom asked.

"Ssshhh."

"The robbery occurred around 4:00 PM when two men posing as police officers entered the premises, held a worker at gunpoint, restrained her and stole the famed Maxmillian dress from the classic film *Peacock Island*."

The reporter angled back and pointed at the building behind him. "The thieves left via the front door of the building. The restrained worker was discovered by another employee. Police are asking any witnesses to contact them with information."

"Holy smokes."

"Baby girl?" Dad said.

Lucie paddled her hand. "I was just there today. Well, not inside, but I was walking Fin right around that time. I met the manager outside."

"*Peacock Island*," Ro said. "Isn't that the sci-fi flick from the sixties? The one where the peacocks take over an island and kill all the humans but one?"

Joey, the sometime sci-fi enthusiast nodded. "That's the one. The survivor wears some dress made by a famous designer. The movie sucks, but people go nuts for the dress."

Lucie met her father's concerned gaze. "I could be a witness."

2

———

Joey flapped his arms. "Oh, Christ! Not again."

"Joseph! Language."

"Sorry, Ma. But this dog-walking gig is a pain. Always with the drama."

Ro made snoring noises, and Joey poked his finger. "And don't you start with the snoring. You know I'm right."

"It's not like she goes looking for trouble. Not her fault she is always—and I mean *always*—in the wrong place."

Dad banged a hand against the table, rattling the silverware. "What the hell are you people talking about?"

"Joe," Mom said, "stay out of it. Lucie will handle it."

She will?

Before Lucie could comment, Mom turned a hard, warning glare on her. Translation: *Don't get your father involved.*

Point there.

"Uh, yeah," Lucie said, "I'll handle it. I really didn't see anything anyway. All I did was talk to the manager."

Ro snapped her fingers. Three times. And pointed one of her perfect nails. "What if the manager was the hostage?"

Really? She had to say that?

Joey flapped his arms again. "Ah, Christ!"

"Everyone calm down." Mom, ever the voice of reason. "Lucie will call that detective friend of hers, tell him she was there but didn't see anything and that'll be that. Case closed."

"What detective friend?" Dad asked, the words flowing like hot lava.

Joey and Ro both looked at her, anticipating her answer. Ro puckered against a smile while Joey had that same wide-eyed *my-father-terrifies-me* look he always wore when Dad got the lava voice.

"It's just someone I know," Lucie said. "He helped with the dognapping case."

And, oh yeah, I might be falling in love with him.

Yeesh. *That* was a revelation. Or was it? For weeks now, every time she saw Tim or talked to him on the phone even, she got this little buzz inside. The flutter. Knowing the upheaval her relationship with Tim would cause—and maybe fear of an eventual broken heart if he dumped her— she'd been hesitant to acknowledge it. But it had been there, burrowing inside, waiting for her to open up to the possibilities of a future with an Irish cop.

Dad waggled his finger at her. "You know how I feel about cops."

Yeah, he only liked the crooked ones he could buy off. But God help her if she said that. Nope. She needed to take the high road. Smooth this out until she could come up with what to do about being a potential witness and about introducing her father to her new boyfriend.

Boyfriend. Huh. Was he? Were they a couple? Exclusively dating? When it came to sex that was sacred ground. Once that happened, they were exclusive whether

Tim liked it or not, because she wasn't into casual hookups.

"Yes, Joe," Mom said. "We're all aware of how you feel about cops."

Time for an intervention before her father lost his cool. Lucie walked back to the table, gathered up a few scattered plates and forks. "Relax, Dad. Everything is fine." She hip-checked Ro's chair on her way to the kitchen. "I have to run out and meet with a potential client. Can I see you a second? To touch base for our meeting tomorrow."

Ro shoved her chair back. "What meet—"

Lucie gritted her teeth, instantly silencing Ro. Who knew that trick worked so well? "Frampton's," Lucie said. "Now. Please."

Ro followed her into the kitchen shaking her head. "Since when do we have a—"

Lucie set the plates on the counter next to the sink and started rinsing. "Shush." Lucie kept her voice somewhere between her regular volume and a whisper. "We don't have a meeting. I'm just . . ."

"Freaking out?"

"Yes! How is it even possible that I was in the area at the exact time of that robbery?"

"Okay, Sister. Just take a breath. They could have the time wrong. I mean, you didn't see anything did you?"

"No. And I even walked around the whole building. Didn't see anyone come out."

"So, you're in the clear. You must have been there right before."

Lucie replayed Fin's walk in her mind. "I talked to the manager. I ran into her out back. Had a whole conversation about Fin and Coco Barknell. She must have been the one to discover the restrained employee. Oh, my God. I was chatting that woman up while people were robbing the place."

"You don't know that. They could have left twenty minutes before."

"No. The newscaster said around four."

From the dining room, Dad yelled, "What are you two whispering about? I hate that whispering."

Finishing with the plate rinse, Lucie turned the faucet off. "Nothing, Dad. Just work stuff."

Ro grabbed her elbow, dragged her closer to the back door. "Even if it was the same time, you didn't see anything. That's all. You didn't see anything. And the manager knows who you are. If the cops want to find you, they will."

"Maybe I should ask Tim about it. I'm on my way to meet him. I should just come clean, right?"

Ro's lips peeled back. "*No!* Why would you do that?"

Uh, because she wanted to be honest? When did the truth become a sin? "Well, why wouldn't I? I like him, and he already told me he likes full disclosure."

"Honestly. My work is never done." Ro huffed then popped her eyes wide. Queen Demented. "Because you *like* this guy. And the last time you got into a dustup you were terrified to tell him, because you thought he'd think you were a scam artist. Plus, you've already told me he worries about his career. He doesn't need his girlfriend bringing heat with his bosses. I say, do both of you a favor, and don't tell him yet. Play dumb. Pretend you never saw that newscast. Then if the cops show up, you can act surprised and *then* tell O'Hottie. That way, you're in the clear. You don't have to bring him into it unnecessarily. He'll thank you for it."

In a twisted way, it made sense. Particularly because she and Tim had discussed the issue of his career and how his superiors would feel about him dating a mob boss's daughter. So far, it hadn't been an issue. But if she kept racking up these criminal involvements, that wouldn't last long.

There'd be no harm in keeping this to herself. Letting it play out.

"Okay," Lucie said. "You're right. No need to panic. Chances are it'll be nothing."

LUCIE PARKED IN THE GARAGE ONE STREET OVER FROM THE custard shop and called Tim to let him know she was there, but would be a few minutes. At which point, he told her to stay put until he got there to walk her.

She liked that about him. The protective nature. The cop in him.

Being a smart girl, she waited in her car until she spotted him come off the garage elevator. He still wore his suit—minus the tie—leading her to believe he'd come straight from work. Otherwise, he'd have changed into jeans. They were alike in that way. They both preferred casual clothing during their downtime.

She hopped out of the car, hit the lock button and met him at the rear bumper.

"Hey, pretty lady."

"Hi, sailor. Want a date?"

Any stress she'd felt on the drive downtown dissolved the second he hit her with his flashing smile. That smile was a wicked aphrodisiac. Every time he leveled it on her, she experienced a hot tingle that made her all sorts of giddy.

He bent over, popped a light kiss on her lips, lingering for just a second, letting her know that if she played her cards right, maybe they'd hit third base again tonight.

She could only hope.

Before he could back away, she gripped the open flap of his suit jacket and deepened the kiss. *Go, Lucie.*

He backed her against the car, brought his hands up to cup her cheeks and the light, playful peck morphed into something altogether different. Something involving tongues and nips and a whole lot of steam.

A car whizzed by, honking at them, and Lucie burst out laughing.

Only slightly awkward.

He angled away, shaking his head at her, but his smile stretched wide. "You're too damned cute, Lucie." He popped another kiss on her lips. "I love spending time with you."

"Ditto that, Detective." She hooked her arm into his. "Now take me for that custard you promised."

They reached the street level, and the frosty wind coming off the lake prickled Lucie's cheeks. Fall had definitely arrived. The good news was evening bumper-to-bumper rush hour had dwindled and didn't require pedestrians to say a novena before they stepped off the curb. Lucie and Tim headed east, keeping pace with the other folks. City walking, Lucie called it. Not slow, but not fast either. She bumped Tim's shoulder. "Thanks for walking me."

He bumped back. "There's no way I'm letting you walk through a parking garage at night. I should have picked you up."

"But that wouldn't have made sense since you live downtown. Why should you drive from here to Franklin and back again?"

He shrugged. "I guess."

The light changed, and he set his hand on her lower back, guiding her across the street. The minute his fingers touched her, even through her jacket, something flickered again. The fuse being relit.

And, yep, she wanted to feel that sucker burn.

He slid his hand from her back, let it dangle at his side. Lucie glanced down.

"Something wrong?" he asked.

"I would like to hold your hand. If that's okay."

Again with the devastating smile. "It's more than okay. I don't want to push you, Lucie."

"What if I want to be pushed? What if it's not a push at all and it feels right and good and . . . easy. You're easy, Tim O'Brien."

"I beg your pardon, madam."

Lucie laughed as they angled around a group of teenagers moving the opposite direction. "You know what I mean."

"Yeah," he said. "I do. You're easy yourself. Being with you, it's comfortable. Like we've been doing it forever."

She'd had forever with Frankie, and they'd gotten too comfortable. They loved each other, but the spark had worn off.

"Sometimes forever becomes a habit," Lucie said.

"Do we feel like a habit to you? It doesn't to me."

Oh, ouch. Not what she meant at all. "No. I just . . . never mind."

Tim stopped walking, drew her closer to the building, away from sidewalk traffic, and wrapped both her hands in his, chasing away the chill.

"I know, Lucie. Why do you think I've been giving you space? I want you to be sure about me. About us."

Without him saying it, she knew what this was. This was about Frankie. Tim wanted assurances that she wasn't planning on leaving for New York anytime soon. And after the time they'd spent together these past couple of months, he deserved an honest answer. One she wanted, desperately, to give him.

"It's over," she said. "With Frankie."

He kept his gaze on her. The cop searching for a tell. "You're sure?"

"Positive. Every time we broke up before there was always this feeling, a lifeline, that kept us connected. We were apart, but not really apart. It's hard to explain, but each time before I knew it wasn't really over, that we'd find our way back. This time there's no lifeline. I haven't talked to him since he left."

"Wow."

"Yep. Part of it is you. I like you. A whole lot. And hanging on to Frankie wouldn't be fair to you. To us. I can't give you all the credit, though. That wouldn't be fair, either. I wouldn't want you thinking you were some kind of rebound. Because you aren't. You're the man who made me realize that I'd been selling myself short."

She pulled her hands free of his, stepped closer and reached under his suit jacket to tug his shirt. "For the first time in years, I feel great. Alive. Like everything is new and fresh, and I love it. You gave me that."

Tim's eyebrows hitched up. She'd surprised him. Good.

"Damn, you're gonna undo me. I knew it that first night we went to dinner."

Was that what she wanted? To have such an effect on him that he'd come apart? No. She wanted this Tim O'Brien. Strong, reliable and fierce. "I don't want to undo you." She grinned. "Not emotionally anyway."

"Ooh, you're a wicked woman."

She held her fingers to her mouth and snorted. "I know. So naughty. It's great fun."

Tim dipped his head and kissed her, sliding his tongue along her lower lip. She shivered, but not from the cold wind. This was all about the man stirring her up.

In ways she desperately needed to be stirred up.

She gripped his suit jacket, folded herself into his big body. She could get used to this—the PDA—with him. No hiding, no worrying about people gossiping about the mob kids uniting like when she was with Frankie.

He pulled back from the kiss, snuggled against her ear. "How about some custard?"

"Yes! It'll be my second dessert tonight. I'm going to get fat."

"That's okay. More for me to grab on to."

"Excellent answer, O'Hottie."

He laughed at her, dropped one arm over her shoulder and strolled toward the custard shop on the next corner.

"So, dear," he said, "how was your day?"

Ugh. The question she'd dreaded since she left the house. The guilt of keeping the robbery from him—and her possible connection to it—might kill her. She should tell him. Just come clean and get it over with since he'd handed her the perfect opportunity.

But Ro was right. Admitting it would involve him, and that could be a conflict of interest. Dating a cop was turning out to be a not-so-easy thing. At least for her, the one who attracted trouble.

Still, a lie by omission was a definite trust-killer for two people so early in a relationship.

Keeping it from him also made her a hypocrite. For years she'd been on her own little soapbox about always telling the truth and never being afraid of honesty.

Now look at her. Slicing and dicing what she wanted the truth to be. She should at least let him decide for himself if her being near the auction house created a possible conflict.

"Lucie?"

She stopped walking, turned to him and earned a few choice swear words from the guy behind them.

"Dude," Tim said, "take it easy."

The jerk kept moving though, and Tim rolled his eyes before looking down at Lucie. "What's up?"

"I'd like to tell you about my day."

"Sure. Are you okay?"

"Oh, yeah. Nothing horrible."

The blast of a train horn—his lieutenant's ringtone—sounded above the chattering pedestrians and street noise, and Lucie suspected her evening was about to come to an end.

"Ah, dammit. Hang on, Luce."

Over the last couple of months, Lucie had grown accustomed to these calls. He'd explained to her early on that even when off-duty, he could be called in at any time. It was part of his world, and, although he'd been casual about the conversation, she'd understood the message. Life with him meant his job and the general public of Chicago came before everything else.

He unclipped the phone from his waist holder, tapped the screen. "O'Brien . . . yes, sir." He glanced at his watch. "Twenty minutes. Give or take. Yes, sir. Got it."

He disconnected and stowed his phone.

"You have to go."

"Yep. Sorry. We caught a case late this afternoon. Not mine, but they need an extra set of hands."

"It's all right." She turned back toward the parking garage. "Walk me back, and I'll drive you to your car."

"I'm sorry, Lucie. I hate cutting the night short."

"Me, too." She poked him on his rock-hard belly. "But you'll make it up to me."

"What did you want to tell me? About your day."

Well, she certainly couldn't tell him now. Not with him rushing off to do heaven-knew-what. He needed to focus on his job, not her.

Tomorrow.

She'd call him in the morning and tell him everything.

That's what she'd do.

Tomorrow.

THE FOLLOWING MORNING, WEARING HER FAVORITE COMFY jeans and pink sweater, Lucie was ready for a day filled with paperwork and Ro meetings. Since she'd arranged to have her two dog walkers cover the pooches so she could catch up on her administrative tasks, she took advantage of a sunny fall morning and walked to Coco Barknell. One of the perks of leasing a shop just a few blocks from home.

At 8:05 she reached the store, spied a smudge on the front window just below the image of the winking poodle in their logo and sneered. Maybe she was a freak about keeping the windows clean, but too bad. She had an image to create here. Potential customers wouldn't want to see a smudgy environment.

Worse, the cleaning company had just been there the night before, supposedly, so clearly they'd been negligent in their duties.

Sighing, Lucie unlocked the front door. "I'll just add that to the list to be handled today."

"Baby girl!"

No, no, no. Key still in the door, she backed up three

steps, swung her head left and spotted her father beelining down the sidewalk. He wore a light, zip-up jacket, dress slacks and a dress shirt, and the sun shined off his salt-and-pepper hair. Hair that he'd let grow an extra inch since returning home.

When she'd seen him an hour ago, he'd set his coffee mug in the sink, kissed her cheek and left for Petey's, the luncheonette two doors down from Coco Barknell where he and his cronies hung out.

For years, according to rumor anyway because Joey and Dad never shared anything related to her father's business, Petey had been receiving a weekly stipend from Joe Rizzo and crew. That little infusion of cash basically allowed them to use the luncheonette as a base of operations.

It also created an opportunity for her father to pop in on her at Coco Barknell anytime he chose. Even if she were in the middle of a meeting or knee deep in a P&L. What her father hadn't quite grasped was the idea that this storefront was now her office and should be treated as such. When she worked as an investment banker, he'd never dream of popping in on her all day long.

Which only told her that her father still thought of Coco Barknell as a hobby. A little side business until she got a *real* job. Well, it had to stop.

And soon.

"Hi, Dad," she said. "What's up?"

"Did you eat yet? Petey is making breakfast. Come eat."

"Thanks, but my day is jam-packed. Can I take a rain check?"

"You gotta eat." He waved toward the store. "Whatever it is, it'll wait. Come with your old man and eat."

Lordy, where was Ro when she needed her?

Time to schmooze. Lucie stepped forward, kissed her father on the cheek. "Dad, I'm busy. This is my work."

He cuffed her under the chin like he used to when she was seven. Some habits really did die hard.

"I can't come down and see my daughter? Since when?"

"Of course you can. But I may not be able to drop everything and go."

He rolled his eyes. Lovely.

"Dad, I'm sorry. I'm swamped."

"Okay. Sure." He lifted his wrist, checked his watch. "I'll come back in an hour."

Obviously, she needed reinforcements on this deal. Tonight she'd recruit Mom to talk to him. Maybe *she'd* crack through that thick skull.

Lucie flicked her thumb at the door where her key ring patiently waited to be removed from the lock. "I have to get to it here. Thanks for coming down."

A whirring noise drew Lucie's attention, and she turned to see a Chevy with more than a few dents and a broken grille double-parking next to Jimmy Two-Toes's Caddy. A short, balding man levered out of the car and shot the cuffs of his sport coat.

"Cop," Dad said.

Another car, a black Dodge Charger that made Lucie's stomach twist, rolled to a stop behind the Chevy.

Maybe it wasn't . . . nope . . . no such luck. Behind the wheel of that Dodge—the one he'd recently started driving after his Crown Vic was totaled when an errant bus hit it —was Tim.

Dear. God.

"And another cop," Dad said. "These bastards won't let up on me."

A nasty bout of nausea attacked, filling her empty stomach, over Tim being referred to as a bastard. He was far from that, and her father would one day know it.

Right now might not be the time, but one day, he'd see what she saw when she looked at Tim.

"Um," she said, "maybe they're not here for you."

"Who else are they here for?"

Still behind the wheel, Tim met her gaze and nodded.

"You know him?"

Obviously, her highly observant father hadn't missed that nod. "I do. That's . . ." *My boyfriend.* "Tim O'Brien. The detective Mom was talking about last night. He's a good guy."

Soon you'll hopefully know how good.

TIM SLID OUT OF HIS CAR AND ONCE AGAIN MADE EYE CONTACT with Lucie. He didn't know what the hell to think. Last night he'd left her and went straight to headquarters, where he was briefed on the robbery of the Maxmillian dress, a funky, tight-fitting, knee-length black number one of the female detectives called "couture." Whatever that meant. And the truly wacky thing was it had feathers all over the bottom. The entire bottom. A veritable skirt of feathers.

Also during the briefing he'd been shown a security video. One that included Lucie chatting it up with the auction-house manager.

If she knew about this robbery—and her proximity to it—she could be a witness. And if she knew all that and hadn't bothered to tell him . . .

That would *upset* him.

A lot.

But he'd stay calm—for now. Not let his brain get crazy.

He followed Gus Bickel, the lead detective on this case, to the curb where Lucie stood, her gaze steady on his. Her father, whom he'd recognized from all the media coverage of his trial, was beside her, shoulders back, a bullish—if that was even a word—look on his face.

The famous Joe Rizzo. Too bad. Investigating a crime was not the way Tim had hoped to meet Lucie's family.

"Ms. Rizzo," Bickel said, badging her as he stepped to the curb. "I'm Detective Gus Bickel. Chicago PD."

"Hello." Lucie shook hands with Gus and then turned to her father. "This is my father. Joe Rizzo."

Mr. Rizzo shook hands with Bickel. Not a bad start.

Bickel pointed at Tim. "You know Detective O'Brien, correct?"

Lucie held his gaze again. "Yes. We're . . . acquainted. Good morning."

Jeez, this was awkward. Last night he'd had his tongue in her mouth and today they were acquaintances? Twelve hours ago she'd given him that speech about not wanting to hide their relationship. Now? He didn't know what the hell to think.

"Good morning, Mr. Rizzo." Tim shook hands with Lucie's father.

"What's up, fellas?" Joe Rizzo wanted to know.

Bickel faced Lucie. "Ms. Rizzo, we're investigating a robbery. Could we go inside and speak to you a moment."

When Lucie made a move to head inside, her dad grabbed her arm. "Hold on."

"Dad, please. Let's just move whatever this is inside."

Ignoring Lucie—which wasn't copacetic on any level—Joe Rizzo eyeballed Bickel. "Does she need a lawyer?"

A lawyer. *Here we go.* Bickel turned to Tim. Yeah, he'd requested to come on this little jaunt because he was "friends" with Lucie. That's what he'd told them. The second his superiors got wind that he was dating Lucie, they'd pull him off this case, and he'd be no help to her. If Lucie was involved, he'd most likely have to remove himself, anyway, but now they were still in fact-finding mode.

"That's up to her," Bickel said.

"I don't need a lawyer," Lucie said.

Her father turned a stony look on her. No shock there. He'd spent most of his adult life speed-dialing attorneys.

"Okay, then," Tim said. "Let's head inside."

And get this the hell over with.

Lucie led Tim and his detective buddy inside with Dad bringing up the rear. The insanity of her life could be summed up by the fact that two detectives showed up, and they weren't looking for her father.

How had she gotten to be the hooligan in the family?

She gestured to the conference area, a dining table Ro had picked up at an estate sale. With the money Ro saved on the table, they'd splurged and bought fancy, leather swivel chairs so they could be comfortable while building their hopefully Fortune 500 company.

"Gentlemen," Lucie said, "would you like anything to drink? I don't have coffee on yet, but I could start a pot."

"I'm fine," Detective Bickel said.

"I'm good," Tim added.

Excellent. Everyone was a happy camper.

"Awright," Dad said, "what the hell kind of bum beef is this?"

Nice, Dad. Prison slang to brighten the day. Lawdy, she might as well curl into a ball and start screaming. Not only had her plan to tell Tim she might be a witness in an armed robbery failed completely, but now she had to face him with her father—the cop hater—present.

Heck of a way to have the two men meet.

But as in every other time things got crazy, she'd roll with it.

"Mr. Rizzo," Tim said, "we have questions for Lucie."

"Ms. Rizzo," Detective Bickel said, "were you near the Bendorf Auction House yesterday?"

And we're off!

"Yes, I was. I walk a dog that lives in the area. Fin. He's an Australian Shepherd. In fact, yesterday I met the manager of the auction house while we were walking."

Bickel made a note on his pad. "Did you see anything unusual?"

Lucie took a second to steal a glance at Tim, who sat casually, hands resting on the chair arms, but that rigid set of his jaw? Not good.

"No, sir. I walked Fin around the entire block and returned him to his home."

"Are you aware there was a robbery at the auction house yesterday?"

Do or die. She could say no. Avoid Tim being mad at her for not admitting she'd been at the scene and preserve the trust between them.

And yet, it would be a lie.

She went back to Tim, made direct eye contact. "Yes, I'm aware. I saw it on the news last night, realized I was in the area around the same time and planned on calling Detective O'Brien this morning."

Okay, so maybe that wasn't altogether true, but it wasn't a lie, either. Just a *flexing* of the truth.

Who was she kidding? Flexing? Before Coco Barknell

there'd been only truths or untruths. No gray area. Now suddenly there was bend.

Whatever. She couldn't think too long about that. A girl had to do what a girl had to do.

Tim's jaw didn't necessarily soften, but those green eyes of his did. At least she'd managed to somewhat explain herself without completely outing their relationship in front of one of his co-workers and—oh, yeah—her father.

"Lucie," Dad said, pulling out his phone, "don't say another word."

But with Tim sitting right there, she knew she would say more. If for no other reason than to assure him she was being honest and cooperative. "It's okay, Dad. I have nothing to hide."

And Tim needs to know that.

"I know you don't, but we're talking armed robbery. I'm shutting this down until I get a lawyer in here."

"Dad!"

"That's all right, Lucie," Tim said, earning himself a scathing look from his detective friend.

Tim was siding with her father?

"Leona?" Dad said into his phone. "It's Joe Rizzo. Willie available?"

Lucie had learned the hard way that Leona was his lawyer's—and Lucie's too after the art-fraud dustup —assistant.

Detective Bickel kept his eyes on Lucie, but stood. "We'll wait."

He wandered a few steps taking in the office space, the furniture, the bolts of fabric in the sewing area, all of it.

Tim, without offering one blip of body language, straightened his tie then set his hands on his thighs, fingers spread wide, but seemingly relaxed. He wouldn't dare say anything more in front of her father and Bickel, but as soon as the place cleared out, Lucie would call him. Explain herself and hope he understood.

Now over by her desk, Bickel continued his perusal of all things Coco Barknell. He could snoop all he liked. He wouldn't find anything. "I have nothing to hide, Detective Bickel."

Still on hold with the lawyer's office, something Lucie found infinitely entertaining, Dad jerked his chin at her. "Don't talk."

Bickel's gaze locked on her desk. After a few seconds, one side of his mouth tilted up into a lazy, smug smile.

"Ms. Rizzo, I know we're waiting on your lawyer. I understand how you feel, but let me ask you about this feather."

Tim didn't move his head, but his gaze shot right to hers.

The feather? What the heck did that have to do with anything?

Bickel reached across her desk, pointed at the pretty peacock feather she'd found the day before near the auction house.

He turned back, that smug smile spreading. "You know that fancy dress has specific feathers. The blue part? The so-called eye. On the stolen dress they're all double-eyed feathers." He held up two fingers. "Two circles instead of one. Very rare." He pointed to the feather on her desk. "This feather right here? Double-eyed. An interesting coincidence that you were on scene at the time of the robbery and are now in possession of a rare double-eyed feather. You see my problem here, Ms. Rizzo? The one where I think you stole that dress."

3

————

"Oh, jeez," Tim muttered.

Lucie snapped her head around, held his stare for a solid five seconds as panic—not the faster-than-a-speeding-bullet kind, but the meandering kind that shredded each bone of each limb—slowly ate through her body.

"Willie?" Dad said, "'Bout damned time. I'm putting you on speaker. I got two detectives here getting on Lucie about some dress that got lifted yesterday." He punched the button on the screen, then waggled the phone. "Say hello to Willie Clay."

Tim attempted not to roll his eyes at Dad's dramatics. "We've met," he said, clearly referring to the last time Lucie got—as the guys at Petey's liked to say—*pinched* for unknowingly storing stolen track suits in her back room. Willie had come to her aid and met Tim in the process.

"Who do we have there?" Willie asked.

Tim finally leaned forward. "Mr. Clay, this is Detective O'Brien. I'm here with Detective Bickel."

He'd raised his voice to that full baritone that Lucie didn't often hear. When with her, on a personal level anyway, his voice took a softer tone, more playful and teasing. When he was in cop mode? That playful teasing turned hard and serious. Commanding. In a twisted way, she liked it. Maybe not when her innocence was in question, but when Tim slid into cop mode, he emanated fierce and powerful and, well, sexy.

Lucie found it wildly intoxicating.

Just not right now.

"Again O'Brien?" Willie said, "What is it with you?"

A sudden lack of air made Lucie's throat expand and she slapped herself on the chest, coughing the whole way. Dad gave her a whack on the back. "You all right? What happened. Need water?"

Tim stood, took one step toward her and stopped. A pained grimace overtook his face and Lucie hated it. Despised every second of this meeting. Not for her. For him. Because he was stuck in the middle of an investigation involving a woman he was dating. She coughed once more and held up her hand. "No, I'm good. Thanks."

"Detectives," Willie said, "what is this about a missing dress?"

Bickel moved closer to the phone, but remained standing, crossing his arms over his chest. Had the man been thirty pounds lighter, that attempt to look tough might have worked. Now, all she saw was bloated belly sitting beneath his crossed arms.

"Counselor, we're investigating an armed robbery at the Bendorf Auction House yesterday. You may have seen it on the news."

"What does this have to do with my client?"

Bickel smirked, then eyed Tim. "Ms. Rizzo was at the scene around the time of the theft. In fact, she spoke with the auction-house manager just before the woman entered the building and found her employee tied up. We came here to discuss this with your client," he uncrossed his arms, waved one hand, "see if she remembered anything unusual." He stopped talking and focused on Lucie. "At least until I found a feather on her desk."

"A feather? I can't wait to hear this one."

Bickel's smile widened. "The bottom of the stolen dress is lined with peacock feathers." He pulled his phone from his pocket, tapped the screen a couple of times and held the phone out to Lucie. "Feathers that look like the one we found on your client's desk."

TIM SAT IN HIS CHAIR, FORCING HIS BODY INTO A SEMICALM state. Not an easy task when all he wanted was to pound something.

How the hell did Lucie continually get into these shit storms? And how the hell did that feather wind up on her desk?

Down deep, he knew she wasn't involved. Knew it. He liked to think of himself as a decent judge of character, and, over these past months, he'd learned a lot about Lucie Rizzo. The first thing being her desire to live a good, honest, legitimate life. Despite her father's criminal history.

"I can explain the feather—"

"No," Willie said. "Don't say anything."

Lucie shook her head so hard it should have concussed her. "It's all right. I want to explain."

"Lucie," her father said, "let the man do his job."

"Dad, I have nothing to hide." She went back to the detectives. "I found the feather on the street yesterday. My company," she gestured to the fabric samples and sketches on the table, "creates pet accessories, mostly dog coats and collars. I was walking Fin yesterday—I can give you his owner's number to confirm that. I found the feather outside the auction house. I thought it was pretty. The colors specifically. They all blend, and I thought it would be fun to create a collar with stones the same colors. I brought the feather back with me to show our designer, Roseanne. That's why I have it."

Bickel took his seat again. "And you had no idea where it came from? Didn't strike you as odd that there was a peacock feather on the sidewalk?"

Ha. Given her lineage, that was about the biggest dumbass question Bickel could ask. In her lifetime, Lucie Rizzo had probably seen enough oddities to last her five thousand years. A peacock feather? That had nothing on life in the Rizzo family.

"Don't answer that," Willie said.

"Detective," she said, "nothing strikes me as odd anymore."

Bam. Tim held his curled hand up to his mouth and coughed to hide the grin. He had to hand it to her, she was fast on her feet.

"Lucie," Tim said, "did you see anyone, aside from the auction-house manager?"

"No."

"Jesus Christ," Willie said. "Joe, what am I doing on this call if she won't listen to me?"

"No other pedestrians? A car pulling away? Nothing?"

Thinking that over, she pursed her lips and stared at the ceiling. "Well, it was the middle of the day. Sure there were people around, but I didn't see anyone carrying a couture dress, if that's what you're asking."

"Detectives," Willie said, "that's enough. She's answered

your questions. I'm shutting this down. For the love of God, Lucie, shut up."

Bickel made a show of rolling his eyes. "Awright. So you pick up this feather and bring it back. Then you see the theft on the news last night. You said you'd planned on calling Detective O'Brien this morning." He turned to Tim. "Assuming that call hadn't come in?"

Bickel had always been in the top ten of Tim's least favorite co-workers. That question just bumped him to a solid number three.

Tim didn't bother answering.

Lucie gritted her teeth. "I'd planned on calling him when I got to the office. And, as you saw, I was just arriving when you pulled up."

"I see," Bickel said.

"We're done here, Detectives," Willie said. "Ms. Rizzo has told you all she knows. Any further contact can come through me."

Bickel rolled out his bottom lip and nodded. "Sure. But for now we're seizing the feather as possible evidence."

Bickel turned to Tim. "I'm gonna grab an evidence envelope and some gloves from my car."

Which left Tim alone with Lucie.

And her father.

Only slightly awkward since Tim had a boatload of questions. Questions he couldn't necessarily ask in front of her father or her lawyer.

The second Bickel walked out, Lucie swiveled her chair toward him.

"Tim—"

He held up his hand. "Don't. Not a word. At least until I unravel myself from this case. Anything you say right now, I have to put in a report, and I sure as hell don't want to take that chance." He stood, straightened his cuffs. "What a cluster."

Unbelievable. When he'd gotten called in the night before, he'd had no idea the case he'd spend most of the night reviewing would involve Lucie. How the hell could he have known? She'd never mentioned it.

Which . . . hang on. He stopped messing with his sleeves.

He'd just told her not to talk. He should leave her be. For both their sakes. But, hell, he needed an answer. Because if she'd seen the news before she'd seen him the night before . . .

"When exactly did you hear about the robbery?"

Joe Rizzo swung his eyes from Lucie to Tim and back to Lucie. "What's going on?"

"Tim—"

The doggie bells on the door jangled, and Bickel entered wearing latex gloves and carrying a paper envelope.

Tim turned away from Lucie, walked to Bickel. "You got this? I gotta get back."

"Yeah, I'm good. We'll huddle up later. See what's what."

Meaning, huddle up about what this feather might mean for one Lucie Rizzo. Daughter of Joe Rizzo, notorious mobster.

Lucie's panic exploded. Forget that slow-moving thing. This time her entire body lit up, all at once, a fierce combustion.

For the first time since they'd started dating, Tim was mad at her. Really mad. He didn't say it—didn't need to. She saw it in his face, the hollowed cheeks, the locked jaw. All of it added up to one handsome cop being more than mildly upset with her.

He'd always told her he wanted honesty, and she'd broken that trust by withholding information.

If she could go back, just hit rewind, she'd do it differently. Too late now.

Would he even believe she'd wanted to tell him the night before?

Bickel finished collecting his evidence, gripped the baggie between his fingers and held it in front of him, making sure she knew exactly what was happening. Gee, thanks for that clarification.

"I'll be in touch," he said.

Dad grunted.

"I'll be here," Lucie said.

Nothing to hide, fella.

The detective strode from the shop, and Dad didn't waste any time. "What the hell's going on with the redheaded guy?"

The Irish cop.

The one she'd planned to introduce to her father. What was it with her plans lately? Every one of them seemed to get incinerated. Not just quietly either. Her plans went up in a fireball.

Well, her dad wasn't stupid and putting him off had never been one of Lucie's strong points. Before now, she'd always had Frankie to run interference. Dad listened to Frankie. It irritated her on many levels, and she'd never reconciled herself to it.

She'd simply given up and let Frankie handle the heavy lifting with Dad.

Only now Frankie was in New York, and Lucie was

dating Tim. Time to put on big girl panties and figure out how to have a meaningful conversation with her father.

She faced him, stared into the very same blue eyes she saw in the mirror. *I can do this.*

"Dad, we're not going to argue about this."

"About what?"

"About what I'm going to tell you. I'm an adult now. I make my own decisions. I need you to respect that."

He angled his head one way, then the other. "Heh?"

"Tim O'Brien. He and I are dating."

Whoosh. There it was. The words just stormed out. After two months of fretting, it hadn't been nearly as hard as she'd thought.

Dad's mouth didn't move. Maybe a bonus there. At the very least, she'd expected yelling. Lots of it.

"Dating? What does that mean?"

What kind of question was that? Her father knew what dating was.

She paddled her hand. "You know. We're seeing each other. We go to dinner, to the movies. Spend time together."

"What about Frankie?"

Frankie. Ah, yes. It all came down to the boy wonder and her father's wish that the two of them get married and pump out oodles of dark-haired, Italian grandchildren. And for the first time, it hit her, that punch of realization. If they'd had this conversation two months ago, they'd already be arguing, and she'd, more than likely, be defensive. But now, after living under the same roof with her dad, watching him adjust to life on the outside again, she got it. Understood her father on a level she'd never imagined.

When she and Frankie had split up, it wasn't only her dreams going up in flames.

Her father's went with them.

She stepped forward, wrapped her arms around him and closed her eyes. He smelled like freshly chopped firewood, that same scent she'd known since she was a child crawling into his lap at family parties or to watch television or tell him about her day. That precious time when she was still his little girl. The time before she'd been old enough to understand his life.

"Dad, I know what you wanted and that you love Frankie. I love him, too. I always will. But we can't make it work. We've tried too hard and too long. It's not fair to either one of us. I'm sorry."

A small sob clawed from her throat, and she breathed in again, focused on her father's scent, took comfort in it and squeezed her eyes tighter, willing the tears to dry up as Dad began patting her back.

"Ssshhh, baby girl. Don't cry. It's all right."

And this, this was what she'd missed all these years. The man who used to hug her—fiercely—and tell her he'd fix it. Whatever it was, he always fixed it. At least until she'd gotten old enough to understand that the one really important thing he needed to straighten out, his lifestyle, he had no desire to change.

After that, their relationship had crumbled, a piece at a time, until she simply couldn't communicate with him.

She backed away, gripped his arms. "Please. I may not always agree with you, but I love you. You need to let me live my life. And right now, if I haven't completely blown it, Tim O'Brien is part of my life."

"How long?"

"Since August. I wanted to introduce you to him, but I was afraid of how you'd react. There's the whole cop thing. And the lack of a vowel at the end of his last name."

Dad laughed. Laughed? Really?

"Lucie, is he good to you?"

"Very."

"He's respectful?"

"Always."

He shrugged. "That's what I care about. Sure, Frankie would have made a great husband, and it didn't hurt that he was Italian. But if a man treats my daughter well, and she likes him, I'll give him a chance. If he screws up, there's gonna be trouble."

"Who are you, and what have you done with my father?"

He waved both hands at her. "Bah!"

Lucie smiled and smacked a kiss on his cheek. "Thank you for understanding. And watching out for me. This time, though, I think I'm the one who screwed up."

4

———

GETTING RID of her father had never been an easy task. Getting rid of him after she'd been questioned by detectives and admitted she'd been dating one of them proved to be darned near impossible.

Lucie sat at her desk watching her father wander around the shop, pick up fabric samples, study the sketches fastened to the wall near Ro's desk and stare down the commercial-grade sewing machine they'd purchased for Mom.

Since Dad's return from prison, he hadn't been a fan of his stay-at-home wife being a working woman. He wanted her home when he got there, whenever that might be, cooking his meals, making his bed, doing his laundry.

Guess what, Dad?

Things had changed.

And Lucie loved it.

When the stare-down dragged on, Lucie wandered over to him and set a hand on his shoulder. "Dad, I have a ton of work."

Gently, she guided him to the door.

"You're kicking me out?"

That sounded rather harsh, but the Rizzo clan had never pulled its punches. "Well, yes. It's my admin day, and with the visit from the detectives, I'm already forty-five minutes behind. And you know as soon as Ro comes storming in here, it'll only get worse."

Because Ro, as much as Lucie adored her, created drama. She couldn't help it. Some days it seemed as if tiny drama gremlins marched into the store behind her. An army of drama.

But Dad laughed. "That girl. She's a pip."

"Yeah. And pairing her with Joey?"

Dad waved a hand. "Forget about it. It'll never be dull."

Two more steps toward the door. *Come on, big guy.*

"All right, all right. I'm goin'. You call if you need anything, though. I'm right down at Petey's."

"I know. Thanks."

Trying not to be too pushy, Lucie swung the door open and restrained herself from waving him out. A girl could only go so far when attempting not to insult her father.

"Good morning," Ro sang as she strutted her stuff from the opposite direction as Dad.

As usual, her BFF was dressed to kill in a tight skirt, an animal-print blouse that barely contained her pushed-up boobs and high heels that elevated her to a minimum of six feet tall. On her shoulder she carried a giant tote bag and a briefcase. God only knew what she had in there.

"Hi."

Ro cruised through the doorway and whipped off her sunglasses. "I see you had a visitor. Again."

"Breakfast at Petey's this time."

"You know you're going to have to give in eventually. He comes down here every day wanting you to eat with him.

Suck it up, Sister. Make your dad happy. Just maybe, if you do, he'll leave you alone."

Hardly. "I don't think that'll happen. Not after the two detectives just left."

"Stop it."

"Our grand plan not to tell Tim about me being at the scene of that robbery failed. Epically."

Ro dumped her briefcase and tote on her desk, and her mouth plummeted. "I don't understand. How?"

"Because my luck stinks. And, well, my detective boyfriend got pulled into the case."

"Stop. *It!*"

"Yep. And my father is no dummy."

"Ohmygod."

"I had to tell him."

"About you and O'Hottie? *No.*"

The thing about Ro was, even with the drama, in desperate times, she made Lucie laugh. The relief valve. Right now was no exception.

Her BFF stood in front of her, hands on hips, eyes popping, her lips curled almost to a sneer. She looked like something out of a comic book. Lucie unleashed a good solid snort of laughter.

"What's funny?"

"I just . . . love you. You help me even when you don't know it."

She paddled her hands, jangling the bangle bracelets stacked on her wrist. "Blah, blah. I'd do anything for you. But what did your dad say about Tim? Poor Joey has been losing sleep worrying about this day."

Joey? How the heck did this become about him? "He has?"

"Sure. He kinda likes Tim. And he's afraid he'll have to kick the crap out of him. It's a burden, Luce."

"He thought . . ." Lucie shook her head. Really, she didn't want to go wherever her mind was about to take her. "Never mind. My family is so twisted."

"Amen to that."

"I think it'll be okay. My dad was surprisingly calm about it. He said as long as Tim treated me well, he didn't have an issue."

"Huh."

"I know, right? Maybe prison actually reformed him."

"Honey, I wouldn't go that far. But, hey, this is a start. Now you don't have to hide him anymore."

No more hiding. The thing she'd just moaned to Tim about last night. No more. It was out there, now.

Only Tim might hate her for keeping her potential-witness status from him.

"Assuming he's still talking to me. Because, let me just say, it was awfully frigid in this room thirty minutes ago."

Ro snapped her fingers. "Only you would have a cop boyfriend that lands a case you're involved in."

"I'm not involved. I was there, but I'm not involved!"

"You and I know that, but, honey, this is the third time that poor guy has seen you wind up in a jackpot. How much can he take?"

Assuming it was a rhetorical question, Lucie didn't answer.

Ro jumped on the task of making coffee, and Lucie grabbed her cell, heading to the back door of the shop. At least in the alley, she might have privacy. If she went out front and one of the guys from Petey's saw her, they'd all wander down to pepper her with questions about the detectives. That mess would take her an hour to break up.

Who had that kind of time?

In the alley all she had to deal with was the stench of garbage. Maybe a rat or two.

Preferable any day.

Two rings in, Tim answered.

"O'Brien."

Typically he answered with, "Hey, pretty lady," or if he was in the middle of something he'd say, "Luce, can I call you back?"

Either way, whenever she called he always knew exactly who it was. Today? *Today* he answered with a completely impersonal, forget-about-dating-this-woman greeting.

"It's me. Lucie."

"Luce, I can't talk now. I'm sorry."

"Okay. But I'm sorry. About this morning. If it was awkward."

He laughed, but the caustic nature sent Lucie's shoulders flying back.

"Awkward," he said. "Even for you, that was nuts."

Um . . . ow. What could she even say? "I'm—"

"When did you know about the robbery?"

Sticky territory. Being a girl who valued honesty, she wouldn't lie to him. Absolutely couldn't. For a man in law enforcement, he'd stood by her when most cops would have bailed.

"I had a plan."

"Dammit, Lucie. We said full disclosure."

"Please. I wanted to tell you last night. I did. I saw it on the news and realized I'd been in the area. I feel like I get in the middle of something illegal, and it's never my fault, and I worry that you won't believe that. Or that you'll lose your job because of who I am."

"Lucie—"

"I wasn't going to tell you I was there. I thought it would be better if you didn't know. But then, when I saw you last night, I couldn't hold it back. That's what I wanted to tell you when you got called in. But I couldn't dump it on you when you had to focus on your job."

"And what? You just weren't going to tell me?"

"No. What I said is true. I planned on calling you first thing this morning. As soon as I got here. Because God knows there's no privacy at my house. But it was too late." She stopped talking for a minute, set one hand on her head and squeezed her eyes closed. "I intended to tell you. Please, believe that."

A horn blast sounded from Tim's end, and he let out a stream of swearing that might have melted her ears. "Get the hell out of the way," he shouted.

Wowie-wow-wow. Mad Tim. Really mad, Tim.

"Crazy friggin' drivers."

Look who's talking. She'd driven with him *plenty* of times. Just short of a madman behind the wheel.

Now was certainly not the time to joke about that. "Are you mad at me?"

"You bet your life I am. Doesn't mean I'm not still nuts about you. I get it. I took off in a hurry last night. I knew you had something on your mind, and I was gonna call you; but I got busy, and then it was too late."

How pathetic would she be if she asked if he'd dump her? With all the things that could possibly go wrong in this scenario, she was worried about the cutie detective breaking up with her? *Grow up, Luce.*

"Tim?"

"Luce, you're thinking too much. I can feel it. Take a breath. I'm a cop, and my girlfriend is a potential witness in a case I'm working. I gotta get with my lieutenant. Explain it to him, and get taken off this thing."

"I'm so sorry."

"I know. I'll call you later. Please, for God's sake, lay low for the rest of the day."

"Incoming," Ro said.

Lucie peeled her eyes from the spreadsheet she'd been scouring for a formula error and found her father opening the shop's door.

Not again.

Third time this morning. Technically, it was afternoon, though.

Dad stopped in the doorway, and the streaming sunshine formed a weird halo around him. Dad and a halo. There's a combo she thought she'd never see. He tapped his watch. "Lunchtime. I'm buying."

"Dad—"

"You know," Ro said, shooting out of her chair, "I could eat. Come on, Lucie. Let's get some lunch."

"But I'm in the middle . . ."

Halfway to the door, Ro spun on that crazy high heel and gritted her teeth. "Now look, we're *all* busy around here, and your father wants to buy us lunch. So, we're going to let him do that, and then we can come back here and finish what we're doing. *Undisturbed.*" She faced Dad. "Isn't that right, Mr. R.? As soon as Lucie and I come down to Petey's for lunch, you'll let us get on with our work. Right?"

And, yowzer. Ro had just laid down the law in spectacular fashion. Lucie couldn't help clenching her butt cheeks, anticipating her father's reaction to being reprimanded. Well, reprimanded in a backhanded sort of way.

"Sure," he said. "I mean, you girls have been at it all morning. You need to eat. You come to Petey's, have a sandwich and then come back to work. I got some stuff to do this afternoon, anyway."

That tore it. With Dad out doing whatever the heck he did during his working hours—she really didn't want to know—Lucie would have an entire afternoon of peace. All she'd have to do is suck-up the next forty-five minutes and go into the dreaded Petey's for a sandwich.

With Dad.

And crew.

The possibility did exist that she'd run into Frankie's father, but she was a desperate woman who needed to get her own father the heck out of her hair.

She bolted up, grabbed her keys and followed Ro to the door.

Once outside, Ro plucked the keys from Lucie and locked up. "Lunch at Petey's," she muttered. "I need a picture of this."

The three of them marched into Petey's, and the aroma of baking bread and cooking meat brought Lucie's taste buds alive. Her dislike of Petey's had nothing to do with the food. Exceptional food actually. Her dislike stemmed from the illegal activity Petey allowed to happen there.

Lucie waved at a few locals seated at a corner table. With only a handful of available seating, Dad's crew of Jimmy Two-Toes, Slip and Lemon sat at two pushed-together tables along the wall.

All of them with their backs to the wall so they could see both the front entrance and the hallway leading to the rear door. Mob guys, like cops, always sat with their backs to the wall. You know, just in case someone tried to kill them.

God help her.

The one apparent upshot? Frankie's father was absent.

Thank you very much.

"Ho!" Jimmy Two-Toes yelled. "Lucie! How you doin'? Petey! Make Lucie a sandwich. Come here. Take my seat. Whaddya want? A pop? Tea? What?"

"Jesus, Jimmy," Lemon said, "Give her a minute. You're all over her."

"What? I'm being nice? I can't be nice? She never comes in."

Oh, boy.

"Helloooo, fellas." Ro offered up a little finger wave.

"Ho!" Jimmy yelled again. "A twofer."

Dear. God.

Dad waved Jimmy back to his chair. "Take it easy. We'll sit in the back so I can talk to the girls. Luce, you want a turkey sandwich?"

How sweet was that? Her dad remembered her obsession with turkey sandwiches.

"Yes, thanks."

"That sounds good," Ro added. "Make it two."

Ten minutes into the meal, Joey's giant head appeared outside the window. He poked his index finger into the glass —*tap-tap-tap*—pointing at Lucie.

What was this, now? Lauren and the other dog walker were handling things today, so it couldn't be dog related.

Lucie pointed at herself and mouthed, "Me?"

Because, after all, the way he and Ro had been going at it, he might be looking for a nooner.

But, nope, he bobbed his head up and down and jerked his thumb for Lucie to step out.

"What the hell is he doing?" Dad motioned for Joey to come inside, but Joey shook his head.

"I swear," Ro said, "he's insane."

Lucie balled her napkin and shoved it under her dish. "Let me see what he needs. I'll be right back." Lucie turned back. "Stay here. Both of you."

Ro threw her hands in the air. "Well, excuse me, bossy."

Great. Now she was mad, too. What a day. Lucie had managed to insult just about everyone she cared about today. And by the looks of it, Joey would be next.

She slipped through the door, walked a few feet so they'd be out of sight.

"What's up?"

Joey nudged his head backward. "Some guy nosing around your shop."

Going up on tiptoes because her brother was the side of a mountain, Lucie peeped over his shoulder. A man, forty-ish, with short, dark hair leaned against a light pole checking his phone. He wore dress slacks and a sport coat. Just business casual enough to still be formal, but not so much that he stood out. "Who is he?"

"Says he's an investigator. What the hell are you into, now?"

"An investigator? From where?"

"Some P.I. firm. I was headed to Petey's, saw him and asked what he wanted. Name's Eric Edwards. Edwards Investigations. And he's looking for you. You want me to get rid of him?"

"No. He could be a potential client. I'll talk to him."

A client. Good luck with that. The way this day was going, she knew better.

"I'll come with you."

Of course he would. Joey had a protective streak longer

than Soldier Field. Typically, it irritated her. He always meant well, but the tendency to be overbearing definitely existed.

This time, she didn't mind so much.

"Yes. Probably a good idea. This has been the craziest day."

Joey shifted, held his arm out for her to walk by. "Why?"

"Two detectives, one of whom was Tim, showed up this morning to ask me about the robbery I may have witnessed yesterday."

"Here we go, again."

"Add Tim meeting Dad for the first time, and it's been a real humdinger."

Joey halted, right there on the sidewalk and flapped his arms. "Come on? That's how he met him?"

"'Fraid so. He took it pretty well. But now that Dad now knows I'm dating an Irish cop, stay alert for an ambush."

"Yeah, thanks for that." As he walked, Joey ran a hand over his right cheek. "I'd hate to have to kick Tim's ass. I really would."

Lucie spun on him. "Hey, no one is kicking anyone's ass."

The man leaning against the light pole glanced up from his phone and focused on them. Apparently, she'd been a wee bit too loud.

"Hello," Lucie said. "I'm Lucia Rizzo."

"Hello." He strode toward her, hand extended. "I'm Eric Edwards."

Lucie grasped his hand, found it somewhat callused, but soft at the same time. Odd that. But, unlike some men, he didn't spend too much time on the handshake. No squeeze, no extended eye contact. No sweaty palm.

Nope. Mr. Edwards was a pro at the handshake.

Lucie slid her hand away and squared her shoulders. "How can I help you?"

His gaze moved to Joey and back. "Can we speak privately?"

"That depends."

"On?"

"What we're talking about." She waggled her thumb at Joey. "This is my brother. If we're discussing business, as in you would like to hire Coco Barknell, I'm happy to speak privately. If this is regarding something else, Joey stays."

Joey inched forward. "What *is* this about?"

Mr. Edwards, no slouch himself in the size department, squared his shoulders. Male posturing. Always entertaining.

"I've been hired by Krandall Insurance to investigate the theft of the Maxmillian dress."

This day. First the detectives and now an investigator.

A burst of voices sounded from behind her, and Lucie angled back, spotted her father hooking the left out of Petey's heading straight for her. Jimmy Two-Toes and Lemon filed in behind, and Ro hustled along in her tight skirt and click-click-clicking heels.

Lucie's stomach plummeted. She was good, but she couldn't handle this bunch. Joey alone could be a challenge. Throw in Dad, his crew, Ro and the investigator and she might as well find a tall building and hurl herself off of it.

"Wait a second." Mr. Edwards cocked his head left as Dad approached. "Is that . . ."

And here we go. As usual, her father's reputation preceded him.

"Yes," Lucie said. "It is. Joe Rizzo. My father."

"Holy crap," Joey said, his eyes plastered to Ro.

Any second now he would either make some comment on Ro's appearance or throw his hand over his heart feigning a heart attack. In a lot of ways, it was sweet. In others it felt too caveman.

But it worked for them.

"Don't do it," Lucie said. "I'll kill you right on this sidewalk."

"Can't help it," he said, eyes still tracking Ro and the various body parts that bounced along with her. "That leopard print. It makes me wild."

Disregarding Mr. Edwards—certain things needed to be done—Lucie stuck her fingers in her ears. "How many times do I have to say I don't want to hear comments like that?"

Joey's mouth moved, but thank a merciful God, she couldn't hear what he said. Except that crew was bearing down on them fast, and the realization that this meeting with Mr. Edwards might possibly be witnessed by all of them sent Lucie's last working nerve into overdrive.

She pulled her hands down, gripped Joey's arm, digging her nails in so he'd know how serious she was about to be.

"Hey," he said, "go easy with the talons."

Mr. Edwards cleared his throat. "Everything okay here?"

Lucie hit him with a cheery smile as she dragged Joey closer to the oncoming crowd.

"Listen to me," she said, her voice deadly calm. "If you love me—forget that—if you like me at all, you'll stop them. Just do your Joey magic and get them all back to Petey's for me. Please."

"What do I get?"

God! They didn't have time for this.

"I don't know. Something."

"I have your word?"

"Joey."

"All right, all right. Don't get your shorts in a wad."

"Thank you. I'll take care of this investigator. Just . . . handle Dad."

"You owe me."

As she headed back to Mr. Edwards, Lucie dug in her pocket for her keys. "I'm sorry about that. Let's go inside where we can talk without distractions."

Inside the shop, Lucie walked to the conference table—that table was seeing some serious action today—and pulled out a chair for Mr. Edwards.

With Mom not here and Ro outside with Joey, the silence of the shop, the sense of calm despite her visitor, washed over Lucie.

If only every day could be silent like this.

She breathed in, enjoyed the moment of silence before sitting forward in her chair. "You said you worked for an insurance company?"

"Yes."

"I see."

"It's standard with an item as valuable as the Maxmillian dress."

"Do you work with the police then?"

Because if he did, he could get her statement from them, and they could all put her out of her misery.

"We work hand in hand to recover the lost item. Consider me an extra set of hands hired by the insurance company. I can devote my full attention. The police have other cases."

Lucie nodded. "That makes sense. Plus, you basically need to figure out if the insurance company should pay the claim or not."

He smiled, not one of those flashy, charming ones, but a half-grin that told her she'd nailed it. Joe Rizzo didn't raise no dummy.

"My goal is to find the truth. If the claim is valid, the owner is reimbursed for the loss. I'm trying to find that dress, Ms. Rizzo."

"I understand. How can I help you?"

The bells on the door jangled, destroying the calm, as Dad marched in with Joey and Ro following. The energy these three brought?

Mind-bending. Lucie breathed in, fought the wave of hyperawareness prickling the back of her neck.

"Uh, Joey?" Lucie said.

He held his hands up. "Hey, I tried. It's not easy."

Mr. Edwards stood and faced Dad and his ornery, squinty eyes. "Hello, Mr. Rizzo. I'm Eric Edwards. I'm a private investigator looking into the theft of the Maxmillian dress."

"Again with this dress? She doesn't know anything. The cops were here this morning."

"Yes, I'm aware. I have a few follow-up questions."

"Dad, it's—"

"This is harassment!"

Joey moved next to Dad and folded his arms, his big body blocking the exit as if there'd be some kind of smackdown right here in Coco Barknell.

That'd be great for business.

Time to pull out the big guns. Or, in this case, the big boobs. Lucie hit Ro with the do-something-now stare. Over the years, they'd perfected their signals and played off of each other well.

Ro sighed and popped the first available button on her blouse. The one that took her from sexy to slutty. "Joey," she said, "can I speak to you a moment?"

Joey got a gander at the enormous amount of cleavage being hurled his way and did a double take.

So easy.

"Outside," Ro said. "Right now. Please."

"I'm in the middle of something here."

Ro went for the next button, and Joey flinched, his entire body spasming. He jumped in front of Ro to block the view of the other men in the room and grabbed her elbow, leading her to the door. On their way out, she slipped her free hand behind her back and gave Lucie a thumbs up.

Two down, one to go.

Awesome teamwork.

Chances of getting Dad out of this room were below slim. In fact, those chances didn't exist. She'd have to, as they used to say in her old office, manage up.

Lucie rose from her chair at the end of the table and scooted over one. Which gave Dad the head of the table and the power position. At least in his mind. Sheer strategic brilliance on her part. "Dad, have a seat. Let's see if we can help Mr. Edwards."

"Ms. Rizzo, around the time of the robbery yesterday, I understand you walked a dog near the auction house."

"Yes. I ran into the auction-house manager."

"I'm aware. I spoke with her this morning." He retrieved a notepad and tablet from his briefcase and fired it up, poking at the screen a couple of times. He set it on the table and spun it to Lucie. "I collected security video. Would you mind taking a look at it? Let me know if you may have seen the men?"

"Sure."

He hit the play button and a grainy video rolled. "These are the two men. They came in through the front."

Lucie checked the time stamp: 4:03. "I was on the other side of the building with Fin. That's right around the time the manager came up and started chatting."

Edwards stopped the video. "Was that unusual?"

"What? The chatting?"

"Yes."

Lucie pondered that. As a dog walker she met people. And with a cute dog? Forget it, everyone stopped. Complete nightmare. Each time someone interrupted, her schedule slowly disintegrated. She'd gone as far as to code the attention-getter dogs and assign them to separate routes. That way the time loss fanned over two or three routes.

"I tend to meet people while on the walks, so no, I wouldn't say that's unusual."

"What about the auction-house manager? Had you met her before?"

"No."

Edwards jotted a note on his notepad—what did that mean?—before starting the video again.

"The two men in the video? Do you recall ever seeing them in the area? Even if it was weeks ago."

Dad sat forward. "You think they were casing the place."

Edwards shrugged, and Lucie went back to the video. Both men wore police uniforms and hats. The taller one's hair dipped below the brim of the hat. That alone would have alerted Lucie to a problem. Most policemen wore close-cropped hair. The overhead view coupled with the hat brims obscured the men's faces, but one was broader in the chest and thicker around the middle. "I'm sorry. I don't ever remember seeing them. It doesn't mean they weren't there, I just don't recall."

"All right." He stopped the video, tucked the tablet away. "Do you do the same route every day? Same timing?"

Dad waggled his finger. "Don't answer that."

"It's okay, Dad. I've already told the police all this, and Mr. Edwards has indicated he works closely with them."

Dad leaned into his elbows and made direct eye contact with Edwards. "I know this drill. Whatever you think about me, my daughter isn't a crook. MBA from Notre Dame. And I don't appreciate you people coming around her business stirring things up. She's a good girl. Leave her alone."

Times like this, she adored her father. They had their differences, but when it came to his baby girl, he didn't like people messing with her.

Edwards mirrored Dad's body language. Had the two men been standing, Lucie imagined they'd be all up in each other's faces by now.

"Mr. Rizzo, I've been hired to do a job. All due respect, I don't care who you are or who your daughter is. I'm charged with locating that dress. The more cooperation I get, the easier that will be."

She'd been around law enforcement enough to know that everyone was a potential suspect. Particularly people at the location of the theft.

And, hello, crimes involving a gun upped the ante on jail time.

Lucie swiveled her head to Dad. "I guess we know what we need to do then."

"What's that?" Edwards asked.

"Figure out what happened to that dress so I can clear my name."

5

———

AFTER DEALING with an overnight burglary and grabbing a quick lunch, Tim headed back to the station. Priority one: tackle his lieutenant who'd been in meetings all damned day. Priority two: get taken off the Maxmillian dress case.

This mess—the wanting to help Lucie, but do his job at the same time—tore him up. Talk about a balancing act.

And that was before factoring in who her father was. His superiors would love one of their detectives dating Joe Rizzo's kid.

Total shit storm.

He'd known it all along, but he hadn't expected his personal and professional life to collide with such gusto.

He glanced around the bullpen at the six empty desks. The other members of his unit must have been making the brass happy by being out on calls. Tim didn't mind. When all the guys were in-house the noise could blow out the walls. Even ancient cement couldn't handle a squad of foul-mouthed and grisly Chicago detectives.

At his desk, he slid his suit jacket off, hung it on the back of his chair, a decent, cushioned one he'd bought himself instead of the crappy metal-framed ones the department provided. Tim's theory was the brass didn't want their detectives too comfortable at their desks, so they gave them the cheapest, spine-destroying chairs they could find. The chairs alone motivated the guys to hit the streets.

Tim didn't have a problem being on the street. He'd never be a desk jockey. A good day for him meant checking in first thing, hitting the road and not returning until the end of the day.

He unbuttoned his shirtsleeves and rolled them while checking Lou's office just ten feet behind him. Bingo. Door open, the man at his desk.

"Lou." He hustled over before someone intercepted. "I need a minute."

"Enter!"

Tim stepped in, pointed at the door. "You mind if I close this?"

Lou eyed him, his dark eyes narrowing slightly in that don't-screw-with-me way his boss had of nonverbally communicating. He dropped his pen on his desk and sat back, hands falling over the armrests of his chair.

"Go ahead. What's up?"

"The Maxmillian dress."

Lou's eyebrows hitched up. "You got something?"

Tim shifted in his seat, kept his gaze steady on his boss while his pulse went to triple time. He set his hands on his thighs, tapped his fingers. Now or never.

Yeah, he had something all right. Not in the way his boss hoped, but he had something. "Other than a potential conflict? No."

Lou pressed his lips tight, his shoulders sloping as he let out a breath. "Don't wreck my day, O'Brien."

No promises.

Tim lifted his fist to his mouth, cleared his throat. "Bickel was heading out to interview a witness this morning."

"Yeah. Joe Rizzo's daughter. That's almost too good to be true."

Tim shoulders locked up, the tension balling tight and knifing a bolt of pain straight to his fingertips. Certain things, he could deal with. Things like ribbing from the guys about his fair skin. Or the Opie nickname Rich Laslo had laid at his feet because someone said, as a kid, he must have looked like the character from *The Andy Griffith Show.*

Yeah. He could deal with all that.

What he couldn't deal with—apparently—were Lucie Rizzo jokes.

He rolled his shoulders, forced the tension away. "Things can be deceiving. I tagged along on the interview. I know Lucie. Figured maybe I could be of some help."

Lou tilted his head. "'Know her' as in you met her once or twice, or more?"

"Uh, more."

Way more. *As in she nearly sucked my tonsils out last night.*

Lou sat forward again. "I see."

"Yeah. Truth is, we're . . . uh . . . seeing each other. Dating, so to speak."

There. Said it. Done deal. He waited. Couple seconds at least, but his boss sat, still studying him, his dark eyes direct, but lacking heat.

Lacking anything really.

"Un-huh," Lou said.

That was it? No lecture? "I saw her last night. Before I got called in to help with the Maxmillian case. So, there's nothing sideways there. I didn't know Lucie was involved until Bickel talked to the auction-house manager."

Still no response. Okay. What the hell? By now, the guy should be nosing around. Asking questions. Feeling him out. At the very least, asking if he'd discussed the case with Lucie privately. At which point, Tim would have to admit they'd had a general conversation about Tim's involvement in the investigation, but nothing specific to chain of evidence.

He had made sure of that.

But Lou just nodded.

"I'm thinking I should probably come off this case. No?"

A solid twenty seconds passed. Who the hell knew twenty seconds could feel so long? Lou rested his elbows on the desk. "The media is all over this damned dress. We got kids dying in the street, and all anyone cares about is a missing dress. Eh. People. Anyways, last I heard, Ms. Rizzo didn't give us much."

"She didn't see anything. She did find the feather on the sidewalk."

"Yeah, I heard. Bickel is processing it." Lou sat back again, drummed his fingers on the armrests of his chair. He relaxed his head back, casting his gaze up. "If we clear her, there's no conflict. If you get any calls or leads, turn them over to Bickel. Let's keep this clean until we confirm her story."

Crap. Not exactly what Tim wanted to hear. He needed off this case. There'd been plenty of cases he didn't like, cases that drove him nearly insane with crazy witnesses, unruly defendants, filthy, unlivable crime scenes. All of it he'd dealt with and never, not once, asked to be taken off a case.

Now? Being stuck between Lucie and his job, he wanted out.

Lou brought his attention back to him. "Unless you got some reason I should feel otherwise?"

Suck this up. "Yes, sir."

"And, O'Brien, I don't think I need to tell you to be sure you know what you're doing with this girl."

And . . . come again? Tim shook his head. Did he just . . . yeah . . . sure did. Plenty of four-letter responses came to mind. Plenty. But, reversing the roles, if Tim were the superior officer and one of his detectives marched into his office announcing he was dating a notorious mobster's daughter, Tim probably would have issued the same warning.

Hell, Tim had issued that warning to himself a few thousand times.

But he had more than a minor itch for Lucie. And when had scratching ever helped?

"Understood, sir."

"Good. Get on the reports from this morning. I'll let you know if anything comes up on this dress."

Tim left the office, grabbed his cell phone from his desk and headed outside for privacy. With that nastiness done, he could talk to Lucie with a clear conscience. He just wouldn't be able to discuss the case.

"Hi," she said.

He hopped down the back steps and strode to the edge of the building, away from any potential eavesdroppers. Call him paranoid. So what? "Hi. How's it going?"

"Um . . ."

"Don't answer that. I just talked to my lieutenant about getting pulled off this case."

"And?"

"No dice. For now, any evidence or info that comes my way, I have to shuttle to Bickel. I need to stay out of it."

"Okay. I understand. I hate that I put you in this position. I'm so sorry."

"Don't worry about it. You were in the wrong place at the wrong time."

"I guess. Anyway, the owner's insurance company hired an investigator. He came to see me around lunchtime."

Not a shocking development. High-value items always warranted an investigation. The fact that they were moving this fast though? That was . . . interesting. "They didn't waste any time."

"The dress is worth millions. Can you blame them?"

"Just so you know, that's standard procedure."

"Well, he made it fairly clear that I'm a suspect."

Tim bit down. He should say something. Anything. Natural instinct was to reassure her. But he couldn't. For both their sakes, he needed to follow his lieutenant's orders. The local press was all over this story. Before long, the entertainment rags would get in on the action. And what was juicier than a missing Maxmillian dress?

Ha. How about a detective involved with a suspect who was also Joe Rizzo's daughter.

Television movie if he'd ever heard of one. And he didn't even watch them. His sisters? They loved 'em.

"These things have a natural order," he said. "Be patient."

Lame response. Piss poor. He squeezed his eyes shut, banged his open hand against his head. Impossible situation.

"I know. I've decided to talk to my family tonight. Sort of a family meeting to figure out how to find the dress and clear my name. Between my mom, dad, Joey and Ro, they know half the state."

"Not a good idea."

"Well, Tim, I can't sit here and do nothing. I've spent most of my adult life trying to prove myself to people. Now I have a business to protect. I can't have my superwealthy clients thinking I'm a thief."

"No one thinks that."

"Really? What would you think? Would you take a chance letting me inside your three-million-dollar home when I might be a co-conspirator in a robbery?"

No. He wouldn't. "Hell no. But this is an armed robbery. We're not talking about gum being lifted from the drugstore. These guys had weapons. If you start chasing them down, who knows what they'll do. I'm not letting you do that. No way."

"You're not *letting* me? Huh. Last I checked, my last name and the legal system aren't a great match. I can't chance it. I need to do what I can to help this investigation along. And that means utilizing my family's contacts."

"Contacts? What contacts? I mean, no offense, Lucie, but your father's contacts . . . let's be nice and call them questionable."

This was a cluster. And he couldn't help. Not if he didn't want to make it a bigger cluster. And possibly lose his job. Life with Lucie Rizzo was slowly killing him. He should walk away. Let her and her nutty family become a memory. He'd told himself that a hundred—a thousand—times.

Lot of good that had done. He simply couldn't do it. Couldn't give her up. She made him laugh. Settled him. Nope. Not giving that up.

"O'Brien!"

Tim reared back to where one of his squad mates stood on the steps waving him inside. "Luce, something's up here. I gotta go. I'll call you later. Relax. Okay? Don't do anything rash."

THAT EVENING, WHILE SHE HAD A CAPTIVE AUDIENCE, MEANING Dad, Joey, Ro and Mom were all still seated at the dining room table, Lucie tapped her fork against her favorite Notre Dame glass. The tapping rose above the chatter at the table, and her father paused his effort to convince Ro to become a republican.

Ro and Dad talking politics. There was something she didn't see every day.

The two of them went silent, her father still grinning from the verbal swordplay and—pow—something pinged at the back of Lucie's neck.

For once, the atmosphere, that lively, frenetic energy that came with her family, brought about a happy, contented feeling. Gone was the embarrassment and shame she often felt when entrenched in her father's legal troubles. Life as Lucie Rizzo was a vicious cycle. For years she had tried to distance herself from her family's reputation, but here she was about to ask for their help.

Which brought an entire other level of shame and guilt. What kind of person can love, but be simultaneously mortified? So confusing.

Her family was crazy.

Straight-up nuts. In a lot of ways, she probably was too, but it didn't need to define her.

For once, she could look at these people, feel her love for them and savor it without any shame or guilt.

"Ho," Dad said, "we were talking. What's with the clinking?"

Coming out of her stupor, Lucie cleared her throat. "Sorry. Since we're all here, let's have a quick family meeting."

Joey, swallowing the last of his dinner pushed his empty plate away and held his hands out. "What meeting?"

"Shush," Ro said, bumping his elbow. "This is important."

"You knew about this?"

Mom hopped up from her spot next to Lucie. "Wait. I made a nice lemon pound cake today. Let me get it."

Ro's jaw dropped. "Oh, my God, with the cake. It has to stop."

"I like cake," Dad said.

Joey nodded. "Me too. Get the cake, Ma."

"I like cake, too." Ro waggled her finger at Dad and Joey. "So does my rear."

Now that was funny.

"Go ahead and laugh," Ro said to Lucie. "It's easy for the skinny one."

Disregarding Ro's plea, Mom ran into the kitchen, grabbed her precious pound cake and brought it back to the table. While Mom sliced, Lucie scanned the room to make sure she had everyone's attention. "I need your help."

Joey, the mama's boy, was handed the first piece of cake. "Who?"

"Everyone."

"Whatever you need, baby girl," Dad said.

Yep. People could say what they wanted about the Rizzos, but they stuck together.

"Thanks, Dad. Just to fill Mom in, Dad was with me today when that investigator from the insurance company showed up. Between him and the police, it's clear that everyone is considered a suspect. And with Coco Barknell growing, we can't afford any negative press. If our high-end clients get wind of this, we're sunk."

"I wouldn't go that far." Ro, the one whose ass was growing, accepted a slice of cake. "But you're right. It's not good for business. Not when I'm talking to national department stores."

"Exactly. But between all of us, we know a lot of people in this city."

Joey swallowed a mouthful of cake. "You want us to put the word out?"

"Well, yes. Quietly. We might come up with something the investigator can use. He said he works closely with the police."

Ro squinted. "You're thinking if we get intel, he'll pass it to the cops."

Intel. Look at Ro going all *Charlie's Angels* on her.

"What about O'Brien?" Joey asked.

"No. He can't be involved. Conflict of interest. I'm afraid he'll get in trouble. Plus, he spoke to his lieutenant today and was told any information he gets should be passed on to another detective."

"Hold it," Dad said. "He can help you. You should use him."

Ew. That sounded . . . harsh. In her father's world, connections were everything. And when connections were made they were to be utilized. Not this time.

"No, Dad. I will not *use* him. If I need advice, I can ask him, but as it pertains to evidence, Tim is not an option. I won't do that."

"Seems to me—"

"No. Tim can't be involved. That's it."

"Hey, who the hell do you think you're talking to?"

"Relax, Joe," Mom said. "She's an adult. She told you what she wanted. Tim is her friend. She decides."

Yay, Mom.

The doorbell rang, still the same chime that Mom had

switched to after Dad had gone to prison. Rumor had it that he wanted the old chime back, but she refused. Even the doorbell was evidence of Mom's newfound independence. Prior to Dad going away, whatever he wanted, he got.

Now?

Not so much.

Ro stood. "Allow me. It'll give me something to do with my hands since I shouldn't be eating this damned cake."

Joey's mouth opened—*please, don't let him say something sexual*—and then immediately closed. *Phew.* Maybe her brother was actually learning some restraint.

"Anyway," Lucie said, "what do you all think? Can we start making some calls? See if anyone knows anything?"

Dad shrugged. "Baby girl, I was on this the minute those cops left this morning. Someone knows something."

"And," Mom added. "I can put the Franklin Press into action. You know nothing gets by those ladies."

As annoying as the Franklin Press—aka the town gossips —could be, they knew how to get a message out.

The bell rang again and Lucie glanced over just as Ro swung the door open. "Well, hello there."

Oh, wow. *Wow, wow, wow.*

At the sight of Tim standing in the doorway, still in his suit from work, his shirt open at the collar and no tie, a burst of excitement plowed through Lucie.

He's here.

She hustled to the door, and something sparked in his deep-green eyes. She liked that about him, that when he looked at her, even with the chaos she constantly inflicted on him, his eyes sparkled.

Ro stepped away and gave him a finger wave. "Nice seeing you, O'Hottie."

"Beat it." Lucie elbowed Ro from the door and huddled closer to Tim. "Hi."

"Hi."

"Is everything okay?"

"Yep."

Lucie smiled. "Good. I wasn't expecting you. It's a nice surprise. A *great* surprise."

"You said you were having a meeting."

After he said he'd have to stay out of the case and knowing that Lucie had planned a family meeting tonight, he'd come over anyway. *Wow, wow, wow.*

She angled back, waved her hand at her crazy crew still at the dining room table. "Yes. We're in the middle of it. I can cut it short though. I don't want you—"

"Tim," Mom called, "have some cake."

He grinned down at Lucie. "I gotta have cake."

"Are you sure you want to deal with this? I mean, cake with my family? It might be easier to take your own eye out."

He eased closer, squeezed her forearm. "It's all good, Luce. Let's do this."

He focused on her, held her stare for a solid ten seconds while the words tumbled in her brain. "But you could get in trouble."

"Not if I'm careful."

He didn't care. He'd risk his job, a job he'd dedicated himself to, worked endless hours for, to help her.

"Oh, my God, Tim O'Brien. You might be the best man I've ever met."

That got a smile out of him. A wicked one. Lucie wished they were alone so she could make those lips do things other than smile. She'd kiss those lips right from his face.

"Hey," Joey yelled. "Are we done with this meeting,

or what?"

Lucie turned back. "Pipe down! And no, we're not done yet. Tim is here to help."

WHAT THE HELL WAS HE DOING?

Tim scooped the last bite of some truly fantastic lemon pound cake into his mouth and savored the buttery flavor melting on his tongue.

Like his family, the Rizzos enjoyed good food. He could live with that. Even if it did cost him an extra thirty minutes in the gym.

Beside him, Lucie jotted notes on a pad she'd retrieved from the sideboard. As always, his girl was supremely organized, listing who would be doing what in her quest to clear her name.

Any sane man in his position—"sane" being the key word—wouldn't be here. To say he was straddling the conflict-of-interest line was an understatement. Maybe he wasn't sharing information with the Rizzos, and maybe they hadn't said anything that would change the outcome of the case, but they were making a plan.

And he wasn't just listening. He was participating. At least in a passive way that allowed him to agree that something was a good or a bad idea.

"Tim," Lucie's father said, "what's the word from the cops about all this?"

Lucie flicked her pencil at him. "No, Dad. He can't."

Tim sat back, assumed his hands-on-thighs relaxed-but-not-too-relaxed position. "She's right, Mr. Rizzo. I can't comment. Not because I don't want to. I do. But if something goes wrong and Lucie is somehow implicated, given the high profile of the Maxmillian dress, the local media would go nuts. Add to that her personal relationship with a detective that's even remotely involved, she'll get eaten alive. It'll hurt her." He looked up at Lucie. "And I won't allow that."

"Oh," Lucie said, "that was a good answer."

"Sure was," Ro said.

Joe Rizzo leaned in, rested his arms on the table and fiddled with the handle of his coffee mug. "How's this gonna work then? Your seeing my daughter and being a cop. I mean, I got my people all over the street on this. My guess? Soon, someone, somewhere is gonna know something about this dress."

That was the thing about criminals, their information network was vast. If only they'd used it on the right side of the law. "Take any relevant information to Detective Bickel."

"Not you."

"Noooo. Not me. Call Bickel."

"Are you nuts or what? You want *me* to go to the cops?"

"Dad!"

Good point. That might be interesting though. A mob boss strolling into headquarters with information regarding an armed robbery.

"It's all right, Lucie. Let's speak hypothetically here. If your dad has a . . . source . . . he'd like to protect, you could go to the insurance company's investigator. As long as he has the proof, and depending on what that proof is, he might not need to reveal where he obtained the information. And, let's face it, the investigator wants to find that dress as much as you do. He wants to go back to his client and prove to them why they don't have to pay out that million-dollar claim. He'd be a great ally for you."

Yeah, definitely straddling that line now. He should just shut the hell up and get out of here.

But Lucie tapped her pencil on the table, her lips slightly puckered as she rolled that idea around. "He gave me his card and told me to call him if anything came up. I could just slide any tips along to him. Call me his confidential informant."

Joe Rizzo pounded his fist on the table hard enough to rattle the china, the utensils and Tim's teeth. "You're no snitch!"

Jeez, this was complicated.

"Joe," Mrs. Rizzo said, "stop that yelling. You're insane. Who said anything about her being a snitch. She's trying to save herself here; and, frankly, you should be agreeing with just about anything, because *your* history isn't exactly helping." Mrs. Rizzo stood, began stacking plates, smacking them together hard enough that they should have shattered. "Do you think they'd be doing this to her if her last name wasn't Rizzo?"

Actually, all of it was standard procedure. Tim wasn't about to let that fly.

Joey shoved up from the table. "I'm out. Meeting over. Time to go."

Mrs. Rizzo, her eyes stricken, looked over at him. "You're leaving?"

"Yes, ma'am. It's about to get seriously ugly in here, and I don't want to be in the middle of it." He slashed his hand across his throat then grabbed the back of Ro's chair. "Let's go, Ro."

Lucie saw the wisdom and scooped up her notepad. "He's right, Mom. We're done here. The investigator is the way to go. No sense arguing about ancillary things that won't do us any good. For now, any and all tips get funneled to me, and I'll get them to the investigator. Problem solved. Now, get to work, people."

6

FIN-THE-STALLER WAS at the top of his game today. By nine thirty he and Lucie had barely hit the halfway mark of his walk. Already, the morning schedule was blown.

And worse, Fin decided to plop his fuzzy butt just feet from the auction house. The scene of the crime.

The morning chill hadn't broken yet; and Lucie tilted her head back, closed her eyes. She drew a long breath of dewy, moist air, focused on it moving down her throat and into her lungs.

I can do this.

She opened her eyes, peered down at Fin, still lounging on the sidewalk. "Here's the deal." She slid his treat bag out of her fanny pack and shook it. "You knock it off with these breaks, and you'll get two extra treats when we get back to your house. Two, Fin. Is that a deal?"

She shook the bag again and—*voilà*—Fin stood. Finally, he understood English.

"Good boy," she gushed, giving him a rub under his chin.

She stowed the treat bag, and Fin whimpered. But she wasn't falling for that trick. No sir. A deal was a deal.

"Let's go, Fin."

If he didn't stop again, in another thirty yards they'd be looping around the corner and heading back. *Please, please, please.* No time to spare after his morning antics.

"Ms. Rizzo?"

Lucie swung her head right, spotted a man walking toward her from the back door of the auction house.

"What now?" she muttered.

Fin pitched himself forward and let out a loud woof. The man halted then stepped back, hands in front of him. "Is he friendly?"

"That depends."

What a load that was. Fin may have had a scary bark, but if the man got within licking distance, Fin would unleash the tongulator. What was it with the dogs she walked? Every darned one of them was a love bug.

What she needed was a scary-ass dog. Maybe then she wouldn't get into these dustups.

The man kept his distance, hands still outstretched. "I'm Lewis Dukane. I own the Maxmillian dress."

What could he want with her?

Fin pitched forward again, and Lucie set her hand on his back, gave a slight squeeze. "Sit, Fin."

Miracle of all miracles, he actually sat. Although, it had been three minutes since his last siesta.

"Hello, Mr. Dukane. I'm very sorry about the dress."

"Yes, thank you. It's a terrible shock. Thankfully, it's insured, but this?" He ran his hand down his face. "I never expected anything like this."

"I'm sure."

"Ms. Rizzo, please, is there anything you remember from the other day? Anything at all? The insurance company won't pay the claim until the investigation is complete. It's so frustrating. I've lost the dress, and the claim is in limbo. I'm stuck."

Wow. Way too much information to tell a stranger. Lucie shook her head. "I'm sorry. I've told the police everything I can. I didn't see the robbery. I was on this side of the building, and the men went out the other side."

"Are you sure? There's nothing that felt off? Estelle told me you walk by here every day. It could be something small. A strange car even."

She'd love to help this man, but . . . nothing. Nothing about that day, aside from talking with the auction-house manager, was different.

"I'm sorry, sir. I told the police and the insurance investigator everything. The only odd thing was chatting with Estelle. Otherwise, it was a normal walk."

But, whoa, fella, the sneer he leveled on her sent all the wrong energy spewing, and Fin hopped to his feet.

"I *see*," Mr. Dukane said, his voice gritty, yet sharp.

Fin responded with a low growl of his own.

All righty, then. Maybe she had a killer on her hands after all.

"Stay, Fin."

He swung his head up, but ignored her command. Nothing new there. Except Mr. Dukane stepped back. *Good job, Fin.*

"It's not that I don't want to help. I do. There's just nothing more I can tell you."

"Unless you're involved."

"Hey!"

"I thought I could appeal to you. Beg for your help.

Obviously, that's not going to happen. Given your family ties, I shouldn't be surprised."

Yep. There it was. The real reason he pounced on her this morning.

Not only did she sense it, but so did Fin. He tilted his snout up and sent three rapid-fire barks Mr. Dukane's way.

"For all I know," Mr. Dukane continued, "maybe the robbers made a deal with you. You pretend you didn't see anything, and you get a cut of whatever they make on the dress. I should have expected it from the likes of you."

Lucie's mouth flew open. Now that was enough. More than enough. She'd been minding her owned darned business, trying to make a living—an honest living—and he had the nerve to insult her and her family.

People. For years she'd been shying away from the gossips, pretending to ignore what people said about her family. Well, no more. No more hiding, no more shrinking away, no more shame. "There is no need for that. *Sir.*"

Fin, bless his devoted soul, lifted his leg.

No.

"Fin!"

Too late. A steady stream of urine soaked Mr. Dukane's pant leg and panic shot right out of Lucie's pores. After a few seconds of stunned silence, the man's eyes bulged and his face twisted, its color deepening. This was so not good. Not good, not good, not good.

Instinctively, Lucie slid in front of Fin. Just in case lunatic Dukane got any violent ideas.

"Teach that dog some manners! Do you know what this suit cost?"

Well, too bad. He deserved it. In fact, she wouldn't mind Fin peeing on Dukane's other leg. *Bad, Lucie. Bad.*

"Hey." She poked a finger at him. "I'm giving you slack.

You've had a tough couple of days, but accusing me of a crime is way out of line. Way out." Fin barked and Lucie squeezed his leash in case he made a leap for it. Right now she was mad enough to let him do it. Just let him take a chunk out of this jerk. "You don't know anything about me. What gives you the right to interrupt my workday with this slander? Be careful, Mr. Dukane, I might just sue you. And then you'll have a much bigger problem than a missing dress. Now, I have work to do. Let's go, Fin."

She stepped around Mr. Dukane, being careful not to come in contact with him. For all she knew, she could bump him and wind up with an assault charge.

Ooh, the rotten bastard. The absolute, bone-deep nerve. She'd like to wrap her hands around that skinny neck of his and just strangle him.

But no.

If she did that, she'd be everything the people in this city thought. The mob princess. All that nonsense about rising above would be a lie. A scam.

But, *God,* the naysayers were never-ending. They just kept coming and coming and coming.

"I'm so tired of people doing this, Fin. I really am."

Breathe. That's all she needed to do. Just keep moving and breathing and the anger would wash away.

Shake it off.

A Chevy with a broken grille turned the corner and—oh, no—slowed as it came closer. She knew that car. Dammit, this day. The driver pulled to the open spot in front of the fire hydrant across the street and peered out at her.

She met the gaze of Detective Bickel and nodded despite the collapsing of her insides. When Bickel didn't move from behind the wheel, Lucie turned her attention back to Fin. "Maybe he's not here for us."

Probably wishful thinking, but a girl could hope.

The dog swung his head up, clearly sensing the rotten energy. It probably shot right through the leash. He nuzzled her leg, running his snout up and down; and she dropped to her knees, right there on the sidewalk, and hugged him. Just wrapped both arms around him and squeezed, and he rewarded her with licks. Her cheeks, her chin, her neck, everywhere he could get. All that love just for her.

At least until her phone rang. Still on her knees and getting tongulated—ooh, that sounded bad—she slipped the phone from her bag. Tim. First Fin and now O'Hottie. Things were picking up. "Sit, Fin." She shoved his rear down, and he went into siesta mode. "Good boy." She tapped the screen. "Hi."

"Good morning. How's your day so far?"

"Don't ask."

"Uh-oh."

"Is it legal for someone to accuse someone else of a crime?"

"It's not even ten o'clock. What the hell happened?"

She'd love to tell him. Absolutely would. Because Tim, being the man he was, would offer some form of comfort. He'd talk her down.

But when it came to this case, he couldn't be involved, and she wasn't about to risk getting him fired. "Forget it."

"Don't do that. Talk to me. It's about the case?"

"Yes. But nothing to do with evidence. It won't move the investigation along."

"Then right now I'm a guy talking to his girlfriend."

Girlfriend. There was that word again. She was his girlfriend, and this a private conversation. She hoped. "Your buddy Detective Bickel is watching me. I think."

"Where are you?"

"By the auction house. I'm walking Fin, and he just pulled up."

Tim made a noise she couldn't quite decipher. "He's probably keeping tabs on you. Adding some pressure."

"Well, it's working. And the owner of the Maxmillian dress was waiting for me at the auction house."

"Really."

A woman heading to the bus stop, stepped over Lucie without even breaking stride. Gotta love city life.

"Sorry," she said, then went back to Tim. "Yes. Mr. Dukane implored me to tell the police everything I know. I told him I had, and he accused me of being in on the robbery. Because, after all, I'm Joe Rizzo's kid."

"Shithead."

"Thank you."

"Did you kick him in the shins?"

"No."

"Want me to?"

Lucie grinned. Tim. Always on her side. "No."

"I could punch him."

Now she laughed. A good, solid gurgle that sent the misery of the last few minutes on the run. "Maybe. Let me think about it."

"You do that. Put Dukane out of your head. He's pissed because the insurance company won't pay his claim right away."

"So he takes it out on me?"

"I didn't say it was right. It's not. Believe me, don't let anything he says get under your skin. You're better than that. You know it, and everyone who loves you knows it."

"Wow. Detective, that was quite a speech."

"Did it work?"

She rolled to the side to stand. At least until Fin,

thinking it was playtime, pounced, the force of his front paws shoving her backward flat on her rear. The dog was an absolute animal. "Off, Fin."

"Luce? You okay?"

She snorted as Fin shoved his snout into her ear and licked. Licked again. Lucie squealed and shoved him away, which only made the lovefest more impassioned. He climbed on top of her, pinning her shoulders to the ground, licking her cheeks—*lick*—nose—*lick*—chin—*lick.*

"Off!"

"Luce?"

"I'm okay. Hang on." She dropped the phone, held Fin at bay with both hands, wiggled from under him and sat up. "Fin, you are just ridiculous."

She picked up the phone, shoved her hair out of her face and smoothed it. "Holy cow, that was crazy. Fin just licked inside my ear."

"Lucky damned dog."

Snort. "Hardy har, Detective."

"You all right now?"

She rolled to her feet, tugged her jacket down and adjusted her fanny pack. "I'll live. You're a terrific guy, Tim O'Brien. I just want you to know that."

"Glad to hear it because you're not getting rid of me anytime soon. I gotta go. I'll call you later. Do me a favor, and don't let anyone else lick inside your ear."

———

At eleven, Lucie marched into Coco Barknell, still feeling the aftereffects of Mr. Dukane's barbs. Tim had done a fine job of distracting her, but every time she thought about that awful encounter, it blurred her vision.

Something had to be done to get this investigation moving faster. Ro sat at her desk, fingers flying across her laptop keyboard, her nails click-click-clicking as they slammed the keys. She'd piled her long hair on top of her head, securing it with one of those eighties-style banana clips. Lucie didn't even know they still made those things. Perched on Ro's nose were the drugstore readers she insisted she needed. Probably just a ruse to make herself look more studious. At least she sprung for the expensive, faux-tortoiseshell frames.

"Hi," Lucie said.

Ro tipped her head down, gave Lucie a stern-librarian stare over the rims of her glasses. "Hey. You're back early."

She tossed her messenger bag on the conference table and slid behind her desk. "I'm preoccupied with this stolen dress, so I had Lauren cover the afternoon walks for me."

"Everything okay? You seem . . . edgy."

"Aside from being accused of being a thief? I'm fine." She slapped her palms on the desk. "No. That's a lie. I hate it that every time something goes wrong people automatically assume the worst of me because I'm a Rizzo."

"Well . . ."

"And don't try to tell me I shouldn't let it bother me. That's crap, and you know it."

Ever the drama queen, Ro swung her hands over her head. "Whoa. Relax, Sister. All I wanted to say was that not all people assume that. And the ones who do don't know you."

"Oh, huh. Sorry. And thank you for being on my side."

"Always. What crawled up your bootie today?"

"Can you believe the owner of that dress was waiting for me when I walked Fin this morning? He marched right up, asked me if there was anything else I remembered and then implied that maybe I was in on it."

Ro sat back, looked at her over the rims of her glasses again. "I'm telling you, men are idiots. That's all I have for you. I'm sorry. If I get started it'll be a bloodbath, and that'll be a great way to ruin a perfectly fine day. And I'm not in the mood to bury a body today. Whoever he is, he's not worth jail time. We're too good for that."

Leave it to Ro to cut right to the heart of the matter. But, yes, she was right. Mr. Dukane *was* a moron.

The rage she'd felt during that encounter had already drained her. And her energy bucket only had so much to spare. With all that had gone on, she was already down to half.

"You're right. I can't let him get to me. Please, give me some good news. Anything. What are you working on?"

"Leads."

Perfect. New business opportunities. "What leads?"

She shrugged. "I'm trolling doggie message boards."

Lucie cracked up. Thank God for Ro making her laugh when, once again, her life had been thrown into a bout of chaos. "That sounds a little twisted."

"Laugh all you want." She slapped her hand on her ever-present spiral notebook and swung it in the air. "I've got three lists going. One with target retailers, one with design ideas and one for wholesalers."

Now that was interesting. "Seriously?"

"Yes. You find all kinds of stuff on message boards. For instance, there are three pet-accessory boutiques downtown that we didn't know about. I mean, Lucie, how did we miss that? This afternoon, I'll take them some samples, see what we can do. And, did you know there's a market for doggie skiwear?"

"Now I know you're joking."

Again with the stern-librarian glare. "I never joke when it comes to revenue. And winter is coming. I'll work with your mom on some new designs. I'm thinking ski jackets— with faux-fur collars for the girls."

A lot of times Lucie humored Ro. This would be one of them. Then again, they'd managed to build a business on blinged-out dog collars and coats. Why should skiwear be any different?

"I bet we could get Jeanette at Sammy Spaniel to put a few pieces out for us as a test run."

Sammy Spaniel, an upscale dog boutique in Chicago, had been Coco Barknell's first retail client.

"Exactly what I was thinking. Great minds." Ro's computer dinged, and she went back to scanning. "A new message."

"Anything good?"

"No. Just some dope trying to pick up women. You can't be too casual about these message boards. There are some real freaks out there."

"Well, sure. It's the Internet. And then if you get into the Deep Web, it gets really crazy. Tons of criminal activity out there. We just don't see it."

Kinda like her completely missing two guys stealing a million-dollar slice of movie history.

Message boards.

"Uh-oh," Ro said. "You have a look. That one you get right before the randomly floating ideas in your brain come together."

Lucie hustled over and shoved Ro from the chair. "Move."

"Knew it." Ro grabbed one of the two guest chairs in

front of the desk and slid it around next to Lucie. "What are you thinking?"

"This message-board thing. You're a genius."

Ro gave her the over-the-rims look again. "As if we didn't know that?"

"I'm talking about our dress investigation. As popular as that dress is, there have to be hundreds of message boards out there. The fans of the movie are rabid. Someone, some-where, has to be talking about this dress going missing."

"I like it, supersleuth."

Lucie did a search for Maxmillian-dress message boards. It took less than three seconds to get over two million results.

"Two million. Yowzer."

"Don't panic. We'll split the list."

Split the list? Was she insane? Well, she was Ro. Ro equaled insanity. Still, they weren't researching one million sites each. "We need to shorten the list."

"Be more specific with your keywords."

Lucie grinned. "Look at you, all Internet savvy."

"Blah, blah. Shut it. Try searching for most popular Maxmillian message boards."

That narrowed them to just over one million, and Lucie held her hands palm out. "Okay. Progress."

The third link on the screen led to the movie fan club's website. She tapped the screen. "If I were a rabid fan looking for info, I'd start at the fan club."

The doggie bells jangled, and Joey walked in. He'd finally ditched his basketball shorts —hello, it's October—for what looked like expensive jeans and a long-sleeved Henley. Her brother had always been handsome. In a caveman sort of way. But recently his looks had changed.

His dark hair was cut shorter, his clothing choices a little sharper, his shave a little closer.

Gee, wonder whose influence that is?

"Hey, handsome," Ro said.

He swung his gaze first to Ro, then to Lucie. "This looks dangerous. What are you nutty broads doing?"

"We, my love—" *My love? Blech.* "—are researching message boards."

"What the hell for?"

"Rabid Maxmillian fans."

Joey rolled his eyes. "You geniuses think you're gonna find that dress on a *message* board?" He stepped closer, shoved Lucie's hands away from the keyboard. "Get the hell off there. Do you know what kind of lunatics hang out on those message boards?"

Lucie scooped up the laptop, clutched it to her chest. "It's not like we're talking to anyone. We're just looking."

"Right. And what if you find something? You gonna tell me you didn't plan on commenting. Maybe throwing some feelers out there. Please. I know you two. If there's trouble, you'll find it."

"Seems to me," Ro said, "we've done pretty darned well when we've teamed up."

"Yeah." Lucie set the laptop down and clicked one of the fan club links. "Here we go. Maxmillian Fan Forum. A chat room devoted to lovers of the Maxmillian couture dress. Let's just see what we've got here."

Joey's phone beeped from somewhere in the vicinity of his pocket, and he checked the screen. "This is Dad. I gotta go. You two want lunch?"

"No," they both said.

The last thing Lucie needed was their father horning in

on this chat-room thing. "Joey, I'm begging you, keep him at Petey's. He keeps popping in here, disrupting our day."

"I know. But give him a break. He's been in a cage for two years. Walking down the street is a big deal right now."

Lucie hadn't considered that. The feeling of being locked away, controlled to the point where you couldn't leave a room, grab a snack from the fridge, open a window.

And all that time she'd been mad at her dad for his life-style, for leaving their mother alone. For humiliating them. Her father was no saint, and maybe that derision had been well earned; but just once, she could have meant it when she'd asked how he'd been feeling.

"Huh," Lucie said. "I never thought of it that way."

"He can be a pain in the ass, but throw him a bone every now and again. Have lunch with him. Or go for coffee."

Lucie turned to Ro, who'd said almost the exact thing to her the day before. "Did you tell him to say that?"

She grinned. "No. He's smart and doesn't need me to tell him things like that."

Joey's phone beeped again. "I gotta go. You two be careful on those message boards. And whatever you do, don't comment."

7

———

"Oн, Sister, I think I got something."

Thank God.

Two hours forty-two minutes and thirty-nine seconds they'd been scouring the Internet. Ro worked the message boards, while Lucie researched all things props and the making of *Peacock Island.*

Lucie shot up from her chair and stormed across the room to Ro's desk, where rays from the early-afternoon sun soaked the front of the room in warmth. "What did you find?"

"Cock Heads."

"*Excuse* me?"

"I found an underground fan club. The Cock Heads."

Lucie gagged. "Ew. That's kinda gross."

"Yeah, well, from what it says on this message board it's a takeoff of the official fan club, The Peacocks. The Peacocks' message board has too many rules—I guess they're prudes—so a group of renegade fans started this little subculture."

"And to piss off the prudes, they called themselves *Cock* Heads?"

"So it seems. But, look at their membership. The second group far outnumbers the official group."

Ro scrolled to the top of the screen and clicked the "home" button. "They have their own website and everything."

"Click on the 'about' button. Let's see what it says."

A screen with a photo of a peacock and several paragraphs popped up. Lucie tapped the screen. "Right here. It says there are ten thousand Cock He—uh, members. Only three thousand belong to the official fan group. That's rather interesting." Another link led to a membership page, and Lucie tapped it. "Click this link."

Another screen with a form to join the group popped up. Along with the form was an invitation to attend a meeting. Free of charge for the first time. Below that a search box. Ro typed in their zip code, and the little hourglass churned for a few seconds before spitting out a list of meetings broken down by town. There had to be thirty locations in the Chicago area alone.

Lucie leaned over Ro's shoulder. "There are meetings all over the place."

"And every day at different times."

"These people make Trekkies look like amateurs. We need more info on them. Maybe go to a meeting."

"Honey," Ro said, "I go to a Cock Head meeting every time I see my rat-bastard, stripper-banging husband and his legion of lawyers."

Oh, ouch. Despite her bravado, the divorce had taken an emotional chunk out of Ro. It was all so . . . unnecessary. The heartbreak, the fighting, the holding on.

Tommy had cheated—not to mention the disgusting, vile way he'd done it—and now he wanted to punish her for leaving him?

Lucie set her hand on Ro's shoulder. "I'm sorry he's putting you through this. Are you any closer to a settlement?"

"Eh. Getting there. He's pissed about Joey. Ironic, isn't it? As if humiliating me in front of our friends and families wasn't worse than me dating a great guy. Stupid stripper-banger." She went back to the computer. "Don't get me started. I'm trying to move on and just thinking about it makes me crazy. Anyhoo, if my BFF wants to go see a bunch of Cock Heads, I'm all for it. You know I love an adventure."

The more Lucie considered the idea, the more it grew on her. "We could just go check it out. Maybe start up a conversation about the dress being stolen. See if we get any good dirt." She pointed to the screen. "Find us a meeting for tonight. Lucie and Ro ride again."

AT SEVEN O'CLOCK SHARP, LUCIE AND RO STROLLED INTO THE Java Pit, a cute little coffee house in an ancient brick building on Chicago's West Side. The place had a cool vibe. Kind of artsy with abstract prints on the walls, but the metal coffee pot and mugs scattered along shelves offered a homey feel.

The place wasn't very large. Only seven tables with a bar and another five stools. A couple sat at the back table, huddled together and giggling.

Lucie paused just inside the doorway, let the aroma of freshly brewed coffee bring her senses alive.

"It smells so good in here. Now I have to have coffee."

"Just make it decaf," Ro said. "You know the regular will keep you up tonight and then you'll be crabby tomorrow. And I'm not dealing with that."

"Good point."

"Can I help you, ladies?" the young guy behind the bar asked.

"Hi," Lucie said. "We're here for the . . . uh . . ."

"Just say it," Ro muttered.

But Lucie couldn't get the words out. They just sat there, on her tongue, ready to be spewed, but . . . no.

She turned to Ro, shook her head and was rewarded with an eye roll that could have knocked the building down. Ro marched toward the bar, swinging her hips and everything else attached to her. "We're here for the *Cock Head* meeting."

And, wow, that was loud. But the cute barista laughed. "Yeah. They're upstairs. Go straight back, and take the stairs up. If you want something to drink, though, you gotta get it here. No service up there."

"Okay," Lucie said. "I'll have a latte."

"Nonfat," Ro said. "Decaf. Make it two."

Lattes in hand, Ro led the charge upstairs. "I can't wait to see what these people look like. The website said some of them come in costume. Costume!"

"What kind of costumes?"

"Replicas of the dress. Peacock headbands. That kind of thing. It looked a little looney."

Lucie grabbed Ro's arm, stopped her midway up the steps. "Did you tell Joey we were coming here?"

"Please, girl. Are you kidding? He would have blown his stack. After we get home, I'll tell him. All I have to do is strip, and he forgets why he was mad."

That information Lucie didn't need, and a little vomit backed up in her throat. *Blech.* "I didn't tell anyone, either. No one knows we're here."

"So? You think a bunch of insane Cock Heads are going

to kidnap us from the second floor of a coffee house? What are they gonna do, toss us out a window?"

When put like that, it did sound far-fetched. But hey, this was Chicago, and Lucie's last name was Rizzo. Anything could happen. "I don't know. They could be dangerous."

"Tell you what, if they are, I have enough anger in me that'll I'll open a can of whoop-ass they won't soon forget. And if they're men, even better. They'll be the Cockless Heads by the time I get done with them."

"Oh, just, ew."

Ro laughed. "Do you want to leave? Say it now, and we're gone. But we schlepped all the way down here, we should at least check it out."

Another good point. This whole damned situation was just . . . unsettling. As a matter of general safety, someone should know where they were. Just in case.

She should text Tim.

That's what she'd do. Just send him a casual text saying hi and that she and Ro were at the Java Pit sharing a coffee. He didn't need to know they were chasing Cock Heads.

She shoved her coffee at Ro and dug through her purse for her phone. "I'm texting Tim. If we come up missing, he'll know where to look first."

"If we come up missing he'll trace your phone. But suit yourself and text him."

Lucie blew raspberries at her, and Ro laughed. After sending the text, Lucie grabbed her coffee and took a breath. "You ready?"

"Waiting on you, sweet cheeks. "

At the top of the steps an open door led to a large rectangular room decorated in the same style as the first floor. Near the windows sat a group of about two dozen folks who'd gathered a series of four-top tables into a weird semicircle so they could all see each other. Other patrons filled in the surrounding tables. Not a bad turnout.

A tall, heavyset woman pushed out of her chair and headed for them.

"Give me strength," Ro whispered.

No fooling there. The woman wore a replica of the Maxmillian dress and a headband with peacock feathers poking at least twelve inches into the air.

"I gotta get a picture," Ro said.

"Ssshhh. Be serious. We have to act like Cock Heads."

"Hello," the woman said, a big smile spreading across her face. "Are you here for the meeting?"

"Um, yes," Lucie said. "We're thinking about joining."

"Ooh." The woman clapped. "Everyone! Potential new members. Let's all be nice."

The crowd raised a cheer, then went back to their individual conversations while the woman focused on Lucie and Ro.

"We always love having new members. I'm Annabelle. Please, come in."

"Thank you."

Lucie fell into step behind Annabelle, who led them toward the group at the far end of the room. As they walked, she pointed to a table with various items, pins, T-shirts, headbands, all sporting peacock feathers.

"We have some spiritwear available for purchase if you'd like one. The headbands are my favorite. They're all a little different. Some are ten dollars. The more elaborate range from thirty to fifty."

Yowzer.

Ro stopped in front of the table and perused the items, her gaze landing on a headband similar to Annabelle's. She picked it up, studied the placement of the feathers. After a few seconds, she flipped the band over, ran her finger along the edge, probably checking for errant glue that held the feathers in place.

She gave Lucie the same stern-librarian look she'd given her earlier in the day, only without the glasses. "The craftsmanship on these is quite good."

"Thank you," Annabelle said. "One of our members makes them. Of course, the feathers aren't the double-eyed, but we do what we can."

Ro held up the headband. "I'll take this one."

"Wonderful. We love enthusiastic new members. That'll be fifty dollars."

A gag broke from Lucie's throat. She slapped her chest, swallowed back the sudden hairball. "Sorry. The acid reflux is a killer."

Ro sighed, but in terms of recoveries, Lucie didn't think she'd done half bad.

"Luce, you should get a headband."

Not a chance. "I'm good. Thanks. Maybe a T-shirt on the way out."

Ro forked over her fifty dollars, while Lucie contemplated the madness of paying so much for something Ro could have whipped out herself in three minutes. Maybe less. Ro was all about getting into character when the two of them did these mini-missions, so Lucie chalked it up to dedication.

When it came to parting with her own hard-earned money, Lucie wasn't nearly as committed to the cause.

Transaction complete, Ro plopped the hideous headband on, gave the feathers a fluff and winked at Lucie. "Let's do this, girlfriend."

"Helloooo, all." Ro did one of her flirty finger waves to the group. "I'm Roseanne and this is my friend Lucie."

All at once the group responded with various greetings. *"Goedeavond. Bonsoir. Shalom."*

An absolute United Nations of Cock Heads. Friendly bunch, though. One of the men, an older gentleman with salt-and-pepper hair and funky, horn-rimmed glasses, grabbed two chairs from an empty table, while the others made room for Lucie and Ro to squeeze in.

Before setting her purse on the floor, Ro checked her phone. "Joey just called me. And texted. He wants to know where we are. Let me text him. That'll keep him at bay for an hour."

Ro fired off her text just as Lucie's phone buzzed from her back pocket. "Whoopsie. Someone is looking for me, too."

She swiped the screen, saw two texts. She must have missed the first one. Tim. Just responding to her incognito if-we-get-kidnapped text and telling her to have fun and call him when she got home. Easy enough. The second message was Joey. Asking where the eff she and Roseanne were.

"Joey texted me, too. Don't tell him where we are."

Ro waved that off. "I told him to keep his pants on, and I'd call him later."

With that, she turned her phone off, shoved it back into her purse and gave the table at large her attention. Already Lucie could see the clusters. The three people huddled together directly across from them, a young couple holding hands, three twenty-something women with green hair. Then there were the two men and two women sitting bolt upright, hands to themselves, staring straight ahead. Obviously, they'd each come to the meeting on their own. Not wanting to stare, Lucie chose not to scan the rest of the group and brought her gaze back to her latte. Might as well have a gulp while Ro did her thing. Within seconds, her BFF worked the table, and chatter erupted all around.

They'd gotten pretty good at these investigations over the last few months. The general system required Ro to chat up the group, asking semileading questions while Lucie quietly observed and committed everything to memory.

They were, in short, a great team.

Annabelle stood and tapped her long nails against one of the water glasses. "Attention, everyone." The group immediately piped down. Even Ro. Lucie might have to put Annabelle on the payroll. "Such a great crowd tonight. And we have guests—this is Roseanne and Lucie. Welcome to the Cock Heads, ladies. We won't introduce everyone, but we have several board members and volunteers here tonight, so we'll let them say hello."

Ten minutes later, they'd gone around the table, and Lucie and Ro had the breakdown of the group. Two fashion students, one movie buff, one bored housewife and, to Lucie's delight, an investment banker. She'd never met him, but still considered him a comrade from her old life in corporate America.

Thank God she'd been downsized out of that mess.

"Annabelle," Ro said, "I just love your dress."

Annabelle beamed. "Thank you, Roseanne. I had it made. I brought the seamstress photos of the original, and, I have to say, she did an excellent job. Even the feathers are pointing in the right direction."

"I noticed that. It really does look like the original."

Okay, Columbo. Stop forcing the dress into the conversation.

Lucie kicked Ro under the table, connected with bone—probably her ankle—and she let out a yelp.

Annabelle's eyebrows shot up. "Problem?"

"No. Sorry. I banged my foot on the chair."

"Speaking of the Max," one of the fashion students said, "have we heard anything new? Any leads?"

Annabelle rotated her head left then right, moving so slow that Lucie found herself mimicking it.

"Nothing yet," she said. "I knew we'd have a big crowd tonight with all the activity surrounding the Max, so I checked with the police before I got here."

As if the police would give some lunatic Cock Head an update? Tim would love that one.

The bored housewife slapped her hand over her head. "I'm miserable over this. That auction has been on my calendar for months. I was so excited. Even if I couldn't bid on the dress, I would have been able to see it. Up close."

Ro leaned forward, swung left and made direct eye contact with the woman. "Honey, I feel your pain. We—Lucie and I—planned on going to the auction as well. We'd even hoped to bid."

Bid? Totally off-leash now.

From the corner of her eye, Lucie spotted the sidelong glance from Ro. Right along with the slight quirk at the corner of her mouth.

Game. On.

"I'm in the middle of a hellacious divorce, and making my husband pay when I won the bid on that dress was going to be my farewell gift to that rat-bastard. Now I have nothing. I'm so angry."

Lucie patted her arm. "I know. But don't fret. The dress *will* be found and we *will* bid on it."

A round of murmurs came from the table at large, some nodded their agreement while others said "hell yeah" and "that's awesome." The bored housewife gave a hearty "Amen!"

Blinking back tears—darn, she was good—Ro sniffed

and gently ran the tips of her fingers underneath her eyes. "You all are so wonderful. This has been *such* a trying time. But I know the dress will be recovered. It just upsets me. I wanted to teach that cheating bastard to have a little respect."

The housewife gasped. "A cheater. Men!"

"Hey." The younger guy at the end of the table held up a hand. "We're not all bad."

"Sorry," the housewife said. "But I get it, Roseanne. One of the moms in my son's playgroup just went through the same thing. We stay at home, cook, clean, pop out babies; but gain a little weight and as soon as some twenty-year-old shows a little interest in our man, it's over."

Lucie hadn't anticipated that speech and wasn't sure it was helping, but—too late now—she'd roll with it.

"Ro has always loved that dress. The auction would have come at a perfect time." Really laying it on, she once again patted Ro's arm. "Don't be sad. Sooner or later, the dress will surface."

"I hope so. I'd do just about anything to have it."

Bam. Mission complete. Ro had just put it out there, sent that sucker straight out into the universe, that she had the means—and the desperation—to do whatever it took to find the dress.

Now all they had to do was wait for the universe to respond.

AFTER THE MEETING ENDED AND RO AND LUCIE FILLED OUT the membership application, they tromped down the stairs and out the front door. A blast of cold wind smacked at Lucie's cheeks, and she zipped her jacket to her neck.

October in Chicago, like every other month, could be tricky. Being a lifelong resident Lucie had learned the fine art of layering.

"Roseanne!"

Whoopsie. The two of them spun back, and found Joey storming straight at them. He sidestepped around a group of people, nearly plowed into a lamppost and bumped a car along the way.

For a big guy, Joey could move.

"Uh-oh," Ro said. "Did you tell him where we were?"

"Heck no."

Before either of them could comment, Joey halted in front of them, his face full of hard angles. The mad face.

"What the hell are you two up to?"

Ro flung a hand toward the coffee shop. "Having coffee. What's your problem?"

The old ricochet move of putting it back on him. Excellent.

"Bzzzzttt. Nice try," he said. "We got a Starbucks ten minutes from your house. There's no way you two are coming all the way here for coffee. And what the hell are you wearing on your head?"

Instead of whipping her headband off, Ro gave the feathers a fluff. "My new headwear."

Oh. Brother.

Lucie stepped forward half an inch and threw her shoulders back. Not that it did any good since she was the petite one in the family. But she had experience when it came to her brother. "How did you know where we were?"

"I called Tim."

Of all the things he could have said, that one set her back. "Are you serious?"

"Yeah. Neither one of you answered. I got worried. We're

in the middle of this dress fiasco, and you two go off the grid. I called, and he told me you were here."

Ro looked at Lucie. "We didn't anticipate that. Good to know for next time."

Joey's mouth flew open. "Screw next time."

One of the Cock Heads' board members, a short, middle-aged man from the meeting, appeared next to Lucie and inserted himself between her and Joey. "Is there a problem here?"

"Hi, Wendel. No. No problem. This is my brother."

Wendel inched closer to Joey and tilted his head up. His own version of getting in his face. "He's getting a little *loud.*"

Under the glow of the street lamp, Joey's face went crimson, and Lucie swore it inflated an inch. That kind of pressure should have blown it clear off his body.

But kudos to her brother for keeping his hands at his sides.

"Who the hell is *this* now?"

Ro grabbed Joey's arm. "Relax. Why do you have to be such an animal?"

She led him away—*phew*—and Lucie blew out a breath. "Sorry, Wendel. He's very protective. Believe me, he means well. I'm so sorry if he made you nervous."

"No. Not at all. I can handle myself. I was concerned he'd get violent with you."

How sweet was this? Wendel, all five feet two and a hundred and thirty pounds of him, wanted to protect them. Who said chivalry was dead? Joey would have flattened him with one shot, but Wendel's willingness to help renewed Lucie's faith in humanity.

"Oh, he's just being my ape of a brother. He's harmless."

At least to his loved ones.

"All right. As long as you're safe. I guess I'll move along

now." Wendel held out his hand. "It was great meeting you, Lucie. I'm on the membership committee and will be loading all of your contact information into the database tonight. Let me know if you have any questions."

"Great. I'll do that. Thanks."

Wendel shuffled off, and a burst of heavy, drowning guilt fell on her. Here this guy thought she and Ro were devoted Cock Heads, and the whole thing had been a scam. A ruse to try and find information about the dress. The Max, as the group called it.

Not only had the meeting been a bust, Ro spent fifty bucks on a ridiculous headband, and they'd lied to these people.

"Luce!"

Feathers bouncing, towering heels barely slowing her down, Ro strutted toward Lucie. Alone.

"Where's Joey?"

"He just left."

"He's mad?"

"Of course. He's so sensitive lately. I love this protective streak in him, but he'll need medication if he keeps up with this constant worrying."

Lucie shrugged. "He loves us."

That made Ro smile. "Yeah, I guess he does. Come on. Let's go home. You can drop me by Joey's. By the time we get there, he'll have cooled off and I'll get naked. He'll forget all about this."

"Honestly, I don't need to hear this stuff. It gives me a visual I don't care for."

"What did Wendel say?"

"He'll add us to the database. I think our mission failed."

Ro linked her arm through Lucie's. "You never know. Something might come up."

SOME MORNINGS—LIKE THIS ONE— WERE MADE FOR LUCIE TO be outdoors.

The bright sun shone in a cloudless sky, and the crisp morning air tickled her cheeks. Perfection.

Buddy, the Wheaten Terrier aka the Wheaten Terrorist, stopped at the corner two blocks from his house and sniffed his favorite tree. He'd peed on that tree so many times, he should have a reserved sign on it.

By this time, already twenty-seven minutes into her first walk of the day, many of the residents on the block had gone to work or school, leaving their precious parking spaces open. Unlike Franklin, people in this neighborhood didn't put lawn chairs or garbage cans in their spot to save it. By five o'clock folks would be rushing home simply to snag parking.

While Buddy busied himself sniffing a rock at the base of his tree, Lucie tilted her head back and inhaled. In Chicago, a morning like this could never be considered cold, but it was enough for her to layer on some long-sleeved shirts and break out her favorite Notre Dame sweatshirt.

Today would be a good day.

Buddy finished sniffing and gave the tree his customary squirt. How that dog had an ounce of urine left in him was just short of a miracle. So far, he'd stopped at every tree, every plant, every leaf.

"Dude," Lucie said, "we need to get to the good stuff here. Give me a nice poop, and we're done."

But Buddy was no dummy. Believing he'd get a longer walk if he held off on a bowel movement, he would wait.

And wait.

And wait.

He knew what she wanted. And he knew that she knew that he knew. This was their own screwy little mind trick that occurred on a daily basis. In the early days, before Lucie had caught on to his scheming ways, she'd walk him until he did his business.

Then she wised up.

Now, the halfway point was exactly at the thirty-minute mark. If they went two miles or two feet, at thirty minutes she turned back.

Mind trick declassified.

Still, some days the little pain in the rear—no pun intended—waited until the last possible second. What he didn't know, and she refused to clue him in on by walking him longer, was if he didn't do his business she'd have to walk him until he did. That was the Coco Barknell customer guarantee.

A bowel movement on every outing.

Lucie's ringing phone destroyed the much-needed peace, and she sighed. The challenge—and excitement—of running a growing accessory line while continuing to service her dog-walking clients had started to string her out. The jam-packed days and constant activity set her brain in a state of slow motion. Every thought seemed to swirl, swirl, swirl falling just short of completion. Almost as if two critical wires needing to connect couldn't . . . quite . . . reach.

Exhaustion tended to do that. There simply wasn't enough Lucie to do it all. Something would have to give.

Her fuzzy brain begged for it.

The phone rang a third time, and she swiped the screen before it went to voicemail. As if it would kill her to allow a call to ring through. Maybe that was the answer. Just letting the calls go when she needed quiet.

Except, then she'd have to return a small mountain of

calls, leaving her with more to do. Yet another vicious cycle in the life of Lucie Rizzo.

"Hello?"

"Is this Lucie?"

Male voice. "Yes. Who's calling please?"

"Uh, Bill. I was at the meeting last night."

Bill. Lucie closed one eye, scrunched her nose and mentally replayed meeting the folks from the night before.

No Bill.

But there'd been a lot of people there, and not everyone had said their name.

Now, the bigger question: how the hell did Bill get her number? According to the membership form Lucie and Ro had filled out, only board members had access to members' contact information. And since all the board members had introduced themselves, it didn't take a genius to figure out that Bill, if he was indeed at the meeting, wasn't a board member.

Dang, she was good at this detective stuff.

"How can I help you, Bill?"

"I can help you."

Yes, folks, the creep factor has just exploded. First rule of engagement, know your enemy.

Of course, she'd just made that first rule up, but it sure sounded weighty. She'd roll with it because, whatever this guy was after, clearly he didn't know who her father was. Or that her new boyfriend was a cop.

Lucie clicked her tongue to get Buddy walking again. He looked up at her and curled his top lip back. Was that a smile or a sneer? He got moving and that's all that mattered.

"All right, Bill, how can you help me?"

Hopefully he wasn't some kind of twisted perv about to launch into dirty phone sex or something. Wouldn't that be great? A Cock Head moonlighting as a phone-sex operator and trolling new members for business. Talk about leads.

"You and your friend are interested in the Max."

The Max. "Well, as Cock Heads, I think we're all interested, aren't we?"

"Eh. Some more than others. You and your friend seemed more interested. Enough to try and bid on it."

Ah-ha! Maybe that meeting hadn't been a bust. But she still didn't know what the heck he wanted.

Buddy trotted to the next tree and started his sniffing ritual again. Hopefully, this would be it. The poop of all poops. "Yes. We'd intended to do that, but now the dress is gone."

"I know where it is."

I know where it is. Blood pounded into Lucie's brain and her vision looped and blurred and, holy cow, she had to close her eyes. *Get it together here, Luce.*

After a second, she opened her eyes, gripped the leash tighter simply for something to hang on to while the blood rush passed. "You know?"

"It's for sale on the black market. I have connections. For a fee, I can hook you up. Maybe get that hot little number in your hands."

Hot little number? Lucie wasn't sure about *that.* In truth, that dress was butt ugly with all those feathers covering the bottom half. Not to mention this would be an illegal transaction. Which they both knew and presumably understood.

But she needed a lead on the dress, and if this guy could give it to her, she'd at least have a starting place. Maybe she'd even pass that information to Tim. That could hardly be considered illegal.

"Are you interested?" Bill asked. "And, just so you know, this is a burn phone. No way to trace it. Don't bother going to the cops. I've got someone inside there, so I'll know and then I'll disappear. They won't believe you anyway. Will they Lucie *Riz-zo.*"

And, whoa. He knew who she was. Meaning, the deal just got a whole lot more serious because this guy would have to be the world's biggest idiot to try anything funky with Joe Rizzo's daughter.

"Yes," she said. "I'm interested."

8

———

Ro stood in front of Lucie's desk, hands on hips, shaking her head hard enough that her boobs bounced. Good thing Joey wasn't here or he'd make some lewd comment that would send Lucie into a meltdown. "Are you crazy?"

Lucie huffed out a breath. What a question to ask someone after a full day of walking dogs on Chicago streets. "Of course, I'm crazy. It shouldn't be a shock. You've been my best friend for twenty years, and you know my family. Enough said. Now, are you going to help me or not?"

"Let me get this straight. Some nutjob calls you up and says if you pay him ten grand he'll put you in touch with whoever stole that dress."

"Not exactly."

Ro laughed. "I do love you. What exactly then?"

"He said he'd hook me up with the person selling the dress. It might not be the actual thief."

Ro made snoring noises. "Whatever. Either way, this sounds like a shakedown. I think you should ignore him."

Oh, no she wouldn't. This lead needed to be followed. They should at least determine if the guy was legit. Well, illegally speaking legit. Lucie shoved three fingers against her forehead. *Focus.* "How is it a shakedown? He's not threatening me. All he's saying is if we want the dress, for $10,000 he'll help us get it."

"And what? You're gonna pay this loser? We don't even know who he is."

Lucie pointed to her mouth. "Watch my lips. I. Am. Not. Paying. Him. But I do want to get to whoever has the dress. I feel like I should tell Tim, but then I don't want to get him into the middle of it."

"So call that other detective."

She'd thought of that. Sure had. But her problem was she didn't trust Detective Bickel. Something about him unnerved her. Maybe it was his willingness to believe she was guilty simply because of her last name. Nothing he'd said indicated that, but she'd been Lucie Rizzo, Mob Princess, all her life. She knew the signs.

And Bickel had a blinking neon one.

"I don't trust him. Plus, Bill told me he had someone inside the PD. If I go to them, he'll bolt."

"You do realize he's probably lying, right?"

"Yes. But I can't risk it. I need to clear my name, and this is the first lead—sort of—that I have."

Hands still on her hips, Ro paced in front of Lucie's desk, her tight skirt limiting her stride. Lucie finally noticed that weight gain she'd been moaning about.

Not mentioning that. No sirrreeeee.

"My other option," Lucie said as Ro completed another lap, "is to call that investigator from the insurance company. We talked about that at our family meeting. He said he works hand-in-hand with the police. I could tell him what we've got, maybe set up a sting operation—"

Ro stopped walking and grinned. "Cop-speak. I love it."

"Pay attention. Please."

"Fine. Of all the options, I think that's the best." She waggled her hand. "If this investigator feels he can trust the cops, let him be the one to pass on the info. I'm telling you though, O'Hottie will be *pissed* if you don't tell him."

All of this, she knew. Still, she wouldn't put Tim in the middle of her legal fiasco. He deserved better. No matter where their relationship went, she respected him too much to leave him exposed to this madness. "It's best if he doesn't know. If something goes wrong, he'll be able to tell his supervisors he had no idea any of it was going on, and it'll be the truth. I don't want him getting in trouble. Or worse, losing his job. Not over me."

The tight-skirted one held up her hands. "It's your life. Don't say I didn't warn you. And, let's not tell Joey about this. If he hears someone is shaking you down, he'll be out of control. Even I won't be able to calm him. Boobs only get a girl so far."

Her brother was great when it came to backing her up, and in the last few months he'd really come to her rescue a few times, but lately his protective gene had gone to hyper-vigilance. Lucie suspected his relationship with Ro had caused it. Ro and Lucie were a team. Joey knew that. What Lucie did, Ro did. And vice versa.

Joey might be a class-A nudge, but when it came to people he cared about, people he loved, he became unstoppable.

His emotional attachment to Ro on top of his loyalty to family would double his firepower.

Emotional firepower.

A punch of realization, that light-bulb moment, hit her. Her brother's recent worse-than-usual looney behavior came into sharper focus. *Holy cow.* How had she not seen it?

Her brother was in love with her best friend.

Which meant, whatever she and Ro did, they needed to keep Joey *and* Tim out of it.

THE FOLLOWING MORNING, ERIC EDWARDS' ASSISTANT ushered Lucie, feeling seriously underdressed in her sneakers, baggy jeans and zip-up hoodie, into his office.

And what an office it was. All rich, well-oiled woods, walls painted the warmest beige and carpeting that her feet, despite the sneakers, sunk half an inch into. The carpeting could double as her bed.

Apparently, the P.I. business paid well.

Dressed in black dress pants, a light-gray shirt—no tie—and a sport coat, Mr. Edwards embodied casual elegance. Simple and well tailored, this man would look equally comfortable in a room full of blue bloods or a homeless shelter. He had that way about him. The ability to adjust to his environment.

He strode around his desk, extended his hand to Lucie and hit her with an easy, sparking smile. Frankie had that smile. The one that could light up a city block. Any nerves or lack of confidence over her attire vanished. Poof. Gone. The man, also like Frankie, without a doubt, knew the power of that smile.

In short, she had his number.

"Ms. Rizzo," he said, "this is a surprise."

You ain't seen nothing yet, pal. After shaking hands, he motioned her to one of the two high-backed leather guest chairs in his office. Rather than move around to his chair, he sat next to her, angling sideways to face her.

Interesting. First the plush office, and now refusing to take the power position by sitting behind his desk.

She might like this guy.

"What can I do for you? I assume this is regarding the Maxmillian dress."

Lucie nodded. "It is. I think I might have some information for you."

She waited, studying his face for the slightest movement—a lifting eyebrow, puckering lips, anything—but if he'd had any reaction to that bit of news, it didn't show. Not one hint.

"Please," he said, "go on."

She shifted left a little, facing him more directly. "I received a phone call last night from someone named Bill. He told me he knew where the dress was."

To that, she finally received a slight narrowing of his eyes. "And this person—Bill—found you how?"

How much she should admit about her investigation, she wasn't quite sure. But if she wanted an ally, someone she could partner with and trust, she'd have to be honest.

She scrunched her nose, bit down on her bottom lip and figured what the heck. Why not? "I'll be honest. I've been investigating. Obviously, I'm a suspect, and I need to clear my name. If my clients begin to believe I might be involved in criminal activity, they'll never let me return to their homes."

"Understandable."

"So, I researched the dress and discovered a fan club—not the official fan club. Sort of an underground one that's not-so-underground anymore."

"The Cock Heads," he said.

Excellent. He was up to speed. Good for him doing his own research. "Exactly. I found them on the Internet and went to a meeting two nights ago. I joined the group, giving them my contact information."

"Okay," he said, clearly wondering where this little adventure might take him.

Well, she'd tell him. "At the meeting, I made it known that my friend and I intended to bid on the dress at the auction. A lie, of course. We just needed them to believe we were Cock Heads."

Mr. Edwards smiled. "I understand."

"Right. Good. Yesterday, I received a call from Bill telling me the dress was on the black market. For ten thousand dollars, he'll connect me with the seller."

"I see."

This was moving along beautifully. Lucie rolled her hand. "And I'm not sure what to do with that information."

"The police?"

"No. My . . . boyfriend . . . is a Chicago PD detective. As crazy as this sounds, I don't want to bring him into this. Not until I have to. He's loosely involved with this case, and the last thing I want is for him to be in the middle."

"Un-huh. That's noble of you, but risky."

"Tim is a good man. He shouldn't lose his job because of his association with me."

Or the Rizzo name.

Mr. Edwards jerked his head. "What is it you want from me?"

"I was hoping I could pass the information to you, and you could either go to the police or maybe investigate it yourself. You know, a lead."

"Which might clear you as well."

Lucie snapped her fingers and then pointed. "Exactly. Can you help me?"

"Ms. Rizzo, anything I can do to serve my client, I'll do."

He rose from his chair, swung around his desk, grabbed a pad and pen from the top right drawer and sat. "Tell me what you have."

Lucie laid it all out for him, the Cock Head meeting, the people she'd met, Wendel coming to their rescue on the street, the phone call, all of it.

Mr. Edwards listened, took notes, interrupted when he had a question, then went back to his notes. When she finished, he held up one finger and reread his notes, dragging his pen along the edge of the notepad as he read.

"The burn phone?"

"He said it couldn't be traced. And it came up as a blocked number. He also said I shouldn't go to the police because he had a contact there."

"Perhaps a lie." The corners of his mouth dipped. "I know a few people in the department. I'll ask around. His name was Bill?"

"Yes. But, please be careful. He said if I go to the police, he'd disappear. And right now he's my only lead to the dress."

"Ms. Rizzo, I think you should prepare yourself that this might be a con."

As if he needed to tell her that? Of all people? "Obviously, I'm not giving him ten thousand dollars. But I was thinking maybe we could set up a meeting, then follow him or something. I'm not crazy enough to do it alone, but if you'd help me, it might work, right?"

He hit her with the light-bulb smile again. Like Frankie's, Mr. Edwards' smiles did double duty. One second charming, the next lady-you're-cuckoo.

"Hey," she said, "it sounds nutty, but it's worth a try."

He jotted a note, dotting his *I* with a flourish. "When is he making contact again?"

"He said I had until eight o'clock tonight to decide. He's calling me then."

"Fine. I'll see what I can dig up before then. Come back here at seven thirty. I'll listen in on the call. From there, we'll make a plan."

AT SEVEN THIRTY THAT EVENING, LUCIE STOOD OUTSIDE MR. Edwards' outer office door waiting for him to answer. She rolled her shoulders and closed her eyes for a few seconds. *Focus.* The stress from the last couple of days dogged her, settled into her muscles like a million baby alien heads.

The door swished open, and Lucie snapped to. "Hello!"

Whoopsie. *A little aggressive there, Luce.* Fatigue did that to her. Sent her mind into overdrive, forced her to push through when really, she just wanted her bed.

Mr. Edwards motioned her inside. "My assistant leaves at five. She always locks the door."

"I'd do the same. You can't see the entrance from your office."

Growing up Joe Rizzo's kid taught her a few things about safety. Particularly when it came to doors. Her father always watched the doors. Just in case someone tried to whack him.

Lucie blew air through her lips and silently cursed the fact that being Joe Rizzo's kid meant being conditioned, unconscious as it might have been, for things like someone killing her father.

They passed his assistant's desk where not a scrap of paper littered the top—excellent organization—and moved into Mr. Edwards' office. Lucie sat in the same chair she'd occupied that morning.

"Whoever this guy is," Mr. Edwards said, "he's good. I

contacted my source in the PD and reached out to a few Cock Heads. I can't find anything on him."

"Leave it to me to get a blackmailer who knows what he's doing."

Mr. Edwards unleashed one of those killer smiles. Not the slick one, but an honest-to-goodness, crinkly eyed one.

Too bad Ro and Joey were doing whatever it was they were doing—*blech*—because Lucie wouldn't mind fixing Ro up with Eric Edwards. He may have been in his forties, but Ro could use a guy like him.

Assuming he wasn't married.

Immediately her gaze shot to his left hand. No ring.

She'd catalogue that for later. If things went bad with Joey, Eric Edwards could be the fallback.

And, wow, the stress must be dissolving her brain. That little mind-travel sent her from hunting a blackmailer to matchmaking.

Lucie gave her head a solid shake, fought off the bone-melting fatigue she'd been carrying in her shoulders and neck all day, but had absolutely refused to give in to. Rizzos didn't give in.

They fought.

Hard.

She sat forward, met Mr. Edwards' gaze. "Well, Mr. Edwards, that just makes the challenge more fun now doesn't it?"

"That it does. And it's Eric. Drop the 'mister' part."

Lucie saluted. Saluting? She was on a roll today. "You got it. What's the plan? We need to flush this creep out."

Another grin drifted across Mr. Edw—Eric's face and he propped his arms on the desktop. "If you're up for it, I think we should call his bluff. Tell him we'll give him the money."

Humina-wha? Where would she get ten thousand

dollars? Lucie's head fell forward, her shoulders slumping with it.

"If you're not comfortable with it . . ."

Comfortable with it? With her last name there weren't a lot of things she couldn't get comfortable with. She straightened up and visualized her tongue rolling back into her mouth. "It's not that. I don't have ten thousand dollars laying around."

"Don't need to. I'm dead certain it's a con. If you give him the ten K, he'll take the money, tell you to wait by the phone and then nothing. Boom. Con completed and you're out ten grand."

People could be such bastards. Evil, scheming bastards. "So what do we do?"

"When he calls, tell him you're in. He'll probably tell you to leave the money somewhere. We're not doing that. Tell him to meet you and ask for proof he can get you the dress."

"What kind of proof?"

Eric shrugged. "Let him figure that out. He'll argue with you, but if he's desperate enough—and I believe he is—he'll agree to a meeting. Then you tell him you're bringing a friend with you for safety."

"You're the friend?"

"I'm the friend. When we get there, we'll tell him he's not getting the money until he shows us the dress."

Oh, wow. *Wow. Wow. Wow.* "And we're not afraid we'll lose him and the dress?"

"My guess is he'll walk away. He'll tell you he'll be in touch, and you'll never hear from him again."

"But what if he does know who has the dress."

"If he does, he'll prove it."

Lucie sat back again, rested her head back and drew a long breath. "There are a lot of ifs."

"You'll have to decide if it's worth it."

To clear her from the suspect list and save her reputation, she'd do it. She'd spent most of her adult life trying to break away from the stigma of her father's ways. She'd worked hard in school, got an MBA, landed a great job and then when that fell apart, started her own business. Everything she'd done was simply to prove she was more than a mob princess.

And she wouldn't let some slimy blackmailer take that from her.

No.

Sir.

She sat up again, pushed her shoulders back and nodded. "I'm in."

9

———

"BLOCKED NUMBER. THIS IS HIM."

Eric nodded. "Put him on speaker."

Lucie poked the screen. "Hello?"

"This is Bill. Am I on speaker?"

You sure are, buddy. "Yes. I'm driving. Sorry."

Bill hesitated, most likely deciding if he believed that line. As for Lucie, she thought it was fairly quick thinking on her part.

"Oh," Bill said. "What about the dress?"

Game. On. "Ten thousand is a lot of money. I'll need proof you can connect me with the seller."

"Believe me, I can connect you."

Eric wrote a note and slid it over to Lucie. PROOF. Lucie held her hands out and Eric picked up the newspaper. Ah. She knew. She'd seen this in movies at least five hundred times.

"Well, Bill," she said, "I'd like to believe you. Still, just to be sure, I'll need some proof."

"What kind of proof?"

"The kind where you put today's newspaper on top of

the dress and send me a photo. You do that, and you have a deal. And no funny stuff."

Eric rolled his eyes and slashed his hand across his neck. Apparently, Lucie's method acting wasn't nearly as superior as Ro's.

Another long moment passed. *Come on already.* She tapped her foot, waiting, waiting, waiting. Wow, she had to pee. As usual. Ever since she and Frankie returned a million dollars' worth of jewels, she'd had this issue with flop-peeing whenever she got nervous.

She gently set the phone on the desk and stood. Maybe it would help extinguish some of her nervous energy. "Bill? You still there?"

"Yes."

"Do we have a deal?"

"I'll send you the photo. It'll take a few minutes, but you'll get it."

Eric gave her two thumbs up. *Yay, Lucie.*

"Good," Lucie said. "Assuming all goes well with the photo, let's discuss the exchange."

More silence. Apparently she was throwing Bill off his game.

"Nothing to discuss," he said. "You'll leave the money where I say."

Eric had nailed that one. Boy, oh, boy, this guy knew his stuff. Lucie could learn from him. She set her hands on either side of the phone and leaned in. "Bill? You do know my last name, right?"

"Uh, yeah. Why?"

"Do you think Joe Rizzo's daughter is really going to leave ten thousand dollars in cash on a park bench? Without some kind of guarantee?"

"If you want the dress you will."

Eric jotted a note on his notepad and held it up. HANG UP!

Hang up? Wha? So much for him knowing his stuff. Had he lost his mind? Why would she hang up? He pointed again then paddled his hand. Finally, he gave up, grabbed the phone and poked out of the call.

"Hey," Lucie said, "what gives?"

"He'll call back. He needs to know he can't push you around. That you're serious."

"But—"

Eric held up five fingers and curled each finger down one at a time. Four, three, two, one . . .

Lucie's phone rang. *Damn the know-it-all.*

Eric grinned. "He wants that ten K."

"Smartass." She scooped up the phone. "Hello?"

"You hung up on me." The shrill in Bill's voice carried and scraped against Lucie's eardrums, making her wince.

Eric rolled his hand. Ooh, right.

"I did. Listen, Bill, I'm not kidding around. I want that dress, but I'm not about to get swindled."

Swindled? Really? God, she was lame. She should have picked a better verb. *Screwed.* Now that would have sounded much tougher.

"So, here's what we'll do. We'll meet somewhere. I'll bring the money, and you'll take me to the person who has the dress. Once you do that, I'll turn over the ten thousand. And, just to be sure I stay safe, I'm bringing a friend."

"No. No friends. How do I know this friend isn't a cop?"

"Bill, be serious. I'm paying you ten thousand dollars for a stolen dress. I'd be arrested right along with you."

"Uh . . ."

Please, don't less this guy be the sharpest knife in the drawer.

Eric whipped his pen up, scrawled another note. YOU'RE LOSING HIM.

"Bill, this is a limited-time offer. I want the dress, but I'm taking a big risk here. We either make this deal in the next ten seconds, or I'm hanging up."

Eric gave her another thumbs up. *Yay, Luce!*

"Five seconds."

"Okay. Okay. Fine. We'll meet."

"After you send me the photo."

"After I send the photo. You'd better be ready with that ten grand, or I'm gone."

"Oh, I'll be ready."

She sure would.

Two trips to the ladies room—*thank you, flop-peeing problem*—and a barely tolerable twenty minutes later, Lucie's phone chimed the arrival of a text. "This is probably it."

Yep. It took a few seconds for the photo to load, but —*holy moly, would you look at that?*

"Well?"

"It's the dress. At least it looks like it. And that's today's *Banner-Herald.*"

She knew this because her father read the newspaper every morning and that morning, while waiting for her coffee to brew, she'd skimmed the article on the front page. Yet another story on corruption in local government. Thieves everywhere.

"Did he send an address?"

Huh? Lucie cocked her head. *Address. Meeting.* Right. "Yes." She rattled off the address. "He said to be there at midnight."

Eric shook his computer's mouse, bringing the screen

alive. "If that address is where I think it is, this should be interesting."

Lucie knew. "It's on the South Side. Vicious neighborhood. Ro calls it the Death Side. I won't walk dogs there. Too dangerous. Particularly at night."

Eric's fingers pounded the keyboard— not the hunt-and-peck method a lot of men used—and a map popped onto the monitor. He zoomed in to street view and a row of one-story warehouses.

"Damn."

"What?"

He tapped the screen. "For-sale sign. The building is empty. Which means there's probably no security or any sort of life there at night. We'll be alone."

This setup—at the very least—sounded sketchy. "So, Bill wants me to come to gangbanger central with ten thousand dollars in the middle of the night?"

They were sure to die. No question. In that neighborhood, people bled out on the street for a pair of sneakers.

And now she had to walk in there carrying a boatload of money?

Not happening.

She shook her head. "I don't like it."

"That makes two of us."

"What do we do?"

"We bring backup."

"He said to come alone. No cops. That's what he said. He'll bolt."

"We're not bringing cops. I'll pull together my team."

His team? She didn't have a clue who his team was. How could she trust them? Any of them? Even Eric. He seemed like a good man, but he had a client to protect. His loyalty was to corporate America.

Not Lucie Rizzo.

Forget his team. She had her own. A team she could trust.

TWO HOURS LATER, LUCIE MARCHED THROUGH RO'S FRONT door wearing skinny, black jeans, a black sweater and her black, leather jacket. The Lucie Rizzo version of Catwoman.

Not surprisingly, she found Joey's humungous body stretched across the recently acquired sectional—most likely acquired for said humongous body—while he took in a Blackhawks game.

"Pass!" he shouted. "Pass!"

And even if she still hadn't *quite* gotten used to her brother making himself at home in Ro's living room, nothing about it struck her as odd. They'd all been friends for years. So all this Ro and Joey constantly together? It all seemed ... well ... normal.

As normal as normal could be in the Rizzo world.

"Hey," she said.

Joey whipped his head around and levered up. "Hey. Why do you look like the SWAT version of Little Orphan Annie?"

Such a jerk. She marched up to him and smacked him on the back of the head. Not hard, but enough for him to know she wasn't in the mood for his caustic humor.

"Where's Ro?"

A few seconds later, Ro swung into the hallway that led from the kitchen. "Hey, girl."

Dressed in gray yoga pants and a body-hugging, hip-length sweater, she was barefoot and carrying a bowl that she shoved at Joey.

"Popcorn? Suh-weet." He grabbed her arm, pulled her down for a lip smack that, with any luck, would be over quick.

Once again, Lucie had become the third man in a two-person band. She looked down at her sneakers, the super-cool Chuck Taylor's she'd swapped out the white laces on so they wouldn't glow in the dark. A smudge marred the front rubber.

She stole a peek at Ro and Joey, whose kiss still dragged on. *Kill me, please.* Lucie's cheeks burned, and she cleared her throat. "Hey! I'm standing right here."

Finally—*thank you, sweet baby Jesus*—Joey pulled back. "Seriously," he said to Ro, "you're the best."

Ro scooted around the edge of the sofa and swatted Joey's sock-clad feet. Immediately, he lifted them, Ro sat and Joey dropped his legs.

To keep her brother focused, Lucie snatched the remote out of his hand and hit the power button.

"Uh, I was watching that."

"I know. But I need you. You can watch the highlights."

Lucie set her messenger bag down and sat in the chair across from Joey and Ro. She'd always loved this chair. Ro described it as a chair-and-a-half, and, with Lucie being of rather diminutive stature, her body curled right into it.

"What's up, Luce?" Ro asked.

"We've had a development on the dress. I need your help."

"We're in."

"Well, more Joey. Ro, I'm not sure you should be involved in this mission."

Ro did one of her famous drama-girl gasps. "We are a *team*. I'm *always* involved."

"I know. But this time it could be dangerous."

"Ah, dammit." Joey shot to a sitting position and waved his arms. "What now? You know, Luce, with Dad on the outside, it's getting harder and harder to keep stuff from him. You're not making it easy."

"I know. And I'm sorry. Believe me. Things just happen to me."

Her brother's dark eyes pinned her like targeted prey. "Well, make it stop. Fast. I can't take it anymore."

Unable to stand the pressure of Joey's stare, Lucie turned to Ro. "The Cock Head meeting wasn't a bust after all."

Ro scooted to the edge of her seat and leaned forward. "Do tell, Sister."

"Yeah, *Sister*," Joey said, "do tell."

Apparently Lucie was getting good at summarizing her exploits, because in less than five minutes she'd wrapped up her dealings with Eric and Bill and their scheduled meeting.

Joey poked a beefy finger. "You're not going."

"Yeah, I am."

"In that neighborhood? Nuh-uh. I'll go."

"You can't. It has to be me, or the guy will bolt. I've already pushed him by telling him I'm bringing Eric Edwards. I can't risk another person."

Joey rolled his eyes. "I'll be Eric."

That stupid, demeaning, you're-an-idiot eye roll drove her to madness.

She clamped her teeth together, counted to three and breathed until her pulse quieted. "No, you won't be Eric," she said. "I made a deal with him, and I'm sticking to it."

"Then, smarty, why the hell are you here?"

This would kill her. More than kill her. She'd spent her entire adult life distancing herself from all things Joe Rizzo, Mob Boss, and now she expected to utilize the very thing she'd found so *disgusting*.

Total hypocrite.

Eh, if it kept her from bleeding out in a warehouse parking lot, she'd accept it.

Lucie dug into her messenger bag for the manila envelope she'd prepped. "We have to meet behind a warehouse." She slid the photos out of the envelope and walked to where Ro and Joey sat. "I printed these from the Internet. It's the back view of the building."

"Desolate," Ro said.

"Yes. The warehouse is empty. Big for-sale sign on the front."

"Which is why they chose it." Joey drummed his finger on one of the pictures. "And I don't like these railroad tracks."

Ditto on that. The tracks, used for freight trains, ran alongside the warehouse so the closest building, store or home to where they'd be meeting was at least half a block.

Ro swirled her finger just above the photo of the tracks. "Joey, you could round up some of the guys and set up a perimeter around this area. That way, if it's an ambush, you'll see it and break it up."

Perimeter? Ro might need to lay off the military action films. Surely, Joey had some kind of equally smart-mouthed comment to that.

But . . . no. He cocked his head, mulling the idea. "It'll be dark. We could use the trees for cover."

Perhaps they'd been watching the films together. "I have to meet the guy at midnight. Can you get something set up by then?"

"For you? Sure. The guys love you. Plus, they're pissed the cops harassed you at the store."

"Oh, please. They didn't harass me."

"Hey, you want help or not? The imaginary harassment is gonna get these guys on board."

"Well, fine. But I don't want them being mad at Tim. He was just doing his job."

Joey waved that off. "Tim can handle it." He checked his watch, the one with the platinum band and ice-blue face that Dad inherited after Grandpa died. For years, Lucie had never seen her father without it. Then he went to prison, and from that first day—the first minute of Dad's absence—Joey wore it. Whether he missed their dad or simply wanted people to know that Joe Rizzo wasn't out of reach, Lucie didn't know. Most likely, a bit of both.

In the two months since Dad had come home, he obviously hadn't asked for his beloved watch back. But that would be typical of their father. If the watch made Joey happy, he'd let him keep it. Simple.

"All right," Joey said. "We have two hours. It'll take a good twenty minutes to get there, and we want to be in place at least an hour early. Which means, I gotta haul ass."

He hopped off the sofa. "I'll call you when I'm on my way there. Text me the address." He turned to Ro. "You stay put."

"I can—"

"Whatever you're gonna say, forget it. I'm not screwing around with you on this one. Bad enough I'm letting my sister do this. You? You'd be collateral damage. Forget it, Roseanne."

Ro scrunched her nose, a sure sign she was about to launch into a full attack.

"It's not happening," Joey said. "If you come anywhere near that warehouse, we're gonna go at it. And I don't care how naked you are. I'll stay pissed for a long time."

Eeep. Lucie peeled her lips back, gave Ro the save-your-self headshake.

"Fine." Ro folded her arms, let out a good solid huff. "The minute it's over, you call me. Both of you."

But Joey had never been accused of being stupid or a fool. He bent low, got nearly nose-to-nose with Ro. "Promise me."

Oh, now that's dirty. Ro didn't make a lot of promises. To her, a promise, like shatterproof glass, should only be used in extreme cases. When she made a promise she never, ever broke it.

"Ro," Lucie said, "just say it. You know how he is. He won't give up, and the longer he stands here, the less time he has to get a posse together."

Ro flapped her arms. "Fine. I promise I will stay here and not go anywhere near that warehouse." She smacked his arm. "Satisfied?"

A lightning-fast smile lit Joey's face, and he smacked another lip-lock on Ro. They had the weirdest foreplay. All steam and sexual energy and, well, Lucie didn't know what to do. Stand there and wait for the fire to burn out? Or tell them to knock it off and get a room?

She tilted her head up and inspected the crown molding. "Any time now, kids."

Joey finally backed up, cuffing Ro lightly under the chin. "Thank you. Now I only have to worry about one of you. I'll call you when we're done." He faced Lucie. "Give me half an hour and you'll be set."

Eleven fifty and Lucie's text alert pinged.

"Joey is in place."

Five minutes earlier, Eric had parked his fancy Lincoln in the desolate warehouse's back lot. They now sat, engine quietly idling, while Lucie scanned the blackness in front of her. The cloud-smothered sky offered no moonlight to illuminate the trees where Joey and posse had strategically placed themselves.

Well, she hoped they'd strategically placed themselves. With this crew, a girl couldn't assume anything.

Eric swept his gaze left to right. "Where are they?"

"Don't know exactly. He didn't want me distracted and looking for them. All I know is they're scattered in the trees. He said there are five of them, and they can see us."

Joining Joey were Slip, Jimmy Two-Toes, Lemon and—God help her—Frankie's father, Al. Later, she'd question the moment of insanity that precluded asking one of Lucie's least favorite people to help on this mission, but all in all, she couldn't say much considering the short notice.

She had to hope the men would do as Joey asked and not tell Dad about this. If they did, the lecture would be like submersion into quicksand.

Slow and agonizing.

Eric rested his head against the seat, but Lucie sensed the high-strung tension rolling from him. He must have been a cop in his prior career. Like Tim, he possessed an edgy stillness even when adrenaline ate him alive.

"I have my team in place on the other side of the building. If our friend Bill tries anything, we've got all angles covered."

"Good. Can we go over the plan again?"

The lights from his dashboard threw shadows across his face as he continued scanning the lot. "When Bill shows up, we wait for him to come to us. We don't get too close to his car."

"What do we tell him about the money?"

"Tell him it's in the trunk. I threw my gym bag back there and stuffed it with fake bricks of money."

"Fake bricks of money? You keep that stuff on hand?"

Eric shrugged. "You never know when it'll come in handy."

"Wow."

"If we have to, we unzip the gym bag and show him. I put fifties on top of the stacks. If he sees the actual stack, we're screwed."

Yikes. She didn't like the sound of that.

"After show-and-tell," Eric said, "we insist he take us to the dress. *Then* we'll give him the ten K."

"Our hope is he takes us to the dress and then your team busts in, right?"

Please let that be the plan.

"Right." Giving up on the tree line, he glanced over at her. "I know you're nervous. You should be, but take a few deep breaths. I've done this before. I think it's a con. I doubt this mope has any connection to the dress."

Off to the right, headlights from an approaching car flashed against the pitch-black parking lot. Lucie sat forward in her seat. As if having her nose pressed against the windshield would make a difference in how much she could actually see.

"This has to be him."

Eric clucked his tongue. "Unless random people drive back here at midnight. Could be a drug dealer."

Ohmygod. Really? She could see the headline now: MOB PRINCESS BLUDGEONED BY STONER.

"Well, thanks for that. I feel so much better now."

The corner of Eric's mouth lifted. "Sorry."

He flipped his lights on and off, and the approaching car

came to a stop three spaces down. The front grille of Bill's—hopefully Bill's—banged-up sedan faced Eric's door.

Eric held his hand up to cut the glare of headlights. "He's making sure we're the only ones here."

"And blinding us."

"That, too. But I see enough to know he's alone."

"Unless someone is crouched down."

"Yes."

Great. Hot stabs jabbed her chest, just hack, hack, hacking away. If a stoned crackhead didn't kill her, her nerves might.

A minute later, headlights still on, the driver's-side door on the other car jerked open, and a man stepped out. Still partially blinded, Lucie couldn't make out details, but the man easily towered over the roof of the car. Tall man. Leather jacket hanging open. Breaths coming in white puffs into the cold night air.

He walked toward them and stopped near the front of his car, his arms loose at his sides.

Gun?

Another glorious thought that sparked hacking stabs. She simply sucked at this criminal stuff.

"Let's go," Eric said.

Lucie followed him from the car, sticking close and hoping Joey had the posse contained.

Everyone, including her, needed to stay calm.

Eric halted about three feet from supposedly-Bill and nodded.

Lucie did the same. "Bill?"

"That's me. Where's the money?"

Up close, with the help of the headlights, the man's features became clear. Total puzzle. Short, dark hair with a touch of gray on the sides gave the impression of middle-aged, but his chubby cheeks and skin that lacked any deep crevices or lines appeared, at most, early thirties.

How-the-heck old was this guy?

Plus, she didn't remember seeing him at the Cock Head meeting. But she'd been fairly hopped up and could have missed him. She supposed.

Eric cleared his throat, the rumble drawing Lucie's gaze up. He slid his eyes toward Bill.

What?

When she didn't answer, he grimaced then faced Bill. "It's in the car. We see the dress, you get the money."

"And who are you again?"

Get in the game here, Luce. If she blew this, her chance at finding that dress and putting an end to this nightmare might go up in flames. "He's a friend of mine," she said. "A *family* friend."

If that didn't scare the crap out of this creep, nothing would. A family friend of the Rizzos could be any number of psychos.

Bill studied Eric for a few seconds, taking in his dress slacks and sport coat. It must have all passed the Bill test because he shifted back to Lucie.

"Show me the money."

Oh, boy. But she and Eric had discussed this. They had a plan.

And heaven help her if that plan went bust.

"I'll get it," Eric said.

Just as he stepped away, a loud *brrring, brrring, brrring* demolished the quiet air, jerking Lucie sideways as Bill fumbled for his phone.

Lucie's own phone rang, and, as much as she itched to check it, she didn't move. *Joey.* Had to be. Tim would be asleep, and Ro knew not to call. And how truly pathetic was it that she could narrow the possibilities to only two people?

Well, three if she counted the drunk who constantly reversed two digits and called looking for a ho named Jules. Leave it to Lucie to have a similar number to a prostitute.

Bill poked at his phone and, still keeping an eye on Lucie, partially turned away. "Hello?"

He was taking a call now? What kind of amateur was this guy? Her phone rang again and with Bill occupied, she peeked at the screen. Ro.

Bill's head snapped around and the hard glare he leveled on her sent a burst of panic ripping up her neck. A stream of swear words flew from his mouth, and Eric stepped in front of Lucie, blocking Bill's direct path.

Hold on here.

"Crap," Bill said, and Lucie peeked around Eric to see him eyeing her with the disdain of a lynching party. "No . . . I'll take care of it."

Lucie's phone rang again. *Dammit, Ro. No time now.*

Bill ended his call and jammed his phone into his jacket pocket hard enough that it should have torn clear through.

One thing was evident. "Bill" and "happy camper" would not be used in the same sentence anytime soon.

He confirmed it by charging back to his car. "Deal's off."

"Hey." Eric held his hands wide. "What the hell?"

But Bill had already reached his car and ripped open the door. "Deal's off! I said no cops."

Cops? What cops? All they had was a bunch of amped-up mob guys. "I didn't call the police," Lucie said.

"No? Then how do the news reporters know you're involved?"

Lucie cocked her head. *News reporters?* "Heh?"

"Watch the news. I'm outta here. It's too hot now. Stupid! We were so close to a deal."

No. *Nuh, nuh, nuh.*

More hot stabs traveled from her stomach into her chest, and she sucked a breath and rushed toward Bill, reaching the car just as he slid in. She hammered her fists on the window, and he leaned right, his eyes bulging. "Back off, crazy!"

The distinct thud of the doors locking filled the momentary silence, and those hot stabs went nuclear, spreading over her body, lighting up her skin. This man, whoever the hell he was, knew where that dress was and that dress would clear her name. *Bastard.* She banged on the window again. "Open this door."

A hand clamped over her arm. Eric. "Lucie, calm down."

"He can't leave. I need that dress." She snapped the door handle then went back to banging on the window. "Open up, you . . . you . . . Cock Head!"

He fired the engine, and she watched as he shifted the car into gear.

"I need that dress!"

A second later, the car shot backward, and Lucie started running, chasing him down.

"Stop him!"

One of her crew or someone on Eric's team could block the driveway. Keep him from getting away.

"Stop him. Please."

Red taillights flashed as the car veered left out of the lot, tires spinning against the pavement leaving the distinct aroma of burned rubber.

"Noooo," Lucie shouted, her voice carrying into the trees, but drowned out by the whistle of a distant train.

Come back. Please. Come back.

She whipped back to Eric, about to plead with him to do something, anything, to find that swindling Cock Head, but he had his phone pressed to his ear and held his hand up.

"You got him?" he said. "Roger that. Stay with him. What? . . . Dammit . . . All right. Stay on it."

Before he even hung up, she was on him, stepping right into his personal space. "What is it?"

He shook his head, let out a long sigh. "One of my guys is on him. Well, he *was* on him. He got caught at a light with a cop sitting on the corner."

Lucie stomped a foot. "Darn it."

"Rotten luck. He couldn't blow through the light without tripping the cop."

Once again, Lucie's phone rang. Ro again. *I've had enough of this.* She jabbed at the speaker button, and a niggling pressure wormed up her index finger. Didn't matter. Nothing mattered right now. Including whatever the hell it was Ro needed. Their only lead to that dress, and clearing Lucie's name, just screeched out of the parking lot.

"Hello?" Ro said, her voice a little more breathy than usual.

"Your house had better be on fire with all these calls."

"Honey, it's worse than that. You were just on the news."

10

———

THE POST-ADRENALINE FOG disappeared like a drunk at an AA meeting.

"The news?"

Bill had just said something about the news, also.

"Yepper," Ro said. "They had your picture and everything."

Eric rolled his eyes, and Lucie understood his frustration on a primal—extremely primal—level. Fighting to control her temper, starting with her toes and working her way up, legs, hands, stomach, arms, all of it, Lucie imagined every muscle resisting tension. *Stay loose. Relax.*

Don't kill your best friend.

When she reached her shoulders, she closed her eyes, blew out a breath.

"Uh, Ro?"

"Yes?"

Ohmygod. The pressure behind Lucie's eyes exploded and she waved her fist. The last ten minutes had just stripped away the measly crumbs of her sanity, and she couldn't stand it anymore, couldn't stand trying to control herself when every flipping thing she'd planned for tonight had gone haywire. No, no, no. She'd had enough of this stupid dress and stupid Bill and the stupid Cock Heads.

She whipped away from Eric and stomped off, trying to hold it together. No good.

She shook the phone in front of her, and the words finally broke free. "Why the *hell* was I on the news?"

"Hey, don't yell at *me*. I'm just the messenger."

Lucie stopped storming the lot. At this rate she'd shatter a knee and wind up on crutches. She bent at the waist, let the cold night air smother that flashing temper. *I can do this.*

Calm. That's all she needed.

She glanced back at Eric who watched her with the inquisitive, studious face of a psychiatrist about to commit his favorite patient.

Welcome to my world, mister.

"I'm sorry," Lucie said to Ro. "You're right."

"All the reporter said was you'd been questioned by police about the robbery. No big deal."

"They named me as a suspect? On the news?"

"Well, it was just the cable channel. I did a quick Internet search and the local station is the only one who has it. Wasn't like it was World News Tonight or anything. I think it's contained."

Contained to the cable channel. *Dear God.*

"Don't panic," Eric said.

Excellent advice. Advice she'd love to take, but just the mention of her last name in relation to a crime would create a media feast.

The phone beeped, and Lucie glanced down at the screen to see Joey's name scrolling across the top. Great. "Ro, I need to call you back. Joey is calling."

Dumping Ro, she tapped the screen. "Joey?"

"What's going on? Did you make the deal? Why'd that guy haul ass?"

"It's a mess, that's why. We're done here. Send the guys home for me, will you? And tell them thank you. I'll stop by Petey's tomorrow and tell them myself, but I can't handle that bunch right now. Please?"

"Luce?"

She closed her eyes. "Yes?"

"Are you okay?"

She snorted. If she said no, he'd be on her in seconds, doing his pushy Joey thing, wanting to bust some heads or whatever else he could think of. If she said, yes, he wouldn't believe her. Her brother knew her moods. They'd spent their lifetimes dealing with each other, learning the subtle nuances of certain looks and tones.

And right now, he knew she wasn't okay. "I will be," she said. "Send the guys home and I'll fill you in, but apparently, the Maxmillian dress and I have made the news."

"Shit."

"Pretty much, yes."

Eric stepped up. "Sounds like the PD leaked it to the press."

"Shit," Joey said again.

"Ro said it's contained to the local channel. The networks don't have it. Let's hope it stays that way."

THE FOLLOWING MORNING, DETERMINED TO MAKE THE DAY A productive one despite the four hours of sleep and the collapse of her reputation, Lucie tromped down Franklin Avenue on her way to Coco Barknell. Having thought ahead the night before, she'd called Lauren, her part-time dog walker, to cover the pooches today.

Unfortunately for Lucie, her plan of spending the morning in her office while she waited for updates on the arrest of Bill and his thieving buddies, hadn't quite worked out.

But that was fine. Being an A-type personality came in handy at times like this because she could focus all her disappointment and anger into the ever-present backup plan. *Plan B, here I come.*

Morning dew hung in the air, and she sucked it all in as she walked. To hell with the exhaustion pressing in. She'd do what she always did and march on.

I'm a Rizzo.

And if nothing else, Rizzos knew how to bounce.

Bounce, bounce, bounce.

Lucie tilted her head up, let the sun warm her cheeks and hooked the right at the corner. Two stores down she'd find Coco Barknell's headquarters and the always-active Petey's nestled in the middle of the block.

"There she is!"

"Ms. Rizzo!"

"Do you have a statement?"

"Ms. Rizzo, look here!"

Lucie froze as a swarm of people, a giant flash mob holding microphones and cameras, swung in her direction. All of them in front of her office, blocking her path.

And charging.

The herd descended, and a seizing panic shot right down her legs, rooting her to the sidewalk. And still they kept coming.

No. Nuh, nuh, nuh. Run.

"Ms. Rizzo! How does it feel to be associated with your father's criminal activity?"

"Ms. Rizzo, where's the dress?"

"Ms. Rizzo, have you spoken to your father?"

Rushing blood blurred her vision, and the stampeding crowd looped and swayed. She rocked back on her heels and blinked. Once, twice, three times. *There we go.*

The whooshing in her head settled into a low hiss, but the mob closed in. Getting closer. She could turn and run, but . . . no. She had a business to mind. The only way to the other side was through them. She shoved one hand in front of her, gripped her messenger bag with the other and pushed into the crowd.

"Step aside, please. No comment. Step aside. Coming through. No comment."

All but one pesky cameraman let her through. The cameraman walked backward, filming as he went while Lucie forged ahead, denying them a statement.

Maybe he could have gotten the hint. No. Freaking. Comment.

Being careful not to bump him—she'd learned that lesson aeons ago when Joey wound up accused of assault for putting his hand on a reporter who'd gotten too close to Dad —she swerved, hustling toward the shop's door.

Head up, Lucie plowed through the crowd, the voices melding, building to a crescendo of unintelligible shouts. A reporter jumped into her path, and she threw her arm out.

"No comment. Please move. No comment."

She cleared a small path to Coco Barknell, and a photographer standing to the left of the doorway snapped pictures. *Click, click, click.*

Look away. Ignore him. A few more feet. That was all she needed.

Two doors down, a crowd began to gather at Petey's. Oh, no. If Dad's crew came outside, she'd have a total mess. They'd take one look at the cameraman bullying her, and someone would lose their mind.

Most likely, her father.

Get inside.

She dug her keys from her front pocket, her fingers shivering as she stabbed at the lock and missed.

"Step back, folks. Step back."

He's here. Lucie whirled around just as Tim pushed through the front row of reporters. *He's here.* Relief poured over her, an instant depressurization. She'd like to kiss him right there in front of the gang of reporters. Wouldn't that be a great lead story?

"Hiya," he said.

His giant hand came around her shoulder and settled over the key still dangling in the lock.

"You're okay," he whispered, unlocking the door.

Tears bubbled in her eyes, and her chest heaved because, holy cow, Tim was here.

Helping her. Taking care of her. *Supporting* her.

"Thank you," she said. "You have no idea ..."

Tim swung the door open. "You're welcome. Let's get inside."

He locked the door behind them—for all the good that did. The reporters and cameramen lined up across the front of the plate-glass window, their hungry eyes peering in.

Her back to the windows, she shook her head. "This place is a total fishbowl. Now they'll stand out there and watch."

Always the calm one, Tim slid his hands into his pockets. "So we'll go in back."

Back room. Inspired thought. She had shades on those

windows, and at the end of the short hallway the hideous old saloon doors had been replaced by a lovely raised paneled pine door. That sucker would shut out the gawkers.

Lucie waved one finger and marched past him. "Perfect."

Tim followed, closing the door behind him, and Lucie bent at the waist, bracing her hands on her thighs.

"So," he said, "good morning to you."

At that, Lucie smiled. *Thank you for bringing me this man.* She straightened up and slapped both hands over her chest. What she wanted, truly, was to step into the fold of his arm, wrap herself around him and just snuggle in.

But with the chaos she'd brought him, he might be here to dump her.

And who could blame him after this reporter fiasco? One thing a cop didn't need was bad press for his girlfriend. This life. She couldn't take it anymore, the running, the proving herself, again and again and again. The tiring emotional zigzagging every time she thought she'd prevail in finally showing people that she'd grown to be an educated and driven woman. A woman who valued independence and honesty and hard work.

Who valued life as a successful—and legitimate— businesswoman.

Yet, here she was, locked in the back room of the old Carlucci's shoe store, just down the street from Petey's, that damned luncheonette where her father ran his illegal activities. And right outside a gaggle of press people wanted her to comment on being a suspect in the theft of a slice of movie history.

No matter what action she took or how much she denied it, the truth would be buried, way down deep, under all that crap she fed herself about rising above. All there, rooted in her.

Lucie Rizzo.

Mob princess.

She sucked in a breath. Wow. *Wow, wow, wow.* All this time, she'd been fighting it. Denying it. Avoiding it.

No use.

She could either buckle under the pressure of the stolen dress, the reporters, the *gossip* or she could fight back.

And one thing about Rizzos, they knew how to fight. Tim stepped forward, eyes slightly narrowed as he studied her face. "Luce? What's happening right now? You look a little nuts."

She bobbed her head. "I'm . . ." What? What did she feel when it came to Tim?

She knew.

The constant worry, the ridiculous self-protection about him dumping her, had to stop. She wanted him in her life. Period. All the rest had to go away.

Tim wrapped his hand around her wrist and squeezed. "Luce, what is it?"

She smiled. "I'm . . . just . . . so happy to see you right now."

———

STANDING IN LUCIE'S QUASI STORAGE/BREAK ROOM, TIM fought the urge to play Superman. Lucie, he'd quickly learned, had signals. Her dipped head and bowed shoulders were the *give-me-a-second* signal.

Still hanging on to her wrist, he waited. His gaze went to a red bolt of fabric sitting amongst other fabric samples, organized by color and pattern, filling half of a shelving unit against the wall. No doubt Lucie had sorted them. Had to love an organized woman. The remaining half of the shelves contained office supplies and dog-related items—poop bags, treats, bolts of fabric, collars—all of it neatly stacked.

They'd maximized the space with the shelving units leaving the opposite end of the room for the countertop complete with a sink, a microwave and coffee pot. A round, oak table with four chairs completed the setup.

A few months ago, the room had basically been a dumping ground for the old owners. Now, the scent of fresh paint still hung in the air, and the newly tiled floors shined. Lucie had made that happen.

Nothing stopped her. Ever.

Except maybe a crowd of reporters.

She lifted her head. The ready signal.

Instinctively, he knew there were things she didn't tell him. He hadn't nailed it yet, but something in her body language—the stiffness maybe—changed when she held something back.

He never stewed over it. For the most part, Lucie defaulted to honesty, and he trusted her. If there were things she didn't tell him, there were reasons. And those reasons, more than likely, had to do with his job and compromising him.

That, he respected. Plenty of people would drag him into their drama knowing full well he could lose his career.

Not Lucie.

She'd never—as much as he sometimes wanted it— need a man to fight her battles.

"Well," he said, pulling her in for a hug. "I'm happy to see you, too." He lingered for a minute, cupped the back of her head in his hand and breathed in the familiar and some- times excruciating cucumber scent of her soap. He wanted her. Physically. Emotionally. Every way. But she hadn't been ready.

He kissed the top of her head before backing away and meeting her gaze. "I'm sorry about the reporters. I heard it on the news this morning and came straight here."

"Did someone leak my name?"

Of course someone leaked her name. The lack of movement on a case that should have been a slam dunk would frustrate any detective. Tim had to figure out which of the detectives had the most to gain from leaking a potential suspect's name. He had a pretty good idea. He'd spotted Bickel's car parked on the corner. The detective sat behind the wheel watching the action as reporters swarmed Lucie, and Tim's blood boiled over at the possibility that Bickel had resorted to using the media to amp up the pressure on Lucie.

In the court of public opinion, people in this town would easily believe Joe Rizzo's daughter was a criminal. Just like her father.

On their first date, she'd told him, laid it right out there, that she struggled to separate herself from her father's reputation.

At first, he'd thought she was being neurotic, worrying too much.

Now? With this latest development, he got it.

And it pissed him off.

Criminals deserved whatever they got. But good people? Honest, hardworking people? They shouldn't be crucified in the press. No matter their last name.

"I'll get into it. See if it came from my department."

If it did, he'd. . . . Hell, he didn't know what he'd do.

Something.

"Okay, thanks." She paused, squeezed her eyes closed.

He should wait again. Let her sort through it. But, hell on earth, how much of this waiting crap could he do?

With one finger, he tipped her face up. "Talk to me."

She blinked once, twice, three times and tried to force her chin down, to look away. To hide.

Nothing doing. He nudged her chin again. "*Talk* to me."

"I feel like . . . there are things I should tell you."

"But?"

"I don't want to involve you."

He smiled. "Thank you. But I'm a big boy. Tell me what you've got, and *I'll* figure out if I should be in the middle."

She pointed to the table and chairs. "We'll need to sit down for this."

At that, Tim laughed. Couldn't help it. Without a doubt, life with Lucie Rizzo would never be boring.

11

———

Lucie slid into the chair Tim pulled out for her then eyed the cold, empty coffee pot. All this without a fresh hit of caffeine. Twisted torture.

If she had to confess, she'd damn sure need coffee. She smacked her hand on the table and hopped out of her chair. "How about some coffee? I'll make it strong, just for you. I swear, I don't know how you drink that sludge."

"Sugar."

"What?"

"I load it up with sugar. And you're stalling."

From the overhead cabinet she grabbed the bag of fancy coffee Ro liked and started scooping. As she prepped the pot, her mind drifted to Sunday dinners when she was a kid.

The memory produced a burst of laughter.

"What's funny?"

She filled the pot with water, getting to eye level and confirming ten cups. "I was thinking about my grandfather. My dad's dad."

Whoopsie, a little too much water. She dumped a wee bit from the pot. Perfect.

"When I was a kid we'd have big family dinners every Sunday. One o'clock. If you were late, too bad, they locked you out. My cousins would all be there, too. Twenty-five people in my gram's basement. After dinner, my grandfather always had to have a cup of coffee. If it didn't land in front of him within five minutes of the plates being removed, he'd start screaming." Lucie cleared her throat, squinted her eyes and channeled Grandpa Joe's deep bass voice. "For the love of Christ, can I get a cup of Sanka?"

O'Hottie laughed, sending her already tortured emotions on a swooning spree.

"How old were you?"

Lucie hit the button on the coffee pot and rested a hip against the counter. "Maybe seven or eight."

She missed those days. Back before she understood what her father did for a living. He'd always been gone at night. Always. Working, Mom would say.

"Sounds like fun."

"It was fun. I was young then." She slid back into her chair, propped her chin in her hand. "Sometimes I want to be seven again. When I was seven, I didn't know what I didn't know."

"You mean about your dad?"

"Back then I was his little girl. I loved spending time with him. You know, he's wicked funny."

The corner of Tim's mouth lifted. "Your dad?"

"Yeah. He tells the best stories, and you never quite know if they're true or not. At least until he gets to the end. If it's not true, at the very end of the story he does this quirking thing with his lips and then we all throw napkins at him because he bamboozled us."

The good stuff.

That's what she needed to hang on to. For years she'd

focused on the negatives, always seeing her father as the villain, the man who'd humiliated his family, the man who'd left his wife alone while he'd spent years—off and on —in jail.

Yes, he was all those unsavory things. No arguing it, but there were good things, too. The roof over their heads, the making sure his wife and kids had money while he was locked up. The unwillingness to allow people to mess with his family.

"I think," she said, "I need to give myself a break on being mad at my father."

"I'd imagine it takes a lot of energy."

"God, you have no idea." She looked up at him, met his gaze, that beautiful green that made her think of warmth and comfort. "I can't do this anymore, Tim."

His head jerked back, his giant shoulders going with it. The stricken look on his face? Not good.

"Luce, what are you saying?"

Oh, no. He thought *she* was dumping *him*. She put her hands up, frantically shook her head. "No, no, no. Not you. God, no."

He dropped his head, let out a grunting laugh. "Phew. That got my attention."

"I'm so sorry. I can't believe you thought . . ." She stopped. Shook the thought away. "Never you. I adore you."

"Well, all right then. Good to know. Ditto on that."

Good to know, indeed. "I worry all the time. I'm a Rizzo, I will always be a Rizzo. I can't get away from it and, honestly, I'm not sure I want to. I need to stop trying to prove myself and just be me. Lucie Rizzo."

Tim sat forward, linked his fingers with hers. "Lucie Rizzo is a hell of a woman. Honey, you can't control your father, or what people say. Focus on what you can control. Take it from a cop, you'll be a lot happier."

"I'm happy now."

"Are you?"

"Yes. With you. I'm happy. These past couple of months I feel . . . lighter. A fresh start. Every day means discovering something new about you. I like it."

"Good. So do I."

"I don't like keeping things from you."

"Again, we agree."

"So, I'll tell you everything. You're a big boy, right?"

He snorted, grinning at her for throwing his words back at him. "I am. Tell me what's on your mind, Luce, and we'll figure it out."

Where to even start?

The Cock Heads.

Really, the craziness began with that first meeting. "The day before yesterday, after you talked me off the ledge about Mr. Dukane, I came back to the shop, and Ro was cruising message boards for leads."

"Roseanne. On a *message* board?"

"I know. I try not to think about her unleashed on the Internet. Anyway, I thought maybe we should do some research on the Maxmillian dress. You know, see if we could get any leads."

"Please, no."

"Hey! I couldn't help it. I was a suspect and didn't even do anything wrong." She paddled her hands. "Anyway, we found a fan group for the movie. The Cock Heads."

Tim's head jutted forward. "The *Cock* Heads?"

"They have a strong membership. Daily meetings all over the city."

"Wow."

"I know. We thought we'd check it out."

"You and Ro?"

Of course, her and Ro. Who else? "Yes. We went to a meeting. That night I texted you that we were out for coffee? We were at the meeting." Before he could say anything she held her hand up. "I didn't lie to you. I knew your boss didn't want you directly involved, and I didn't want to compromise that. It was easier not to tell you. Then if something came up, you'd have full deniability. That was my intention."

She waited a few seconds, her heart pounding under Tim's steady gaze. Most likely searching for the lie.

No lies here. Just life with Lucie Rizzo.

When Tim didn't speak, she forged ahead. "The meeting was uneventful. At least until the next morning."

"Why do I think this will hurt?"

"It's not that bad. I got a call from someone named Bill. He said he was at the meeting and could hook us up—oh, hang on, I left out the part about the meeting where Ro mentioned she'd planned on bidding on the dress at the auction."

"And me without blood pressure meds."

Ha. Fatalist humor. She pinched his cheek. "You're funny. So, the next day, this Bill calls me and says that for ten thousand dollars he can hook me up with someone who has the dress."

"Oh, Luce."

"Don't panic. I wasn't about to give this nut ten grand."

"You should have told me about it."

"I wanted to, but—"

"I know. You were worried. Forget it. Tell me the rest."

The rest. This part could be difficult. She'd just have to stick to the truth. The truth always prevailed. "I thought about going to your detective friend. Bickel."

"He's not my friend."

"Whatever. I didn't go to him because Bill told me he had a contact at the police, and if I went to them he'd know. I couldn't risk that dress disappearing."

"Understood. What happened with Bill?"

As the man in her life, and knowing him and his alpha tendencies, Tim might get a smidge upset that she'd sought help from Eric, clearly another alpha and one investigating the same crime.

"Don't get mad."

He sat forward, leaned into his arms and gently rapped his knuckles on the table, his jaw flexing a couple of times.

She might be pushing the good and patient detective to his limits. "I'm sorry."

"It's all right. And something you should know. If I get mad, I'll get over it. I don't hang on to crap. Tell me what you did."

This man. Always with the right answer. "I went to Eric Edwards." When he didn't respond, she rolled her hand. "The P.I."

"The one working for the insurance company?"

"Yes. Remember we talked about that at the family meeting? That I could funnel leads through him? Well, I did. I thought he'd be the safest bet. He wasn't a cop, and he stood to gain from finding the dress."

To her surprise, Tim didn't yell. For a second he didn't even speak. All he did was flop out his bottom lip. "Okay. I follow that logic. I'm the one who suggested it in the first place."

"Seriously," she said, "I might love you."

A flashing smile whipped across his face and her hormones wailed.

"Ooh, I like the sound of that."

Hang in with me, big boy, and you'll like more than that.

Whatever Tim was thinking—and Lucie hoped it was filthy—he shook it off. "Luce, you distract me when you say things like that. Not that I mind, but . . ."

"We need to focus."

"Yes. So, you went to the investigator. Then what?"

"We set up a meeting with Bill."

"For the record, now I'm starting to get mad."

Nuh, nuh, nuh, nuh. "It went bust! The cable channel broke that damned story last night, and Bill took off. He said things were too hot around me. And that was that."

Perhaps she'd filtered out a few irrelevant details, like Joey and the posse, but more aggravation wouldn't do him any good. For the most part, she'd given him the facts he needed.

"Now, the press is at my door, Bill is gone, and I don't know what to do. I mean, can this get any worse?"

The back door flew open, and in stepped Ro, Joey, Dad and his cronies, Slip, Lemon and Jimmy Two-Toes.

And Frankie's father.

"Luce," Tim said, "I think it just got worse."

"WHAT THE HELL IS GOING ON?"

Her father stood in the middle of the break room, hands on hips, his face so red it took on a blue tint.

When Lucie pushed out of her seat, Tim did the same, standing behind her while she faced the crowd. This back room was only so big and with all these people clogging it up, the walls closed in, making her head throb.

"Dad," she said, "please calm down."

"We got cameras all over the street."

Ro elbowed Joey. "And they're for Lucie. Who'd have seen that one coming?"

Joey snorted and the two of them made googly eyes at each other. Lucie stuck her finger in her mouth and gagged.

"Sorry," Ro said. "Couldn't resist."

"Well, try to control yourself."

Dad eyeballed Lucie then Ro. "You two about done?"

Lucie straightened up. "I know it looks bad . . ."

"Looks bad? Ha! You think? We gotta get rid of them."

Slip and Lemon muttered something about bats and skulls, and Lucie angled back to Tim. "You didn't hear that."

"What?"

What a guy. Now she had to clear everyone but Dad, Joey and Ro out of the room. The rest of the lunatics had to go.

"Guys," she said, "would you mind going around front and making sure everything is calm out there?"

She met Dad's gaze, opened her eyes wide and nudged her head. *Come on, Dad, take a hint.* "She's right. Don't get nuts, though. Stay calm. Don't put your mitts on anyone. You hear?"

The men filed out, and, whether from the burst of fresh air through the open door or the increased space, Lucie's head stopped pounding.

At least now she could think. "We need to get rid of the reporters, and we know from Dad's experience they won't leave until I comment."

Joey threw his arms up. "Comment? What the hell are you gonna say?"

"I don't know, Joey, that's what I need to decide."

Still standing beside her, Tim shifted sideways into Lucie's view. Maybe simply so she could see him and reinforce his presence. Whatever the reason, it worked.

"What do you think?" she asked him. "About commenting?"

He lifted one shoulder. "It's a risk. The first thing I'd tell you is to check with your lawyer. Anything you say will be heard by cops, too."

"I have nothing to hide. Whatever I say, it'll be the truth. How can that be bad?"

"Personally," Ro said, "I think she should do it. Maybe it'll knock something loose."

"A reward," Dad said.

"What?"

"We'll offer a reward."

Yes! A reward. Someone, somewhere knew who stole that dress, and, with the economy being what it was, a nice reward might entice someone.

Someone like Bill who'd just tried to weasel ten thousand dollars from her. His little scheme failed, but money motivated him. If he knew where that dress was, a reward might encourage his cooperation.

"Ten thousand dollars."

"Whoa," Dad said. "Heck of a reward."

"I know, but we need it to be enough for people to jump at it. Ten thousand dollars is a lot of money to some people. Heck, right now it's a fortune to me."

One by one, she went around the room, scanning the faces of the people closest to her, gauging their reactions. What she got was a mix of *your screws aren't loose, they're gone* and *you're brilliant.*

"Sister," Ro said, "if I had that kind of money, I'd give it to you. The stripper-banger has me on a tight budget."

Joey gave her a hard look then faced Lucie. "I'll give it to you."

"I'll do it," Dad said.

Now Joey and Dad were going to argue?

Joey shook his head. "You can't. You're on parole. You don't think the parole board will wanna know where that ten K came from?"

The blue tint to Dad's cheeks went full-blown purple, and Lucie backed up a step anticipating the blast of anger about to spew.

Joey ran his hands over his face. He hated—despised—when Dad's temper flared in his direction. "Look, I know you want to give her the money, but think about cause and effect here. You—" He broke off, looked up at the ceiling.

Dad curled his fingers into tight balls. "What? Say it."

"You don't need anyone sniffing around asking questions about where you got the ten grand. And I have cash. I don't even have to go to the bank."

At some point, Joey would use this against her. How many times had they argued over the fact that he didn't trust banks? He had his money spread over five different banks and only kept enough in each account to show a legitimate income that came from the bar he supposedly worked at. The rest of his money he kept stashed somewhere. More than likely in a wall because under the mattress seemed so cliché.

Dad mulled it over, squinting, rolling his lips in and out, the whole deal. Really, Lucie didn't see what there was to think about. God help her for saying it, but Joey was right. Her father putting up the money would only fuel the gossip.

"Dad, you know I hate to say it, but I agree with Joey. I'd rather keep you out of it as much as we can." She faced Joey. "Thank you."

And then, she took three steps closer and did something she didn't do nearly enough. She wrapped her ginormous brother in a hug. As much as her short arms could get the job done, anyway.

"Sometimes I want to kill you," she said, "but I know I can always depend on you. That's a gift."

A burst of affection ripped from her core, and she closed her eyes, took a second and savored the rare quiet moment with her loud-mouthed brother. For kicks, and because it felt right, she smacked a kiss on his cheek.

"I love you, Joey."

"He's a pain in the ass," Ro said, "but you can't help but love him."

"Wow," Tim said. "Tough crowd."

Lucie swung back and smiled at him. "Are you okay with this whole reward idea? I want your opinion."

"It's not the worst idea ever. But you need to call your lawyer. Have him draft a statement. I'm telling you, anything you say will be scrutinized."

Dad held up his phone. "I'll call Willie."

"I like this idea," Ro said. "You put the reward out there and then we go back to the Cock Heads."

"Ho," Dad hollered. "What's with the language?"

The perplexed look Ro gave him? Priceless. Lucie chomped on her bottom lip. Beside her, Tim, also attempting to hide his amusement, lifted his hand over his mouth and coughed.

How the man justified letting himself get involved with Lucie's craziness, she'd never know. But he took it in stride, finding humor where most would see dysfunction.

"Dad," Lucie said, "the Cock Heads is a fan club for *Peacock Island.* That's the movie the missing dress was in."

Her father shook his head while scrolling his contacts for Willie's number. "They could have picked a better name. That's all I'm saying."

Lucie went back to Ro. "It's a good idea. The Co—going to another meeting. I'll make the statement about the reward and then we'll find a meeting and see if anyone reaches out. We can also ask about my buddy Bill. Maybe someone knows him."

"Hold up," Tim said. "The meeting is one thing. Bill? Now you're pushing it. This guy could be dangerous."

Joey waggled a finger. "He's right. You're not going alone. I'll go with you."

The drama queen sighed. "You can't. If Wilber—"

"It's Wendel."

Ro drilled Lucie with a look. "Whatever. If *Wendel* sees you, after you scared the be-jesus out of him the other night, who knows what he'll do. You might get us kicked out."

"Willie?" Dad said. "It's Joe. I need you on something ASAP. Call me back." Dad ended the call. "Voicemail. He'll call back fast. Always does."

Because he knows a cash cow when he sees it.

"I'll go to the meeting with you," Tim said. "They don't know me."

Um, had he forgotten his boss told him to avoid direct involvement in the case? "You can't."

"Yeah, I can. All I'm doing is crashing a meeting. If something pops, I'll call Bickel. This is legwork."

"That's what you're going with? Really?"

"It's a fine line, but yes, that's what I'm going with." He smacked his hands together. "Now, you need to get this impromptu press conference going. I can't go out there with you, but I'll be right here if you need me." He tweaked her nose. "Then, pretty lady, I have to get my ass to work before I really do get fired."

Oh, this man. Always there for her, no matter what,

offering the one thing she'd always wanted from her partner. Unconditional support.

All of them, her best friend, her lunatic brother, her Irish cop of a boyfriend and even her father, the man she found it so easy to fight with.

Her peeps.

All there for her.

She smiled, and Joey held his hands out. "What?"

"Nothing. You guys are an awesome team. It's a little crazy."

"But it's our crazy," Ro said.

Lucie tugged on the front of Tim's shirt. "Thanks for staying."

"You bet."

She faced her crew. "Now, listen up, dream team, let's have a press conference."

Fifteen minutes after giving Dad's filthy-expensive lawyer the plan, he spit out a statement that said little more than she had nothing to do with the theft and, in her ongoing effort to prove her innocence, would offer a ten-thousand-dollar reward for the dress's return.

The man wasn't happy, but he'd given her something short and simple to read and demanded that she do so without improvising even one syllable.

She'd certainly try, but Lucie couldn't stay silent. No more running.

After disappearing to the front of the store five minutes earlier, Ro marched back into the room, hair and arms flying.

"Here." She shoved a sheet of paper at Lucie. "I typed the statement for you."

"Are the reporters still out there?"

"Oh, yeah. Slip and Lemon are standing in front of the windows like a couple of commandos. All they need are automatic weapons and headbands."

Lawdy! That would be a spectacle. Just thinking about it made Lucie's bladder fill. She needed to get this over with. Just give the statement and shoo the reporters away before one of the hotheads on Dad's crew went berserk and pummeled something.

Or someone.

Lucie waved the statement. "For crying out loud, let's just do this so we can all get back to work."

She had a business to run, and the last few days had cost her. Between the downtime and having to call in her part-timers for backup, her P&L had disintegrated.

Ro held out a tube of lipstick. "Soft blush. It's a good color for you."

Lipstick. That's what concerned her?

"Don't look at me like that. You have no idea how the camera washes you out. You'll be thanking me when your pretty soft blush lips are on World News Tonight."

12

———

T HE SECOND J OEY swung the shop's door open a gaggle of voices exploded from the sidewalk.

Lucie froze in the doorway, the sound of the crowd smothering her. She stepped back half an inch, took in the row of reporters and flashing cameras just in front of her, and blinked. *Just get it done.*

Directly in front of her, barely three feet away, stood Debbie Deline from the local cable channel. She wore her signature red coat and matching lipstick, microphone at the ready.

Joey propped his foot at the base of the door and leaned forward. "You okay? I can do it if you want. Reporters love me."

Not the one who'd charged him with assault. She waved him off. "I'm fine. It's just a little . . . shocking."

"Eh, you got this. I'll be right here. And Ro, too. You even got Dad and a cop in the back room. Perfect setup."

The dream team.

Her father, not wanting to cause more of a spectacle—

something she needed to thank him for later—had opted to stay inside with Tim.

The straight-laced cop and the mob boss.

All kinds of twisted.

Lucie stepped out of the doorway, nodding at Slip and Lemon, who'd moved closer and spread their arms. A human rope keeping the reporters at bay.

"Lucie! Look here."

Nope. Not doing that. She raised her head, though, and again blinked at the flashes. She kept her head high. That's what Rizzos did, they moved forward, marched on.

Didn't let anyone see them sweat.

She held up her hand. "I'm not going to yell over you. I have a statement. If you want to hear it, you'll quiet down—"

"Lucie!"

"—and stop yelling at me." A few long seconds passed, and the crowd finally quieted. "Thank you."

She looked down at the statement, ready to read, but something felt . . . off, insincere even, about a prepared speech. Heck, she hadn't even written the thing. She wanted to win these people over, as much as she could anyway, and show them that she had nothing to hide. If she read the statement, something *crafted,* why would anyone believe her to be genuine?

Folding the paper, she tucked it back into her pocket. She had the gist of it anyway. Willy might have a heart attack, but winging it, speaking from the heart, had always been Lucie's way, and she couldn't change that now.

Joey stepped up beside her. "Uh, what's up?"

"Doing it my way." She faced the murmuring crowd. "Good morning, I'm Lucia Rizzo. Most of you know that already, or you wouldn't be standing in front of my business. I won't be taking any questions, but I will say that any speculation regarding my involvement with the stolen Maxmillian dress is unwarranted. To prove that, I am offering a ten-thousand-dollar reward for the return of the dress. A tip hotline will be set up in the next hour, and information can be found on the Coco Barknell website." Lucie pointed to the website address beneath the logo on the plate-glass window. "Thank you."

She pivoted to the door, but the crowd erupted, everyone shouting questions.

"Ignore them," Joey said. "Keep walking. They'll shut up in a minute."

A loud whistle sounded, and the crowd did, indeed, shut up. "The party is over."

Dad's voice. Outside.

Lucie spun back just as the crowd, seemingly in sync, shifted left.

Joey stepped back, craned his neck to see. "Crazy son of a gun. He must have gone through the alley."

"Joe," a reporter yelled, "how's it feel to be on the outside again?"

"How do you think it feels?" Dad joked.

Lucie peeked around the mountain known as Joey to where her father stood, smiling at the crowd, arms loose at his sides. "He shouldn't be out there."

"Joe, do you have an ankle monitor?"

"Joe, look here!"

On and on it went, people shouting questions, trying to lure her father into saying something stupid—they should know better—and begging for a photo.

"What's he doing?"

Joey shook his head. "Well, kiddo, I think he's drawing fire." He turned back, jerked his thumb toward the store.

"Inside. Before these vultures figure out they've got a two-for-one."

When Lucie didn't move, he gave her a light shove. "Go."

"Joey, he can't stay there."

"I know. You get inside, and I'll take care of him."

Her father, a man who'd just been released from prison, who probably still had federal agents watching him, had just taken over her press conference, creating the spectacle none of them wanted, so she could escape the reporters.

He'd done that for her.

Ro opened the shop door. "Get inside. Joey, take care of that hot mess."

Lucie hustled through the door. "I can't believe he's doing that."

Ro shrugged. "I can. He's your dad. When has he ever let anyone hassle you?"

As complicated as their relationship had been, as much as she couldn't reconcile what he did for a living, and made it no secret she didn't approve—and never would—he'd still thrown himself into the fray.

For her. To protect her.

Because that's what parents did. They protected their children. No matter what.

Dad marched through the front door of Coco Barknell with Joey behind him shooing reporters and photographers away.

With his middle finger.

With everything that had just gone on here, the thing that would most definitely make the evening news would be Joey flipping off the media.

Lucie lunged for her father, but Ro grabbed her arm. "Save it. Everyone in the break room. Let's not give this crowd a photo op."

Joey locked the front door, and the four of them headed down the corridor. Lucie shoved open the door. Tim stood on the far side of the room, head down, hands in pockets. At the ruckus coming through the door, he snapped to.

"How'd it go?"

"Fine. Until my father threw himself into the grinder." She whirled on him. "Dad, I love you for doing that, but that was *dangerous.*"

He waved both hands. "Ah, I was having fun with them."

Tim swung his head between Lucie and her father. "What happened? And for the record, I told him not to go."

"One thing you'll learn, the men in my family are stubborn. He occupied them for me. He was an ace."

Her dad shrugged. "After a while, you get used to this garbage."

"By the way," Joey said, "when Willy sees that news clip he's going to go ape-shit because you blew off his statement."

Ew. She hadn't considered Willie watching the news.

"Well, I'll deal with that later. I couldn't do it. I wanted to be sincere."

Beside her, Tim let out a breath. "Luce, seriously?"

Now the detective sided with the defense lawyer? Nothing today had gone even slightly the way she'd have expected.

"Everyone knock it off. The message was the same. It was just in my words. Not his."

Her cell phone rang. Dear God, could this be him? "Oh, don't even tell me." She slid the phone from her back pocket. A 312 number, but not Willie's. "Hmmm ..."

"Who is it?" Tim asked.

"I don't know. Let's find out."

After all, she did just make an offer of a ten-thousand-dollar reward.

"Hello?"

"You're crazy!"

And this was news? "Who is this?"

"It's Lewis Dukane. There's a slew of reporters banging on my door and calling my office. And the rabid Peacock fans. I just got a call from a Cock Head, whatever the hell that is, wanting to know about some reward you mentioned on a news report. What reward?"

Holy cow. Someone must have broadcast her statement already. Yes!

"Mr. Dukane—"

"Oh, hell," Tim said.

"Mr. Dukane, calm down. We're on the same side here. We both want to find the dress, right? This is the way to do it."

"Luce, hang up. Don't talk to him."

She waved Tim off. Getting the owner of the dress on Team Lucie could only help her.

"Ms. Rizzo, I don't have time for your shenanigans."

According to her research, Mr. Dukane owned a chain of wine bars in Chicago, New York and California. She'd give him credit for building a successful business, but he didn't need to be rude. "You know," she said, "I'm trying to help here. This is your dress. I'd think you'd be a little more appreciative of my efforts. Considering you're not putting up the reward money."

Joey huddled closer. "That's telling him, tough guy."

"Help?" Mr. Dukane said. "By sending legions of people

my way? That's how you help? Who is going to field all these calls?"

So maybe she hadn't anticipated reporters and fans flocking to Mr. Dukane.

My bad.

And those Cock Heads, they could be rabid.

"I certainly apologize for that, sir. I told everyone to go to my website for information. I didn't realize we'd receive this kind of reaction. But, hey, maybe we'll get a solid lead out of this, and the dress will be recovered. Wouldn't that be great?"

"You dumb twit!"

From the first moments she'd met this man, he'd been horrendous to her. Right here, right now, it would stop. "Rudeness. That is uncalled—"

Click. The line went dead. Lucie held the phone in front of her and shook it wildly. "Idiot!"

Joey burst out laughing. Ro slapped him—hard—on the arm. Dad narrowed his eyes and Tim watched the whole thing with a detached amusement that tilted his mouth into a half-hidden grin.

"What a jerk," Lucie said. "He hung up on me."

"Who was that?" This from Dad, whose narrowed eyes and locked jaw told her all she needed to know about what he was thinking.

"He's the owner of the dress."

"How'd he get your number?"

"I don't know. Maybe from the auction house. Or it's on the Coco Barknell website. The upshot is, our little impromptu press conference worked. The bad news is he's getting slammed with calls and reporters showing up at his door."

Ro peeled her lips back. "Ew."

"Yeah. Not happy." She turned to Tim. "I kinda feel bad."

"Don't. He's an ass. Arrogant as all hell. Everybody owes him a living, that type of thing."

In her limited dealings with him, she could see that.

Tim's phone rang. The dreaded train horn. "That's your boss. I'm so sorry I've kept you."

The phone rang again, but he reached for her, squeezed her arm. "It's okay. But I gotta take this."

He made a move to drop a kiss on her but stopped. Probably the audience scaring him off. As tempted as she was to finish it, to just hop up and lay a smooch on him, she wouldn't. Clearly, he wasn't yet comfortable kissing her in front of her father, and she wouldn't rush him.

Instead, she pecked him on the cheek. Nice compromise. "Go talk to your boss. Thank you for everything. I'll call you later."

"Don't forget we have a Cock Head meeting to attend."

———

LUCIE, TIM AND RO ARRANGED TO MEET AT A CAFE AROUND the corner from the Java Pit at six o'clock. They'd grab a quick bite, draft a plan and then hit the Cock Head meeting at seven.

At 5:50, Lucie and Ro nabbed a parking spot near the coffee shop and hoofed it to the cafe. Darkness descended, bringing a crisp wind that prickled Lucie's cheeks as they walked. At the corner traffic light, she tilted her head back at an array of twinkling stars splashed across the black sky. Such a perfect night for a walk.

With a hunky detective.

With any luck, her pain-in-the-butt brother would show up later to take Ro home and Lucie and Tim could sneak off for a few minutes. She'd barely seen him all week, and the realization brought her back to those miserable times when she and Frankie had been broken up and loneliness consumed her.

Oddly, she never felt lonely when away from Tim. Somehow, even in such an early stage of their relationship, she felt . . . at ease.

Not comfortable, but safe.

At the cafe, Ro held the door open, but having been cooped up all day while lying low from the few reporters still loitering in front of the shop, Lucie needed air.

And a few minutes alone.

Her BFF eyed her. "What's wrong?"

"Nothing. Why?"

"I know you. You've got a spooked look. Spill it, Sister."

Such a gift—mostly—to have a friend who knew her so well. And cared enough to ask what her problem was.

Lucie took two steps, wrapped her arms around Ro and squeezed. "Thank you. But really, I'm good. I've gotten too used to being outside with the dogs every day."

"Ah. You didn't get that today."

Lucie backed away and tapped her nose. "You guessed it. I need air and a few minutes by myself. That's all. Get us a table, and I'll wait for Tim."

Ro grinned. "Okay, but no sneaking off to make out."

Lucie snorted. "We'll try to control ourselves."

No promises though.

An empty bench, courtesy of the cafe, sat in front of the building. Lucie plopped onto it, fighting the urge to check her phone. A few minutes of being disconnected might give her a much-needed energy boost.

Hunting down stolen memorabilia could wear a girl down.

She rested her head back against the brick building. The cold from the hard surface traveled into her neck and shoulders. She inhaled, held the breath for a few seconds and let it go again. Her own Lucie version of speed meditating.

"Hey, pretty lady."

Tim's voice. She opened her eyes to the hunkmeister standing right in front of her, his lovely green eyes sparking and heating her cheeks.

And hello? She hadn't even heard him walk up. He could have been a mugger and here she was zoning out on a city street.

I need sleep.

"Hi." She rose from the bench, tugged on his suit jacket. "You snuck up on me."

"You looked peaceful. Sorry if I scared you."

"You could never scare me. In fact, with you, it's the reverse."

"And that's a good thing, I hope."

"Safety is a very good thing. You look like you have something on your mind."

He made a grunting noise, ran one finger under her chin and kissed her. Soft and long and . . . *oh, my, my, my.*

He'd kissed her before, plenty of times, but this one? Total panty dropper. A slow brush of lips that left her more than a little gooey. She snuggled closer, and the heat of his body curved around her.

Safety.

Finally, he pulled back from the kiss. "It occurs to me," he said, "that you haven't seen where I live."

This is it. For weeks she'd been thinking about when he'd finally make his move. When she'd be ready for him to do so.

He'd been upfront about making sure she was over

Frankie. When Tim O'Brien took a woman to bed, he didn't want the Ghost of Boyfriends Past in there with them.

Well, she was ready. "In fact, I haven't."

"It's only three miles from here, would you like to?"

"Now?"

He laughed. "After the meeting." He leaned in, nuzzled her ear. "I have to warn you, I might get handsy."

"Wouldn't that be conduct unbecoming an officer?"

"Only if I'm lucky."

She swatted him on the chest. "That's . . ."

"What?"

A great idea. As much as she wanted to scold him, why bother? They'd been playing this game, teasing each other with sexual innuendos, for the past two weeks, getting closer and closer to this moment.

She could either think it to death—as she usually did—or let it happen.

"I'd like that," she said. "I'll text Joey. Tell him to come and get Ro."

"We could drive her home."

"Holy crap, Detective, you must really need to get some if you're willing to drive to Franklin and back."

Tim cracked up, threw his arm over her shoulder and steered her toward the door. "Or maybe it's just the woman. Ever think of that, smartass?"

Again, she smiled up at him. "Coming from you, that's a great compliment." She dug her phone from her jacket pocket and went to work on texting Joey. "Now, let's get the big man down here so you and I can get busy tonight."

AFTER DINNER, LUCIE CHECKED HER TEXTS TO SEE IF JOEY HAD

responded. He typically responded within minutes, but in the hour they'd been at the cafe, he'd gone radio silent.

Which meant her bookie of a brother must have been glued to a barstool sweating out a close game. And she hated that. As smart as he was—way smarter than her, if she were being honest—he could do so much more with his life. Heck, if he'd leave bookie-ing behind, she'd give him full time at Coco Barknell. He'd supervise the dog walking while she oversaw the accessory line. Crazy as he made her, he was reliable and knew how to take charge of an operation. With him and Ro helping, maybe Coco Barknell could actually grow into that Fortune 500 company she dreamed of.

Tim stood, scooped up the check and walked to the counter to pay while Lucie and Ro made their way outside.

"I like him," Ro said. "I miss mouthing off to Frankie, but O'Hottie? I think he's good for you."

Lucie linked her arm through Ro's. "I think so, too. He makes me feel happy and relaxed."

"Yeah, yeah, that's all good, but I wish you'd have sex with him and give me the details. I just know there's a great body under those suits."

"Maybe tomorrow I'll give you a little something."

Ro halted, narrowed her eyes. "Don't tease me."

Lucie clucked her tongue. "If my brother would text me back and tell me he'll pick you up tonight, you might just get your wish."

"Stop. It."

Lucie laughed. Ro. So easy. "He wants me to go home with him after the Cock Head meeting. I texted Joey. He hasn't answered."

Ro ripped her arm free and dug into her giant purse. "You're going. Believe it."

On the street, a car cruised by, slowing as it neared, the

driver obviously anticipating the score of a parking spot via Lucie and Ro. Lucie waved the driver on. *Sorry, pal.*

"The Hawks are on," Ro said. "But I'll get his attention." She shot off a text with an evil grin quirking one side of her mouth. "I love doing this to him."

"Seriously, you two are sick."

"I know. But it's fun."

Tim stepped out of the restaurant, his suit coat blowing open as a gust of wind took hold of it. Lucie's gaze landed on the center of his chest, wandered up to where the top button hung open after he'd ditched his tie.

With any luck, in a couple of hours, she'd know what hid under that shirt.

Ro leaned closer, got right up to Lucie's ear. "Now whose the sick one?"

"Oh, just shut it."

Tim stepped between them, held both arms out. "Ladies, shall we?"

The two of them linked arms with him, and they headed west toward the Java Pit. As they walked, Ro's phone went off, and she pulled her arm free.

Please, let that be Joey.

"Well, well," she said, "looks like you two lovebirds are in business. Joey will be here in an hour." She shoved the phone back into her purse and grabbed hold of Tim's arm again. "O'Hottie, you owe me."

Dear God.

"Fair enough," Tim said.

Inside the Java Pit, they greeted the cute barista from their previous visit. Knowing the guy probably counted on his tips, Lucie ordered a round of coffees, and they headed upstairs.

"Brace yourself," she said to Tim, "The lady that ran the

meeting the other night wore a replica dress, and it was a sight."

"I'll say," Ro added. "Darn it! I forgot my headband."

"You'll survive. We'll introduce Tim as my boyfriend. If Wendel is here, Ro, you do your thing and get some conversation going. I'll break off and ask him about Bill. See if he knows him."

Tim stopped in the middle of the staircase. "Are we sure Wendel and Bill aren't partners?"

Ro's eyebrows shot up.

Could that be? No wonder he was the detective.

Lucie cocked her head. "He did tell me he'd load our contact information into the database."

Someone entered the staircase, their heavy shoes clunking against the creaky wooden steps as they climbed.

Not wanting to be overheard, Lucie jerked her chin to the top of the stairs. "I guess we'll find out."

As with the other night, Annabelle, once again in the replica Maxmillian dress, greeted them.

She waved at them from her spot near the spiritwear table, once again strewn with postcards, headbands and various other items. She smiled at Tim, then shifted her gaze to Lucie and Ro, narrowing her eyes enough that Lucie figured Annabelle had seen the news. "I have to say, after seeing that news clip of you, I'm surprised to see you two back."

"Hi, Annabelle," Lucie said. "I'm sure it was a shock, but I had nothing to do with the theft. Which is why I offered that reward. I'm searching for the real thief. And we're here to see if anyone might have heard anything."

Beside her, Tim cleared his throat, and she set her hand on his arm. "This is my boyfriend, Tim."

And, wow, as exciting as it was, the word "boyfriend"

coming from her mouth and not followed by the name "Frankie" would take a minute to get used to.

Change. Always hard.

"Hello, Tim," Annabelle said. "Welcome to the Cock Heads. Please feel free to look over the items on the table. Plenty of information there. And that reminds me." She picked up a stack of flyers and turned back to the group. "Everyone, make sure you take one of these. It's the schedule of events for the Cock Head Convention. Great lineup this year!"

Tim glanced down at Lucie, raised an eyebrow. Yep, they had a convention.

"Oh, I'll take one." Ro snatched one from the stack. "I swear, people, if someone doesn't find that dress soon, I may have to get violent."

"Yow," Tim said.

"Buckle up, big boy. You haven't seen her in action. Her method acting should win her an Oscar."

Ro flopped her ginormous purse onto the table and dropped into a chair with a huff. "Please, someone give me good news."

The bored housewife from the other night sat forward. "Well, I don't know if it's good news or not, but Annabelle is right. The lineup for the convention looks amazing. I heard they're going to have a peacock parade. Right through the hotel ballroom!"

"That's gotta be a health-code violation," Tim muttered.

Lucie elbowed him, then scanned the two dozen folks in attendance, hoping to find Bill among them. Not that she'd be that lucky, but a girl could dream. She recognized some people from the other night—*hello, Wendel*—but no Bill.

Hey, that was a stretch anyway. She wasn't even sure he'd

been here the other night. She certainly didn't remember seeing him.

Besides, the guy would be nuts to show up after their deal had gone bad. Then again, how sane could the man be when making shady deals with Cock Heads?

The upshot tonight was the chair beside Wendel was open. "Okay." She tugged on Tim's sleeve. "The balding guy is Wendel. I'll grab the open seat next to him, and you pull up a chair. We'll see if he knows anything."

"Got it."

"Wendel," she said, "hi. How are you?"

"Hello, Lucie." He stood, shook her hand and quickly brought his attention to Tim. "You brought a friend."

"I did. This is my boyfriend, Tim."

Second time saying it was much easier. Maybe she needed to practice. Practice, practice, practice.

The two men shook hands, and Tim snagged a chair from one of the open tables.

Lucie hung her purse on the back of her chair and scanned the room. "Wow. It's great to see so many people at the meeting."

"We usually get a good crowd, but with the convention starting, everyone wants to figure out which panels will be the best."

"There's a lot to see, huh?"

"You really need to map out a plan for it."

"I'm telling you," Ro said from the other side of the table. "The problem with this dress not being found is the black market. If it gets sold there, we'll never see it again. *Ever.*"

The housewife gasped. "But why?"

"Because that's how the black market works. Buyers don't want to get caught with stolen merchandise, so they hide it in a vault. For them it's more about the hunt. Once they get it, they're happy just knowing they have it. They'll grab a glass of wine and go sit in the vault with it. Then—" she swiped her hands together "—the vault is locked again. It's disgusting. And worse, let's put it on the table here, people, if that happens, Lucie might never be cleared."

Ugh. *Thanks for that, Ro.*

A round of muttering about the press conference rose from the folks around the table, and Lucie took that as her cue to fess up to the group.

"Everyone," she said, "I just told Annabelle, but I want all of you to know as well that I had nothing to do with the robbery. I was simply walking one of my clients—I'm a dogwalker—around the time the robbery occurred. That's why I offered the reward. I'm trying to clear my name."

"Did you get any calls for the reward?" a man called from one of the tables near the wall.

Oh, they'd gotten calls. So far, though, it sounded like crackpots. Still, maybe something would come of it. "Nothing solid yet. I'm hopeful, though."

Two seats down from Ro, a man Lucie didn't recognize waggled his finger. "She's right. There's a huge market for memorabilia of this level. If the dress isn't recovered, you people are sunk."

"We people?" Ro said.

Uh-oh.

"What are you saying? You don't care about the dress?"

"Sure I care. *You're* obsessed."

Lucie turned to Tim. "Oh. Crap."

"On it." He sat forward. "Listen, I can understand the outrage. As an art collector, it galls me. Nothing we can do about it." He picked up one of the convention flyers and waved it. "I've never been. Anyone have any tips?"

Across from him, Ro—obviously craving the smackdown Tim had just thwarted—harrumphed. Lucie rolled her eyes. Later, she'd remind her partner about the benefits of staying on topic.

A multitasking woman at the end of the table set her knitting down. "Personally, I like to see all the exhibitors first. A lot of merchandise gets sold, and if you don't get there early, you miss out. I do the exhibitors first and then the panel discussions and parties."

Lucie perked up. "Parties?"

"Oh, those are the best. They even have food at some of them. You get to mingle and meet people who were involved with the original film."

"Holy cow," Lucie said, "they're still alive?"

Tim made a noise from deep in his throat. *Whoopsie.* She leaned closer, lowered her voice. "Was that rude? I mean, the film is fifty years old. How many people can be left?"

This time O'Hottie laughed and gave her a smooch on the cheek. "You're so damned cute."

"I'm just saying . . ."

The smackdown guy pointed at Ro. "Talk about the hunt and capture. You should see the stuff that gets moved at this convention. Huge deals are made behind closed doors. You ladies really want to find that dress, that's the place to look."

Huge deals. Excellent. That's what they were here for. Tim perused the convention flyer. Well, pretended to peruse. She knew him well enough to know when he relaxed, his body went loose and his shoulders dropped. Right now, those shoulders were stiff enough to divert bullets.

"Do tell," Ro said. "In addition to helping my friend Lucie here, I'm trying to screw my rat-bastard husband in a divorce. Money is no object."

Tim inched closer to Lucie. "She could be mentally unstable."

"You're just figuring that out? Why do you think she and Joey work? They're both lunatics."

"Good point." Satisfied with her answer, Tim went back to pretending to ignore the conversation happening across the table.

"From what I've heard," the man told Ro, "they don't bring the high-value items onto the floor. All that stuff is sold through back rooms."

"How does that work?"

The guy shrugged. "I guess you tell someone what you're looking for and word gets out. I think they find you if they have what you want."

Annabelle checked her watch, cleared her throat and set her hands on the table clearly ready to start the meeting.

Ro held her finger up. "Hold on. This is good. So, all I need to do is put the word out that I'm interested in buying the Max and if it's being sold on the black market, I might have a shot at it?"

Annabelle cleared her throat again. "I don't think this is appropriate."

Good luck, girlfriend. Inappropriate or not, Lucie refused to let Annabelle shut this down. "Annabelle, I agree. But on the flip side, if the dress is being sold in a shady deal, and Roseanne is able to uncover its whereabouts; the dress could be returned, and the thieves incarcerated."

And I'm off the hook.

The bored housewife perked up. "And if we all helped her, we'd get credit for finding the dress."

Lucie could see the headline: Cock Head Heroes.

Ro smacked both hands on the table. "Yes! People would love us."

"Uh," Tim said.

Lucie elbowed him again. "Shut it, you."

She didn't need her cop boyfriend warning them about danger. She needed that dress found.

He opened his mouth, obviously about to argue, but she pinched his forearm.

"Ow," he said.

"Do you *want* me to be someone's prison bitch? I was kinda saving that for you."

Tim paused then gave her a hard look. "Uh . . . wow . . . okay . . . I guess we'll discuss it later."

I guess we will.

Chatter erupted around the table, everyone talking over each other about solving the mystery, media attention, being honored at the Academy Awards—total stretch there, but whatever.

Lucie stood and held up her hands. "Gang, let's pipe down. I love all these ideas, but truly, this could be danger-ous. I think being impact players in the dress's recovery would only bring more attention to the importance of the Cock Heads. But we can't get hurt in the process."

"She's right," the bored housewife said.

A round of agreements followed and the noise kicked up again, scraping against Lucie's ears. "Quiet down a second. I have a plan."

13

———

AFTER DEPUTIZING the Cock Heads for the convention and instructing them to phone or text her if anyone heard anything about a sale involving the Max, Lucie turned the meeting back to Annabelle while Tim shot lasers from his eyes.

The hot, Irish detective wasn't happy. Worse, she agreed with him. Inciting a bunch of crazed Cock Heads might get any number of people hurt.

Which she'd warned them about. They were not, under any circumstances, to try and make deals on their own. All they needed to do was bring Lucie the information and all of it would be turned over to the police.

Still, these Cock Heads were an unpredictable bunch.

Now, standing in front of the coffee shop, where the evening temperature had dropped a good ten degrees in the ninety minutes they'd been inside, Lucie's nerves started to sizzle. The cold air prickled her cheeks, and she shoved her hands into her trench-coat pockets while waiting for Joey to pull around the corner.

"Luce," Tim said, "I could kill you."

Ro swung a look at him, then Lucie and wisely stepped away, pretending to check her phone.

Lucie faced Tim. "I know. I'm sorry."

He dipped his head. "You're sorry? What if one of those people gets hurt?"

"They won't. They're reasonable."

"They're running around with peacock feathers on their heads. How reasonable can they be?"

She held up a finger. "Think about the knowledge they have. Your department has art-fraud experts, right?"

"They're trained police officers."

"But they have informants. Regular citizens that feed them information."

She should know, considering her father had been convicted with the help of a confidential informant—a CI.

To this, Tim had no argument. And he knew it.

He stared up at the sky, shaking his head for a few seconds before meeting her gaze again. "Well played."

"Thank you." She linked her arm through his and squeezed close. "I know you're worried, but Ro and I are good at this. Unfortunately. I can control it. I promise."

"As much as I'd like to believe that, I have to call my lieutenant. I *have* to. He'll get a couple of extra people in the place."

Wait. Extra detectives? "The police will be there anyway. Why do we need more?"

"It's an investigation into the theft of a million-dollar piece of memorabilia, that's why. Not that I should have told you that, but hell, at least I know you'll be somewhat safe."

"Are you mad at me?"

"Yes. You'll make it up to me."

Yay, Lucie.

Where was Joey? He'd texted ten minutes earlier with

his ETA. They certainly weren't going to leave Ro alone while they went off to play house.

Humping-bunnies house, anyway. A low, deep yearning squeezed her belly and moved lower, settling in a place that hadn't seen one darned bit of activity since Frankie left.

In the months he'd been gone, she'd been okay without sex. Well, relatively speaking. She'd been grieving her relationship with Frankie, and, as much as she was attracted to Tim, she'd hadn't been ready for intimacy with someone new.

Someone different.

And Tim O'Brien, with his height and big shoulders that could probably support a mountain, was definitely different.

Lucie snuck a peek at him, the one who'd obviously been watching her.

A wicked smile split his lips.

My God. I might do him right on this sidewalk.

She whipped around to Ro. "Have we heard from Joey?"

"Look at you in such a hurry. Relax. He'll be here."

Joey's Jeep finally swung around the corner. He double-parked in front of the shop and, from inside the car, opened the passenger's side door.

Lucie moved to the edge of the sidewalk and peered in. "Thanks for coming. Tim and I are, uh, gonna grab a bite."

They sure were.

"No problem." Joey leaned right and pointed at Tim. "Are you doing my sister?"

"Joey!"

Tim bent at the waist and met his gaze. "Dude, you really want to know?"

Good answer.

"Just ignore him." Ro slid into the car. "You two have fun. Luce, tell your folks you're staying at my house tonight.

Stay out late for once in your life. Change things up. Be a slut."

Still bent over, Lucie tilted her head to Tim. "The people in my life are all nuts. You know that right?"

"Yep. From my perspective, it keeps things interesting."

Excellent response. Lucie went back to Joey and Ro. "Be careful going home. I'll see you tomorrow."

Ro offered up one of her flirty finger waves. "Toodles. Have fun, you two."

They would indeed.

TIM MADE A RIGHT OFF OF TAYLOR STREET IN LITTLE ITALY onto a quiet, tree-lined block packed with parked cars. In the darkness, modest street lamps threw light over the three-story brick homes stacked together like soldiers in formation.

"If we get lucky," he said, "we'll find a spot on the block. If not, we're hoofing it from the honey hole."

"The honey hole?"

"Two streets up. I always find a spot there. It's the whorehouse of parking. Always one available."

Lucie laughed. "In Franklin, we just put garbage cans in the spaces. A practice, I might add, I don't partake in. Unless it's winter and we've just shoveled out the spot. Then all bets are off."

"Damn, you're cute, Lucie."

He reached the end of the block and hooked a right. "I'm gonna do one more pass."

"There was a guy walking."

"Yep. He lives two doors down. Night owl."

"I like this neighborhood."

"Me, too. I moved here two years ago. Buddy of mine got a job out west and needed to sublet. Rent's on the high side, but the location is aces."

"With Taylor Street right there? No kidding."

Growing up, the Rizzos shared weekly meals at Santa Lucia, her father's favorite restaurant, and one Lucie suspected she might have been named after. In the warmer months, they'd eat and then wander Taylor Street to, as Mom put it, work off dinner.

Back then Dad hadn't been around much, and the walks were probably more about her mother wanting to hoard time spent as a family.

Tim made the second turn onto his street as a car vacated a spot at the opposite end. "Bingo. You bring me good luck, Luce."

He zipped into the spot easily. Even if he did give the car behind him a nudge. Again, in Lucie's opinion, not unusual when it came to city parking.

"Whoops" he said, "call it a love tap."

After parking, he wandered to the rear of the car, bent low and, using the flashlight on his phone, checked for damage to the other car.

"You barely tapped it," Lucie said. "There can't be any damage."

"Doesn't hurt to check."

A man with a conscience. She liked that about him. A lot of people would simply assume there'd been no damage and walk away.

He stuck his phone in his jacket pocket and held his hand to Lucie. She'd gotten used to holding hands with him. Given the time they'd spent walking from parking spaces there'd been ample opportunity to partake.

She slid her hand into his, let the familiar warmth of his

much larger fingers lace with hers. She lifted their hands, kissed the back of his. "Thank you."

"For what?"

"I'm safe with you."

He shrugged. "I'm crazy about you. Why wouldn't I want you safe?"

Because Frankie was crazy about her, too, and she had never felt safe with him. No. That wasn't fair. He'd been protective of her when it came to her physical safety—catching her when she tripped on the sidewalk or slipped on ice. He'd always watched over her in that way.

He'd just never taken her side when it came to his family. And that had left her . . . alone.

With Tim? Never alone. He was Team Lucie all the way. And he proved it every day, even when it could risk the job he loved.

Lucie popped up to tiptoes and dropped a quick kiss on his lips. "I just wanted you to know."

He smiled at her, tickled her under the chin with his free hand. "It's cold out here."

"Sure is. Whaddya say, big fella? Wanna warm me up?"

"Honey," he said, "if that's your idea of dirty talk, we have work to do."

He led her to a stately brick home with arched windows, a concrete stoop, and a four-foot patch of grass bordered with day lilies.

"I like the landscaping. Nice touch."

"Yeah. It's the lady upstairs. The landlord takes care of the grass and Mrs. Hendry tends to the plants. The lilies are nice. I guess. But I can't find the point of the grass. It's not like we can play ball on that grass."

Men.

"Ambiance, my love. Ambiance."

He pulled his hand free, ran it down her back and guided her up the steps. "I like the sound of that."

"Ambiance?"

"No. The 'my love' part."

Ah. That. She could backtrack, deny, deny, deny and tell him it just slipped out. That she'd gotten caught up.

People did that. People who weren't Lucie.

People like Lucie *didn't* say those things.

An overhead light illuminated the lock as Tim messed with his keys. Lucie focused on the thick, oak door. The rich, green paint had a chic distressed vibe to it. She took it all in, every scrape and crack and nick.

All the changes in the last few months hit her. Frankie leaving, the loneliness and hurt in the beginning and then, slowly, allowing Tim and the joy and ease of him—the laughter—into her heart.

In a lot of ways, he'd saved her.

And for a girl who never needed or wanted a man to save her, that was saying something.

He pushed the door open and waved her in. "I'm on the first floor. Easy access."

She stepped into the hallway. Stairs on the left led to the upper floors. To the right was a short hallway and another door.

Tim's door.

She waited for him to check the lock behind them— again with the safety—and when he turned back she grabbed his arm, held him there a second.

"I love you."

Dear. *God.* A burst of panic shredded her chest, cutting off her air. *Too soon.* Why, why, *why* had she said that?

Because it was true. And no one should ever be afraid of that.

If Tim rejected her, so be it. She'd live with it. Even if he didn't feel the same, being the man he was, somehow she didn't believe her admission would send him hiking.

"I'm sorry," she blurted.

Tim's jaw flopped open. "You're sorry that you love me?"

She slapped her hand over her mouth, and Tim cracked up. How many different ways could she blow this?

If Ro were here, she'd be screaming by now. She held her hands up. "No. I just . . ." She glanced back at the front door. Pondered running through it.

"Hey." He gently tugged on a few strands of her hair. "Just what?"

"I don't know." She waved at that damned door. "Got caught up."

"So, it's not true?"

"Yes."

Tim tipped his head back, muttered a "help me" and faced her again. "You're killing me right now."

"I'm sorry."

He held up a finger. "Clarify. Yes, it's not true that you love me or yes, it *is* true?"

She shook her head. That question of how many ways she could screw this up? Apparently a lot. "I do love you. Absolutely. No question. I don't want you to freak out."

"I'm not the one freaking out."

Point there.

"I am, in fact, quite comfortable with it. No need to kill it with conversation or feel awkward. It's all good."

What did that mean? Did he agree? Love her, too? What? But she wouldn't ask. No way. If he didn't love her, the humiliation would be complete. "Okay."

Brilliant.

He jerked his thumb toward his apartment. "You wanna go inside?"

So he hadn't said it back. So what? Three seconds ago she'd gone on a full-bore internal lecture about how it wasn't important if he didn't feel the same. She'd done this, created this moment between them, and damned if she'd go psycho on him and ruin their plans for the evening.

Besides, she could use some sex with a hot guy.

She nodded. "You bet."

"Good."

He walked to his apartment door, unlocked it and pushed it open, holding it for her. Inside, a light from the corridor threw shadows into a room with hardwood floors. Probably the living room.

"Welcome," he said.

Again, she nodded, stepping into the barely lit room.

"And, Lucie?"

For someone who didn't want to talk, why was he talking? She turned, met his gaze. "Yes?"

"I love you, too."

TIM STOOD IN THE DOORWAY AND WAITED FOR LUCIE TO SAY something. Damn the darkness because he couldn't see anything in her body language.

Usually, he'd tag her mood in seconds. She was easy that way. Her haunting blue eyes gave it away every time. Now? He had nothing. Zippo.

From now on, he'd leave on the damned living-room lights.

And then she launched herself at him. Just sprinted the few feet between them and leaped.

Her body connected with his just as he got his arms out, and the force—a hundred pounds was a hundred pounds—sent him crashing into the open door.

Shoving her tongue in his mouth helped break the chaos. In a big way.

He clamped his hands over her ass to keep her from slipping. If her tongue in his mouth didn't give him an erection, well, her legs around him just did.

She pulled back, and the side of her mouth quirked enough to make him think about sex and lots of it. Damn, he was nuts about her.

Every time he was around her his world opened up to all sorts of possibilities.

With her, he was invincible.

A beast.

Untouchable.

She rocked her hips against him. "Hello, you."

"You started it. And I'm not apologizing."

"Please, don't." But she smacked his shoulder. Hard.

"Ow. What's that for?"

"For making me sweat that whole I-love-you thing, that's what."

He moved away from the door, kicked it shut and locked it with one hand because he didn't intend on coming back to do it later.

She'd be lucky if he let her out of bed to pee.

"I didn't make you sweat it. I was surprised. And then you went psycho on me, and I couldn't figure out if you loved me or not. I had to regroup."

"*Regroup?* Did you just say that to me?"

Shit. Were they going to fight about this? Now?

No. They weren't. He smacked her on the ass, and she dropped her legs, made a move to stand. *No way, sweetheart.*

He bent low, grabbed hold and—upsie-daisy—boosted her over his shoulder.

"Eeep!"

At his bedroom, he kicked the slightly ajar door open. "We're not fighting over the fact that I love you. I've been waiting on you to say it. Hell, Lucie, I knew I loved you after our first date. You weren't ready for me. I've been telling myself that. While waiting. On you. So, yeah, I needed to figure out how to not make an ass out of myself when I told you I loved you for the first time. Deal with it."

"Okay," she said. "That's better."

Dodged one there.

"Glad to hear it. By the way, my bed is a king. And we're gonna use every inch of it."

"Eeep," she said again, this time the word coming on a long slow, breath and without the squeak from a second ago.

This time, she knew exactly what was happening.

Tim tossed her on his bed, and—*wow, wow, wow*—Lucie totally loved that.

Due to her diminutive size, most people treated her like delicate china. Something that would shatter when bumped or pushed too hard.

Guess what, kids? She didn't shatter.

Most of the time anyway.

And Tim, after only a few months, understood that in a way Frankie never had.

She hopped to her knees and poked her finger at him. "Out of those clothes, sailor. You're about to get laid."

Even as she said it, she couldn't hold back the giggle. And that got *him* going and here they were, the two of them in his darkened bedroom, about to rip each other's clothes off for the first time, laughing at each other.

Perfection.

"We're really twisted, Tim."

"What's your point?"

He tossed his suit jacket away. Where it landed, she didn't know and didn't care. When he reached for his shirt buttons, she swatted his hands away. "Me, me, me."

He dropped his hands, ran them over her waist, down her hips to the front of her jeans. He popped the snap and worked the zipper low, low, low.

Come to me, O'Hottie.

Zipper done, he hooked his thumbs over the waistband of her jeans and let his warm fingers slide over her skin. Her hormones whooped it up.

Months she'd been without physical touch—skin to skin with a man—and now, with Tim, she ached for more. For the heat and friction and companionship that came with intimacy.

O'Hottie wasn't the only one about to get laid.

Clothes gone, Tim scooped her up, ripped the comforter and sheet back and set her back down, moving over her and propping on his elbows. He dragged one thumb over the side of her face, looping it in circles, round and round and round all the while, watching her, studying her face and her eyes and her lips.

Wow, wow, wow.

"You won't crush me," she said. Seductive brilliance.

He smiled down at her, kissed her lightly—three quick taps—on the lips that held his attention for the last ten seconds. "I know. I'm just looking. Been thinking about this a while."

Me, too.

He dipped his head down, kissed her neck as his weight, all that muscle and warmth, settled on her. Wrapped around her in his nice Tim cocoon, once again that feeling, that enormous sense of security that came with him, hit her.

She dragged her nails up his back, over the hard planes of his shoulders and over his neck, drawing him closer, wanting to feast on his beautiful mouth.

He reached left, slid the nightstand drawer open. "Gotta ... um."

Condom. Another thing she hadn't had to worry about in a long time. She was on the pill, but they'd have the whole safe-sex conversation later. When they also had the conversation about exclusivity.

Because Lucie wasn't into multiple partners.

She hoped he'd understood that. He had to. Right?

He rolled off of her, turned his back and went to work on the condom. "I hate these damned things."

That made two of them.

Later.

He turned back to her, smiling through the darkness, and she saw it, *felt* it. For the first time really let herself experience the buzzing tingle that invaded her body when he looked at her.

He loved her.

Loved her.

She bolted up and kissed him, mashing her bare breasts against his chest, loving the tickling hair in the middle of his torso.

Man's man.

Then she shoved him backward. Taking control in a way she'd never allowed herself. Control meant confidence, in her body, in her looks, in her relationship.

Something she suddenly realized she'd been sorely lacking.

She straddled Tim's hips, and that silly grin of his poured over his face. *He likes it.* Her heart pounded, and she leaned forward, ran her hands up his chest, over his shoulders and kissed him lightly. "I love you."

He gripped her thighs, let her adjust herself and thrust, and—*wow*—the feel of him inside her made her gasp.

"Helloooo, Lucie."

"Helloooo, O'Hottie."

She rolled her hips, moving with him, bringing him deeper and deeper. Amazing. The two people who couldn't be more opposite in lifestyle and looks, somehow found common ground.

Lucie leaned back, brought him fully inside her while his hands and gaze roamed over her body, exploring every inch and—funny thing—she didn't freak out. Didn't dip her head in embarrassment, didn't wonder what he saw, didn't draw comparisons to his perfection and her lack of perfection.

Thank you.

Tim clamped his hands at her hips, gritted his teeth and she shifted, making him groan because, yes, his orgasm was about to hit. And she'd done it. She'd brought him to that edge.

Then she was on her back, flipped right over while Tim stared straight down at her, a wicked smile in place. She knew what he wanted. He wanted her on the edge, too. She brought her legs up higher and . . . perfection. *Right there.*

"Luce?"

She swung her head, needing the silence as her body came alive, every nerve ending exploding with pleasure and release.

She opened her eyes, stared up at Tim, the big shoulders, the green eyes that twinkled when he looked at her. Something in his expression changed, hardened. *Hanging on.* She reached up, dragged her fingertips over his chest. *Boom.* The orgasm took hold, and he cried out. Something inside her churned, and she pumped her hips and whipped her head sideways and waited—*please, please, please*—until finally, finally, she let go into a swirl of bright lights and release.

So good.

Tim sank into her, his full weight pressing her into the mattress, shooing away the cold.

With him, she'd never be cold.

Or alone.

Whatever their differences Tim O'Brien might be the best thing to ever happen to her.

Lucie woke up to the sun slanting between the blinds. Tim needed drapes.

Of course, she wouldn't tell him that on day-one post–I love you, but if she were going to spend overnights, this invasive sun problem needed to be rectified.

She closed her eyes, burrowed under his comforter. The scent of his soap lingered on the sheets, and a little squee went on a rampage in her brain.

A noise sounded from outside the bedroom, and she rolled over. No Tim. From across the hall came the muted splash of running water.

The water stopped, and the bathroom door swung open to reveal an extremely naked Tim. Yowzer, the man had a body. All long legs and sculpted, roping muscles that she'd explored every inch of last night. And . . . wow . . . her cheeks burned.

"Morning, sunshine." He crossed the hall and tossed the towel in his hand into the hamper by his bedroom door. "Sorry I woke you."

"You didn't." She patted the spot next to her. "Since you're naked and all, come back to bed."

A lightning-quick smile flashed. "You have no idea how much I'd like to."

Ah, the early sting of rejection . . . "But?"

"Just got called out. Robbery."

"I see."

He walked toward her, dropped onto the bed and stretched out next to her while Lucie tried to keep her eyes above his shoulders.

"I was going to let you sleep, but if you want I can run you back to your car." He kissed her then ran one finger over her shoulder down to the rise of her breast. "Or you can stay here. Whatever you want."

At the moment, she couldn't have what she wanted. And, yes, apparently she'd turned into the slut Ro had suggested she try to be. Who knew it could be such fun?

Well, with Tim anyway. She had no interest in being with anyone else. "Damn."

"What?"

She shook her head. "Here I thought I was living life on the wild side and turning into a slut. Turns out, I just like having sex with hot, Irish detectives."

"Plenty more sex for the Irish detective sounds *great*."

He kissed her again, and she ran her hand up his thigh hoping she could coax him into some naughtiness. *Slut. Te-he!*

Tim ruined the whole thing by clamping on to her wrist.

"Luce, I can't. I'm already late. Tonight though, you'll be in trouble."

"Promises, promises."

"Oh, don't worry." He rolled off the bed, walked to the dresser and starting at the top worked his way through three drawers. T-shirt, boxer briefs and socks. He tossed them on the bed and moved to the closet where his shirts hung on one side. Sorted by color. White, cream, light blue, pin stripes.

An organized hunk. It was like the Holy Grail of hormonal overload.

He grabbed a white shirt, hung it on the closet knob and moved on to suits, also sorted by color. His long fingers moved over the hangers, searching, searching, searching and . . . bingo. Navy suit. The tie came next. A nice red one with blue accents.

She'd missed this. The comfort of watching her man in his space, completing his morning routine. The normalcy of it. She curled into her pillow, drew a long breath and wished they could stay right there, in Tim's room, just the two of them enjoying a day off.

"Maybe one of these weekends we can go somewhere. Get out of the city for a couple of days," Lucie said.

"Works for me. One of the guys has a cabin in Wisconsin."

"Really?"

He sat on the edge of the bed, slid his boxers, pants and T-shirt on. "Yeah. It's not fancy; but it's on a lake, and it's quiet."

"Oh, I'd love that."

He stood again, zipped his pants and grabbed his belt off the dresser. "Then we'll do it."

He came back to her, bent over and kissed her. A quick

peck on the lips. Yep. She definitely liked starting the day like this.

"Luce, as much as I love the sight of you in my bed, if you want me to drive you to your car, you gotta get moving. Otherwise, sleep a couple more hours and take a cab."

"Would you mind? If I stayed?"

"Nope."

He trusted her alone in his home. A place where he kept all kinds of personal things. Secrets maybe.

Yep, this slut thing might work out just fine.

She tossed the covers off. "I'd love to sleep, but it'll be a busy day. We have a Cock Head Convention to attend."

For whatever reason, Tim burst out laughing. "That name. Seriously, after the night we just had, it conjures all sorts of things in a man's imagination."

On her way to the bathroom, she smacked him on the butt. "See me later, big boy."

"Be careful at that convention today. Anything can happen at those things. Robberies, rapes."

Rapes? Seriously? She turned back to him, flapped her arms. "Wow, that's a lovely thought. You're such a cop."

"I'm just saying. People start drinking and make bad decisions. Make sure Joey and Ro stay with you."

"Fine. I'm going to call Eric, too. See if he'll help us look around. And maybe I'll ask a few questions, but it's not a SWAT operation."

At least she hoped it wasn't a SWAT operation. From what she'd seen of the Cock Heads, anything was possible.

14

———

LUCIE STEPPED into the hotel ballroom and froze.

Ro plowed into her, sending Lucie sprawling forward nearly taking out a woman in a peacock-feather hat. Joey snagged her arm in one of his giant mitts.

"Whoa, Luce," Ro shouted above the noise, testing the confines of the ballroom. "I'm sorry, I didn't see you stop. I was distracted."

Lucie righted herself, tugged on her long-sleeved T-shirt and adjusted her vest, which she'd hoped she wouldn't roast in but could already feel sweat beads rolling down her spine.

The sweat bubbled up the second they'd stepped into thirty-thousand square feet of ballroom stuffed shoulder to shoulder with people.

Some proudly wearing their Cock Head gear.

And the noise. Holy cow. Lucie stuck her fingers in her ears to block the yammering in the confined space.

"Boy," Ro said, "those Cock Heads weren't kidding when they said the place was a madhouse."

Lucie scanned the area directly in front of her where

rows and rows of vendors hawked their wares. Potential customers weaved through the rows, squeezing in and out, craning their necks for a glimpse of the offerings. Incredible.

Rows.

Rows.

Rows.

Of stuff.

Panic curled inside her, twisting in her belly. Her brother tilted forward, craning his neck so he could look at her.

"Don't freak."

"You're kidding, right?" She flipped her palms up. "The place is a zoo. How the hell are we going to get through this? One of the women last night said all the good stuff goes early."

Her phone vibrated, and she whipped it out of her vest pocket. Eric. Texting to say he was already there, working the aisles. Nothing unusual yet.

Oh, *that* was amusing. Wasn't this whole thing unusual?

A middle-aged man stormed by them wearing jeans, a black T-shirt proclaiming him to be a Cock Head and a baseball cap adorned with peacock feathers. He bumped Ro as he ran past.

Ro whipped around. "Hey, take it easy." She fluffed her hair and turned back to Lucie. "These Cock Heads are nutballs. Which is why you need to put what that woman last night said out of your head. We're talking about a million-dollar dress here. Not some ten-dollar stuffed peacock. Trust me, we *will* leave here with answers today. I love you too much to have this fail."

"Damn," Joey said, "that's hot. I get worked up when you're like this."

Ohmygod. Total overshare. Lucie shoved her fingers in her ears again. "Joey!"

Making things worse, Ro wrapped her hand around Joey's neck, mashed herself against him and kissed him. And probably tongues were involved.

Lucie rubbed the heels of her hands into her eyes. Good. They hadn't popped out.

"Let me know when you two are done."

"Honey," Ro said, "if I could help it, we'd never be done."

At that, Lucie laughed. Joey and Ro, they were either the worst couple ever or perfection. Time would tell.

"Now," Ro said, "before I do your brother in the middle of this cattle drive—"

"Technically it's a peacock drive," Joey said. "I'd definitely do you here, though."

Lucie gripped two handfuls of her hair and yanked. "Please. We need a plan. It's only nine thirty and this place is mobbed. In another hour, it'll be worse. I think we should split up."

"No way," Joey said. "Your boyfriend called this morning. He's freaking out about you running around here. He thinks it could be dangerous. No splitting up."

"Oh, my God." Ro charged toward one of the tables in the row ahead of them. "Look!"

The dress?

Could they have gotten that lucky? Lucie rushed to catch up just as Ro scooped something off the table and held it up, cooing over it.

Lucie's shoulders dropped, that momentary excitement plummeting like cement from a tall building.

"Peacock earmuffs." Ro rubbed the feathers against her cheek. "These are just darling. Luce, I'm totally seeing peacock accessories in our doggie future."

Ro rummaged through her giant tote bag, eventually pulling out a twenty and handing it over.

Now they were shopping? Everyone needed to focus. Sure, there was a lot of activity, but this crew—Lucie included—needed to settle down and concentrate on their mission.

She locked onto Ro's arm and dragged her back to where Joey stood.

Ro waved the earmuffs at him, pulled her arm free of Lucie's grip and set her new purchase on her head for Joey to see. "How cute are these?"

Joey whistled. "Those are something all right."

A woman carrying a stack of flyers walked along the edge of the rows. "Maps. Anyone need a map? Maps here."

Yes. Lucie threw both hands up. "I'll take one."

The woman wandered over and slid a couple of papers off the top of her stack. "Here you go. Can I help you find anything? There's a system here."

"We're looking for the Max memorabilia."

"Oh, well, that's everywhere if you want T-shirts or something. But if you're looking for replicas of the dress, those will all be in the back corner." The woman pointed to the far left corner of the ballroom. "Just head that way. You can't miss them."

At least now they had a direction. When the woman left, Lucie faced her partners. "We'll start with the knockoffs. See what we can find. If nothing else, it's a starting point."

"Atta girl," Ro said. "Come on. We've got this."

Always one to take the initiative, Joey pushed through the crowd, clearing a path like a human lawn mower. Having King Kong as a brother offered perks. The biggest being people generally stepped aside when he wanted to pass.

Still, with the size of this crowd, it took ten minutes to finally reach the back corner where racks and racks of black dresses lined the wall. Forty years ago, Italian widows would have had a field day in this place.

"Jeez," Joey said, "there's enough black in here to fill a funeral parlor."

Lucie smacked his arm. "That's what I was thinking. Well, sort of."

"Knock it off, you two." Ro hefted her tote higher on her shoulder. "I'm going in."

Going in? What did she plan on doing? Lucie scooted up behind her, and they charged into the crowd, heads down, full speed.

"Lady! Chill. There's a line!"

"I don't want your table." Ro pointed to the next table. "I'm going there. Dumbass!"

Nice.

Lucie tugged on the back of her blouse. "Let's not start a riot. Okay? Trying to lie low here."

"You broads are wacky." Joey angled around and planted himself directly in front of them. "Just let me do it."

"Folks," he called, his deep voice rising above the crowd noise, "where's the line?"

A petite woman barely bigger than Lucie and standing four deep raised her hand. "Back here."

Joey held his hands out. "There you go. The wait shouldn't be that long."

The three of them moved to the back of the line, Joey standing guard behind them making sure people didn't plow them over. Lucie's phone vibrated. Another text. What now?

She checked it, found an unknown 312 number and punched the message.

THIS IS WILLIAM FROM THE MEETING LAST NIGHT. NOTHING TO REPORT. WE'RE ALL ON ALERT.

Ro peeked over her shoulder. "Who is it?"

"William. He's a Cock Head from the meeting. Nothing to report."

"Then why is he texting?"

As if she should know? Lucie waved the phone. "No idea. Checking in, I guess."

"Lunatic Cock Heads," Ro muttered.

"Hey, they're trying."

A guy wearing a black, button-down shirt and a pair of dress slacks wandered by, his eyes glued to Ro's rear.

Of course, the leather skirt and stilettos didn't exactly blend with this crowd.

"Dude," Joey said to the guy, "eyes up before I take them out for you."

Then he grinned. *Grinned.*

The man raised his fist for a bump. "Sorry, man. Couldn't help it."

"I hear ya, Brother."

Only Joey could threaten to remove a man's eyes and then make friends with him. Lucie stuck her finger down her throat and gagged.

"I know," Ro said. "Males. They might as well have their own country with the language they speak."

The two people at the front of the line moved off without making a purchase. *Thank you very much.* In a few minutes they'd be—*hang on.*

Lucie slid up on tiptoes so she could speak to Ro without screaming. "Um, do you have a plan? I mean you just jumped on this line."

"No, I don't have a plan. You said you wanted to start back here, so I dove in."

No plan. Total mess. "Glad I asked."

Ro snorted and added the eye-roll kicker.

Lucie held up her hands. "I've got this. Follow my lead."

The woman in front of them purchased a peacock-feather headband and one of the replica dresses, which the vendor left on the hanger and pulled a dry-cleaning bag over. Nice touch there.

When the woman left, Lucie stepped up. "Hello."

An older man with long, gray sideburns and a bushy mustache manned the table while a woman—his wife maybe—fiddled with the dresses on the racks. The man smiled at her. Not unusual. People tended to immediately respond to her with an aw-how-cute-are-you look. Most of the time, she despised it. Right now, she'd use it.

"How can I help you?"

"The dresses. Do you have any that have the double-eyed feathers like the original?"

"Real ones?"

Ro leaned in, hit the man with a flirty smile. "She won't say it, but we have money to spend. Rat-bastard, soon-to-be-ex-husband to screw."

She winked and the man's face went deadpan. Just . . . nothing. Not a smile or even a smirk to be found. Lucie may have detected a bit of terror by the slightly raised eyebrows.

"Uh, no," he said, darting his gaze from Ro to Lucie. "No real ones. I could probably get you dyed feathers, and my wife can make the dress. There'd be a custom tailoring charge."

For the drama, Lucie made a pouty face. "I was hoping to get it today."

"Today?" The man puckered, ran one hand down the side of his face. "I could make some calls, see if I could find one for you. I don't know if anyone here would have one. Check with Rudy. Two tables down. He'd be the only one. If he doesn't have it, come back and I'll see what I can do."

A lead. Maybe Ro was right, and they'd actually leave here with some good intel. "Great. Thank you."

Behind them a woman lurched forward, shoved from the crowd. She righted herself and spun backward. "Hey, watch it!"

"It wasn't me, lady."

Lucie glanced right. The jerk yelling was the same guy who'd given Ro the business about cutting the line a few minutes earlier.

"What is with this guy?"

"He's an ass," Ro said, "that's what."

Once again Lucie's phone vibrated. Her phone was blowing up with texts. Another Cock Head with nothing to report. Who reported in with nothing? Why bother?

Whatever.

"You shoved me," the lady in the aisle yelled, her voice packing some serious mean. Lucie looked up from her phone.

The guy jerked his thumb at the chubby, thirty-something nerd next to him. The nerd wore a T-shirt proudly proclaiming him to be a Cock Head and one of those hideous peacock-feathered baseball caps. Someone here had to be selling those things.

"Yeah," the nerd said, "because you shoved me."

The first guy—the ass—gritted his teeth. "Newsflash, genius. There's a shitload of people here. Kinda hard not to get pushed."

"No need for that kind of foul language," the nerd said. "But what should I expect from rude people?"

"Uh-oh," Ro muttered.

Joey sighed. "Fellas, let's keep moving. No one is hurt. No harm done."

Huh, this being-in-love thing might be mellowing her

brother out, because when had *he* ever been the voice of reason?

"Rude?" the guy said. "How was I rude when you pushed me? Fatass."

The nerd's cheeks turned a twisty shade of purplish-red. He scrunched his nose and raised his fists, pumping them in front of his face.

"What?" the jerk said. "You gonna hit me?" He tapped his chin. "Go ahead, fat boy. Right here."

Boom! Crunching bone sounded above the crowd noise, and Lucie reared back, closing her eyes, almost afraid to look. The nerd had clocked him. Right there on the chin. Walloped him.

Good for him. Not that she condoned fighting, but that guy? Totally deserved it.

"Ohmygod," Ro said. "Cock fight."

"Ah, dammit." Joey's voice.

Lucie opened her eyes just as the jerky guy fell into a crowd of onlookers.

"Cock Head down!" someone in the crowd yelled. "Cock Head down!"

The place went wild, the noise kicking up another decibel. A group of Cock Heads began a chant of "fight, fight, fight." If that continued, they'd have even more of a riot.

Lucie held up her hands. "Stop chanting! Please, stop."

In front of her, Joey grabbed hold of the seething nerd, who attempted to outmuscle him.

Good luck, buddy.

"Hang on, dude," Joey said. "I don't blame you for wanting to kick his ass, but trust me, this guy'll have you arrested. Been there done that."

Two security guards pushed through the growing crowd demanding people step back and let them through.

The first security guard stepped up just as the jerky guy roared back, fists flying.

"Joey," Lucie screamed.

Joey raised his elbow and—*whap*—the guy ran straight into it, his nose taking the full thrust. *Ouch.* Not only did he have a possibly broken jaw, he might need a new nose to boot.

The guy's eyes rolled back, and he crumpled to the floor.

"Thank you," the nerd cried, hugging Joey.

Ro shook her head. "Craziest cock fight ever. Who wins a fight and acts like that? He should be strutting."

"Everyone hold still," the security guard yelled.

Joey immediately put his hands up while the guards tended to the nerd and the bloodied jerk on the floor.

Lucie's phone buzzed from her back pocket. What now? But since her part-timers were filling in for her, she'd better answer. An issue with one of the dogs wouldn't help. She checked the screen.

Tim.

Come on. Why would he be calling now? She couldn't answer it. Couldn't. Not with all this chaos. She'd let things settle down and then call him.

"Who is that?" Ro asked.

"Tim."

"Oh, boy."

"I know. Unbelievable timing."

Still in her hand, the phone buzzed again. Incoming text. She knew who that would be. Considering she'd just ignored his call. She tapped the little envelope and, yep, Tim's text flashed across the screen.

CALL JUST CAME OVER RADIO ABOUT A FIGHT AT THE CONVENTION. PLEASE (PLEASE) TELL ME YOU'RE NOT INVOLVED.

Being a truth-dedicated person she tapped out the only message she could.

SORRY. :)

———

Lucie Rizzo attracted trouble like a three-time felon. Maybe four-time.

Tim stood in the hotel lobby, arms crossed, listening to a cop explain what he knew about the altercation that took place inside the ballroom.

Ten minutes earlier, he'd heard Lucie's side of the story. A story that included Joey actually stopping the fight instead of starting it.

Best news so far.

Now if Tim could get this cop to shut up, he'd ask him to check the security footage that should prove Joey's innocence.

Before, of course, he broke someone's nose. Which resulted with him handcuffed in the back of a squad outside the lobby doors.

Never a dull moment with this Rizzo bunch.

The cop took a breath, and Tim refused to let that opportunity pass.

"Do me a favor," he said. "Let's look at the security footage. I talked to a few witnesses, and they say Joey Rizzo tried to break this thing up."

The cop laughed. "Joe Rizzo's kid and you don't think he's mixed up in this?"

Tim fought the urge to remind this cop that the system they were sworn by was built on the basic premise of inno-cent until proven guilty. No matter the suspect's last name.

Instead, Tim held up his hand before the guy said

anything else classified as stupid-to-the-*n*th. "Based on what he says, his sister says and the five hundred people who witnessed the altercation say, I think he's being straight with us. Let's look at the surveillance video and see."

The corner of the cop's mouth lifted into a smirk. "Sure, *Detective*."

Sarcasm. Even better. Tim bit down, locking his jaw before he popped off. Last thing he needed was a beef with this cop. As it was, Tim's lieutenant would probably give him a rip for even being on scene. The boss had been in a meeting when Lucie's text came through and Tim took it as a sign. A big one that avoided him having to ask permission to check things out at the Cock Heads convention. Getting into it with a beat cop wouldn't help.

His phone beeped. He nabbed it from his suit pocket. Lucie texting from where she watched him—ten feet away —do his thing with the cop.

EVERYTHING OKAY?

If he had anything to say about it, it would be. And then the two of them would have a conversation about her slowly killing him. A molecule at a time.

"Listen," Tim said to the cop, "I'm gonna talk to the sister again. I'll meet you in the security office in five."

The cop walked off, probably pissy about being ordered around by a detective. Well, too bad. Tim wanted this situation dealt with so he could get back to his own cases.

And avoid his boss's wrath as much as humanly possible.

Lucie started toward him and stopped—probably unsure if she should approach—but he closed the distance between them.

"I'm so sorry," she said.

"Yeah. Me, too. We're gonna look at the surveillance video."

"Good. You'll see Joey tried to break up the fight."

"Then he'll be released, and you can all go home."

"But..."

No flipping buts. She needed to get the hell out of here. But Lucie stared up at him, all big blue eyes and cute face and, once again, he was toast.

As hard as she made it to stay mad, he couldn't give in. She had to stop putting herself into situations that could cause her harm. End of story.

"You need to go home," he said. "You shouldn't be here, running this investigation of yours. One of you could have gotten hurt in that fight. What if one of those guys had a gun or a knife? Your brother could be in a morgue now."

"It was a random thing. We didn't start it. We were just in the wrong place—"

"At the wrong time. I know. That happens with you. A lot."

She scrunched her nose and growled—*growled*—at him.

So damned cute. And infuriating. The two sides of Lucie. *Killing me.*

"It's not as if I can help it, Tim."

"Maybe you can't, but you make it worse by turning into super sleuth. The other night with this Bill character should have scared the crap out of you. What's it going to take?"

He stepped back, squeezed his eyes shut and winced. This would be life with Lucie Rizzo. From the day he'd met her, she'd been getting caught up in nonsense.

And he wasn't good at nonsense.

He got his head together, opened his eyes. "I'm not arguing about this now. Let's get the situation handled. I'm heading upstairs to look at video. Hopefully, when I come down, your brother will be free to go, and all of you will head home. That's all I got, Luce."

LUCIE WANDERED TO A BENCH AT THE FAR SIDE OF THE LOBBY, away from the crowd of gawkers trying to get the scoop on the guy locked in the back of the police car.

My fault.

If she hadn't been here, Joey and Ro wouldn't have been either. Tim was right. They could have all gotten hurt. At the time, she simply thought they would blend in and ask a few questions.

No one should have gotten hurt. Or arrested.

Dad would go crazy when he heard this. *Won't that be fun?*

Ro stepped up to the bench, her leather skirt and blouse still in perfect order even after being in the middle of a brawl.

But Ro had that warrior instinct, the ability to rebound quickly, while Lucie needed time to stew. To think things over, study the options.

"What's up, Sister?"

Lucie propped her elbows on her thighs and cupped one hand under her chin. "Aside from Joey being locked in a police car in handcuffs, this whole excursion being a bust *and* Tim mad at me? Not a lot."

Ro shrugged. "Eh, sounds like a fairly normal day in the life of a Rizzo. You need to buck up. We're not done scouting this place, and Joey will be free as soon as your boyfriend clears this up. Speaking of your boyfriend, he'll get over it. They always do."

"He shouldn't have to get over it. He shouldn't even *be* in this position."

"What position? He's helping get your brother out of a jam. He's a nice guy, and that's what nice guys do. What's your problem?"

What's her problem? Did she not see the issue here? "You mean other than he's a cop and I'm Joe Rizzo's kid? Or maybe the person he's trying to get out of that jam is also Joe Rizzo's kid?"

"Oh, boo-hoo."

Didn't that just sound like Joey. How many times had he said that to her over the years? Only with Joey it usually had an "effing" between the "boo" and the "hoo."

Lucie sat up, held her hands out. "Boo-hoo nothing. It's true. How will this relationship ever work with that setup?"

"It works because you want it to work. That's how. Tim's not griping about you being a Rizzo. Tim's griping because you're investigating. Let's not make this about poor Lucie with her mobbed up family. Let's make this about Joey possibly getting arrested when he's innocent."

Lucie dropped her hands, bolted upright and stared. Holy cow, Ro—her BFF, her closest confidant who always, always took Lucie's side—had just blasted her. Royally.

Ten seconds of brutal silence sat between them.

Eventually, Ro let out a long sigh. "Damn, that was harsh."

Yes. It was. And so deserved.

Joey might be headed to jail, and Lucie was moaning about her boyfriend. "Ro—"

"I'm sorry that came out like that."

About to say something, she held out her hands, but let them fall again.

"What?"

"As soon as something goes wrong you fall back on the mob princess thing. I hate to see that. You're so much more. Does it suck? Sure, but you're better than that, and you know it. But, dammit, Luce, every time I think you're moving beyond your daddy hang-ups, something in your brain flips and you backslide."

"You're right."

"Huh?"

Lucie smiled, pointed to her mouth. "Pay attention. You. Are. Right. I do let the Rizzo reputation get to me. I'm getting better, though. You said it yourself."

Ro sat on the bench, nudging Lucie a bit. "Move over. Make room for my *giant* ass."

Lucie snorted. This was the magic of Lucie and Ro. They'd been friends twenty years. They bickered, they fought, they'd even called each other names on a rare few occasions. But they always came back to each other. And usually, that coming back involved an awkward joke, a moment of sarcasm.

Self-deprecating humor.

The mother of all reset buttons.

Ro smiled, giving Lucie a shoulder bump. "You are getting better. I think Tim has a lot to do with that. But, Luce, you have to give him a chance. He's going to be mad at you sometimes. It doesn't mean he's running because you're a Rizzo. If he cared about who your dad is, he wouldn't be here in the first place. I know you know that."

"I'm scared."

There, she said it. For the first time in years, the man in her life wasn't Frankie. Comfortable Frankie, who understood the intricacies of *the life.*

"Of course you are. It's a new relationship and it's important to you. He's different and there's no comfort zone when something is new. You're used to the same old thing. Which kinda sucks, don't you think?"

"When the same old thing doesn't work, yes."

"So, buck up. You've got a great guy, let him be pissed when he has a right to be. Don't fall back and make excuses because you're afraid. That's just dumb. And you're not dumb."

All righty then.

"Don't be mad at me," Ro said. "I love you, and I don't want to see you blow a good thing."

Lucie nodded. "I'm not mad. It's just not easy to hear." She smacked her hands against her thighs and stood. "Thank you."

"For yelling at you?"

"Yes. And for always being truthful. Even when it hurts. You're the best friend a girl could have. Now, let's go check on my brother."

15

———

Lucie pushed through the revolving lobby door and spotted the patrol car still sitting in the no-parking zone in front of the hotel. A cop leaned against the back quarter panel, obviously standing guard, while chatting with the bellman.

Inside the vehicle, Joey shot her a thumbs up. A task enabled by Tim telling the cops, who'd initially cuffed Joey behind his back, that they could move the cuffs to the front.

A cab pulled in front of the patrol car and a tall blonde with legs longer than Ro's slid from the backseat. If Lucie needed a reminder that the Maxmillian dress had catapulted her into crisis mode, the blonde had just given it to her.

The woman wore a replica Max that hung on her lean frame, and Lucie nearly vomited. She'd so had it with this dress.

"Great," Ro said, "another Cock Head."

"I know. I'm sick of them."

But the woman offered a pleasant smile, and the immediate guilt dropped on Lucie.

"And worse, she's *nice.*"

"But the dress is a little big. She should have at least had it taken in. We can hold that against her."

As the woman approached, her skinny heel caught in a sidewalk crack, and she stopped to wiggle it loose. Lucie stepped forward to help and . . . whoa. She gripped Ro's arm.

"Ow. Nails, nails, *nails!*"

Lucie clenched her teeth. "Ssshhh. Look at the feathers. The feathers. Quick."

The blonde got her heel free, composed herself and sauntered by.

"It's got the double-eyes," Ro said.

"Yes."

Lucie followed the woman, her gaze swiftly moving over the bottom of the dress.

All double-eyed feathers.

Ro fell in beside her. "What are we doing?"

"I don't know."

"Oh-kay. That's a little wacky."

"I know, but the feathers. All the knockoffs have had single-eye feathers."

And this one didn't. This one had the double-eyes. Of course, they could be dyed. The dress would be more expensive to create with dyed double-eyed feathers, but a rabid collector, one who would be found at the convention, might be willing to spend the extra money.

Only one way to find out.

"Luce, they're probably fake."

"Maybe. But if so, they'd probably all be similar, right? Each one perfectly uniform. I need to get closer and see."

The woman strolled through the lobby toward an elevator bank.

"She's going upstairs," Ro said. "She's probably a guest. What are we gonna do? Ambush her?"

Not a bad idea.

"Excuse me," Lucie called, running to catch up to the woman.

The blonde kept walking but glanced back. *Yes, you.*

Lucie caught up. "Hi. Sorry to bother you, but your dress is amazing. My friend—" she gestured to Ro hustling up behind her, "—and I are here trying to find one like it. With the double-eyed feathers."

"Double-eyed?"

"Yes. The eyes."

The blonde let out a little laugh, and what kind of Cock Head was she that she didn't even know what the double-eyes were? The thing that made the damned dress so famous were the double-eyed feathers. *Come on!*

"She doesn't know," Ro said.

The woman pulled back, her gaze pinging between Ro and Lucie. Panic.

Lucie conjured what she hoped was a reassuring smile and pointed at the feathers. "The feathers on your dress are double-eyed. See that blue circle in the middle? That's the eye. Your feathers have two. Just like the original dress. It's what makes the dress so valuable. Most of the dresses here only have one eye."

"Oh," the woman said. "Well, I don't know about any of that. The dress isn't mine. I'm a model."

A model. What the heck? How strange. Lucie had no idea what to do with that and turned to Ro, who made snoring noises.

"My work is never done," she muttered before facing the blonde. "Are you modeling the dress at one of the convention events?"

"Um, I really can't say. I'm the model."

Yes, we know that.

The blonde backed away, pointed to the elevator. "I need to go, or I'll be late. Sorry I couldn't help you."

Lucie offered up a friendly wave. "Sure. No problem."

But as the woman headed for the elevator those double-eyed feathers damn-near winked—taunted—and Lucie's mind reeled. *Don't lose her.* So far, they hadn't seen any replica dresses with the double-eyes. And the vendor from the ballroom told her they were difficult to find.

Yet, one had just sauntered right by them.

The blonde reached the elevator bank and pushed the button.

Follow her.

Lucie started walking.

"Uh, where we going?"

"I don't know. We can't lose her."

"We can't—"

"Ssshhh. Don't spook her. We're following her."

"And you don't think that'll spook her?"

Point there. "Let me think."

"Please do. Because this is batshit cray-cray."

At the elevators, the blonde glanced back, saw Lucie and Ro coming and got that wide-eyed, freaked look again.

"We're guests here," Lucie said. "We were on our way up when we spotted you."

"Ah."

The lame excuse seemed to relax the woman, and Lucie gave herself credit for pulling off the lie. Who said she was a terrible liar?

Inside the elevator, the smell of old sweat and funk blasted her senses, not to mention the violin version of "Beat It" streaming through the overhead speakers. Really? They put *that* song to violins?

The blonde punched the number twelve. "What floor?"

"Oh, look at that," Lucie said. "We're twelve, too."

Lucie stood behind the woman, studying the back of the dress, the perfect stitching on the seams, each one uniform and, yes, the feathers. The eyes specifically, that bright blue that reminded her of the Caribbean and the vacation she sorely needed. Maybe she and Tim could take that vacation.

Tim. Soon he'd be finished in surveillance and find her extremely absent from the lobby. Already mad at her, this little trip would completely infuriate him.

End run.

That's what Joey always said. She whipped out her phone, waggled it at Ro. "Letting Tim know where to meet us."

Wink, wink.

"Oh, that'll make him much less irritable. I'm sure."

Whatever. *Everyone's a comedian today.*

She fired off the message to Tim.

JUST FOLLOWED A COCK HEAD WEARING A DRESS WITH DOUBLE-EYED FEATHERS. 12TH FLOOR.

At least he'd know where to start looking.

Lucie shoved her phone in her back pocket, catching a glimpse of one of the feathers as she moved.

Wait.

The double-eye. One was larger than the other. And slightly oblong. Not round.

On every knockoff she'd seen the eyes were round.

Could be nothing. An accident. A fluke. She checked the feather to the right of the imperfect one. It looked similar, but again, the eyes weren't uniform.

She slapped her hand over her mouth, and Ro gave her a "what now?" look.

The doors slid open, and the woman stepped off and —*no, no, no*—stopped to check her phone.

Damn. Lucie and Ro had to keep moving or they'd look like the stalkers they were.

"Ow," Ro cried.

Lucie spun back just as her BFF threw herself across the elevator threshold. Her body pitched forward, angling sideways. Her hair flew, her arms pinwheeled and—*crash*—she hit the carpet, landing flat on her rear.

What the . . . At least she hadn't landed on tile or wood.

The blonde snapped her head sideways and gasped.

"These stupid shoes," Ro cried. "I'm going to break an ankle in them."

Okay. This had to be an act. Another Oscar-worthy performance to delay so they could see where the woman was headed.

Lucie dropped to her knees. "Are you all right? What happened?"

"Should I call for help?" The woman pointed at the small table against the wall with fresh flowers. "I don't see a phone, but I'm just going to room 1222. I could run down there and call."

1222. *Thank you, very much.*

Ro rolled to her knees, sticking her butt up as she shifted to her elbows. "I think I'm okay."

"Get up slowly. Can you walk?"

"I'll let you know in a second." Ro looked up at the blonde. "Thanks for offering to help, but I think I'm good. We're just down the hall here. Lucie can help me get there."

The blonde cocked her head. "I do need to get to my appointment. As long as you're okay."

They all said their good-byes, and the blonde strode down the corridor, checking room numbers as she went.

Once out of earshot, Lucie squatted next to Ro. "Please tell me you're faking this injury."

"Obviously. I do know how to walk in my own shoes. I knew we'd be screwed when we stepped out of that elevator and had nowhere to go. And I was good, too. Wasn't I?"

"You sure were. Let's keep it going. I'll help you up, and you hobble around a bit. Maybe make noises or whatever."

"Then what?"

"I have no idea. But it'll probably include knocking on the door of 1222."

TIM STOOD IN THE LOBBY READING LUCIE'S TEXT MESSAGE FOR the fifth time. And for the fifth time, the pounding at his temples went to epic levels.

Stop reading it, dumbass.

Getting aggravated over and over wouldn't help him avoid a heart attack, which, without a doubt, would happen with Lucie Rizzo in his life.

"Detective?" the cop said. "Am I cutting this guy loose?"

Tim shoved his phone in his pocket. "Yeah. Let him go. Anyone gives you any heat, the security video shows him trying to break up the fight."

"It's your ass."

Yeah. Sure is.

The cop took his time getting to the patrol car, and Tim fought another wave of aggravation.

No wonder Lucie got tired of life as Joe Rizzo's kid.

The second Joey was out of the car and free of cuffs, he pushed through the lobby doors and hauled over to Tim. "Where are they?"

"Twelfth floor."

"Why?"

"As if I know?"

Joey grunted. "Swear to God, between the two of them, I'm gonna die young."

"Right there with ya, pal."

A rush of people piled out of one of the large ballrooms into the lobby. Session ending. Half the crowd moved toward the elevators.

"Hurry up," Tim said. "We gotta beat them."

If it came down to it, he'd hoof it to twelve rather than wait in line.

They rode the packed elevator, stopping at the third floor—the first of six stops—to let an elderly woman off. Joey stepped off, held his hand out to the woman so she didn't trip, and the old lady cooed up at him.

Next stop. Floor number five. A woman and her six—*six*—arguing kids got off. Well, the mom and five of the kids got off. The sixth thought it would be funny to not get off. The guy at the front stuck his hand over the door to hold it open while the mom negotiated with the kid, and Tim's blood pressure climbed.

"If I stroke out," he said to Joey, "tell your sister I freed you."

Joey rolled his eyes. "I'll do that."

Finally, the kid got off. *I'm never having kids.* At least not pain-in-the-ass ones.

At the eleventh floor, with only a handful of people still in the car, an elderly couple shuffled forward. Tim pushed the button to hold the doors open for them. "Can I help you at all?"

"Oh, we're fine," the woman said. "Thank you."

The man stopped just before stepping off, and his wife gripped his hand. "It's okay. It's not a step. Just put your foot out." The woman turned back to Tim. "His eyesight is bad."

"Not that bad," the man yelled, and Tim couldn't fight the smile ripping at his lips.

Joey gently held the man's other arm. "I've got him."

The woman let go and steadied herself against the side of the elevator as she stepped off. "Why thank you, young man."

"You folks need help getting to your room or anything?"

"We're fine," the man barked.

Joey peeled his lips back and held his arms up. Tim put his free hand over his mouth. These Rizzos. Flipping funny. The woman waved Joey off, and he hopped back on the elevator.

"Thank you, boys. May God bless you."

The doors slid closed and Tim blew out a heavy breath. "God better bless your sister when I get a hold of her. She's got to stop. She's slowly killing me."

"*You?* I've been doing this with her since that first dogjacking. You got nothin' on me."

Finally, the elevator dinged, and the doors slid open to Lucie helping Roseanne off the floor.

"What the hell?" Joey hollered.

Lucie's head snapped up. "Oh, hi."

"Don't get your boxers in a wad," Ro said from the floor.

Then it all went to hell with their screaming.

Tim cut away to Lucie, almost relieved Ro and Joey were occupied and out of his hair. "Luce, I told you to stay put. How is being on twelve staying put?"

"No time for that now. We have action in 1222."

Action? Tim snorted. "What action?"

"The woman in the Max knockoff went in there."

"There's a million of those knockoffs around here."

Lucie wagged her finger. "Not with double-eyed feathers there's not."

"Huh?"

"The double-eyed feathers on the original Max are extremely rare. Even the knockoffs don't have those feathers. You can get some that are dyed, but the eyes—the blue part in the middle—are all uniform. The dress we just saw? The feathers were double-eyed and totally not uniform."

"Meaning, it's a really good knockoff or—"

"The real thing."

BAM. JUST THAT QUICK, TIM'S JAW SOFTENED, AND HE LOST the tight look from tracking her to the twelfth floor. The realization that she might have found the Max must have hit.

Well, good for him.

"I'm sorry I didn't stay put," Lucie said, "but I couldn't risk losing that dress. Even if it's not the real thing, it's a damned expensive knockoff. Maybe the person who owns it can give us a lead."

"Which room?"

"1222."

Tim swung back to Joey and Ro, still squaring off in front of the elevator. At least Ro was on her feet, and they weren't yelling anymore. "You two stay here."

Joey gave him a hard stare. "What now?"

"Stay here with Lucie and Ro. I'm going down to 1222."

Oh, no he wasn't. Not without her anyway. "Hang on one second."

"No, Luce. You need to stay here."

"What if my mysterious Bill is there? You've never seen him and won't recognize him."

Before Tim could respond, voices carried from the hallway. They turned to where a man emerged from what looked like room 1222. He shook hands with another man who'd also entered the hallway.

Lucie's lungs stopped. They, in fact, might have collapsed—no air. She simply could not suck a breath.

In the hallway, chatting up his guest, an easy smile drifting across his face, was a seemingly content man. A satisfied man. A man free of stress.

Free of a missing Maxmillian dress.

Lewis Dukane.

The bastard owner of the Max.

Lucie gaped at him, her jaw too heavy for her to clamp it shut.

Tim squeezed her arm. "Luce?"

"It's him."

"Who?"

"Lewis Dukane."

Tim's head whipped sideways, and Lucie ducked behind him before Dukane got a glimpse of her. "What do we do?"

The second man said something about calling to confirm the transfer, and Lucie stared up at Tim, hoping he had some sort of plan.

Tim nudged her sideways. "He's coming. Not Dukane. The other guy."

Seconds later the man walked by, nodding at Lucie as he went.

Tim waited until Dukane's guest left the corridor. "When he gets on the elevator, I'm knocking on that door." He pulled his phone from his suit pocket. "First, I'm getting one of those cops from downstairs up here."

"Is that necessary?"

"No idea. But I'm not going in there alone. And you aren't coming with me."

"Tim—"

"Forget it, Luce."

He held up one finger to shush her while he spoke into his phone then punched out of the call. "He's on his way."

"I think—"

"Wait," he said. "I love you, I do, but you are not going into that room. You will stay out here. Where it's safe. Where you won't be impeding an investigation. Got that?"

So much for understanding and comforting Tim. "You're being a little overbearing."

"Lucie, you haven't seen overbearing. If I have to, I'll lock you in the back of that squad I just hauled your brother from."

He wouldn't . . .

He propped his hands on his hips, brushing his suit jacket open and revealing the gun holstered at his waist. "Bet on it."

Whoa, with flashing the gun. *Message received, Detective.*

Joey swung into the corridor. "Hey, do we have a plan or what?"

Tim dropped his hands, buttoned the suit up. "Yes. The plan is I have a cop on his way up here. I'm going into that room. You three stay here. Call it overwatch."

"Whatever," Joey said. "I just wanna get the hell out of here."

Ro ducked around the corner, scooting along behind him. "Luce, we should head back to the ballroom and find some of our Cock Head friends. See if anyone has heard anything about the dress being here."

Tim smacked both palms against his forehead. *Fwap.* "What does it take to get you two to stop? When is it enough? Because I'm happy to lock both of you up."

Ro curled her lip. "Your boyfriend gets a little dramatic."

The elevator dinged, and Tim looked over. "Please be a cop in there. Please."

The doors swished open, and out stepped the cop who'd detained Joey. Wishes apparently did come true.

"Excellent." Tim pointed at the cop. "You're with me. We're going to room 1222. The owner of the Maxmillian dress—you know, the stolen one—is in there. Something's hinky."

"Cool," the cop said.

Cool for him maybe. All Lucie got to do was stand around and watch while her blood simmered.

No fun.

"Joey," Tim poked his finger. "I need you to stay here. Keep an eye out for anyone coming off that elevator. Got it?"

"Sir, yes, sir."

Joey saluted, and the two men made their way down the hall. Lucie gritted her teeth and ignored the pain lancing into her gums. *Darn it.* This just made her skin fry.

"That sucks eggs," she said.

"Ooh." Joey held his hands up and waggled them. "Goody-two-shoes on the verge of swearing."

Her brother. The jerk. They'd been doing so well today, and he chooses now to harass her? "Joey?"

"Yes?"

"Fuck you."

Ro burst out laughing. "Wowie! Atta, girl, Luce. I swear, you Rizzos are a rip. I just love you guys."

Tim and the cop reached the door. The cop stood to the side, away from the peephole, and Tim knocked.

When the door came open, Tim flashed his badge and stepped into the doorway. The element of surprise. *Well, played.*

The cop followed Tim into the room, and the door closed behind them.

"I can't stand it," Lucie said. "I have to listen in."

Joey grabbed her arm. "Tim said to stay here. Don't piss him off."

"All I'm doing is listening. I promise I won't go in." She pulled free and squeezed his hand. "I promise."

"I'll go with her," Ro said. "Kinda curious myself."

"When he gets pissed, don't say I didn't warn you."

Ro waved him off. "Blah, blah." She caught up with Lucie and tugged on the back of her shirt. "You're sure about this, right? As much as I hate to admit it, Joey has a point."

"All we're doing is eavesdropping. With Tim and the cop inside, what could happen?"

16

———

Lucie and Ro lined up on either side of the door, heads angled so they could listen.

Muffled voices came from inside, the words running together in a blur. Dang it, none of it made sense. She met Ro's gaze, hoping maybe her BFF could make out some of the words. A lifetime of friendship gave them the ability to instantly know what the other was thinking. A talent that made them good business partners as well as friends.

Understanding the message, Ro shook her head.

From behind Ro, another door ker-clunked, and a dark-haired man wearing jeans and a zip-up hoodie double-checked the door handle, making sure the lock engaged. Never hurt to be cautious.

The man turned and—whoa. His face, the chubby cheeks, the smooth, wrinkle-free skin. *Him.*

He stopped and stared at Lucie. Her immediate recognition, the cold stab in her chest, sparked an insane blood rush.

"Bill," she said, her voice low and growling.

Now they had him. *Trapped.*

She sidestepped, partially blocking Bill's path. Living up to girl code, Ro filled the space beside her. If he wanted out, he'd have to deal with a Gucci-clad, soon-to-be-ex-wife of a stripper-banger and a partially psychotic Rizzo.

He's cooked.

"I knew you'd be here," Lucie said. "What? Did you make a side deal with the owner? Ransomed his dress?"

Bill burst into a sprint—*no, no, no*—coming straight at them. Lucie and Ro angled forward, setting their feet like a couple of defensive tackles.

"Go ahead," Ro said, "give me a reason."

Bill reached them, holding both hands out and aiming for the slight opening between them.

Boom. He blasted them, sending Ro flying, her feet coming right off the floor. Momentum carried her back, back, back . . .

"Ooofff!"

She pancaked. Flat on her rear staring straight up at the ceiling, she choked out a breath. Seeing her sprawled on the floor, helpless, all because of this same man who'd tormented her, released something in Lucie's brain. Something protective and angry and *violent*.

Lucie sprinted, her feet pounding the carpet, giving chase toward the elevator. "Joey. Grab him! Ro down, Ro down, Ro down."

Joey's giant body swung around the corner and—*fwap*—Bill nailed him. Or Joey nailed Bill, because the loose flesh on Bill's body smacked against six feet four of solid muscle and bounced back.

Take that.

He crumpled to the floor, landing on his belly.

"What the—"

But Lucie kept running. Right there. Right there. And she wanted a piece of him.

He made a move to get up, and Lucie leaped. Just—*voom*—she sailed for a second, landing hard on his back. Air shot from her mouth and her ribcage may have shattered, but she was on the bastard and swinging.

Now he'd pay.

"Lucie," Joey said, "are you nuts or what?"

Oh, she was beyond nuts.

Bill rose to his hands and knees with Lucie still on his back. She gripped the back of his T-shirt, squeezing until the neck tightened and he gagged.

"Crazy witch. Get off me."

He crawled toward the elevator, giving Lucie a horsey ride as he went. She smacked the back of his head—*whap, whap, whap*—squeezing her legs around his back, trying to knee him hard enough to inflict pain.

"Are you *kidding* me?"

Tim.

But Lucie was too far gone now. The rage had set in, full psychosis, and she wanted this man bloody.

A pair of cordovan shoes appeared just in front of them, blocking Bill from crawling any farther, and Lucie raised her head.

Tim's fair skin suddenly glowed a fierce red, and his eyes shot green lasers. He set his hands on his hips, tap-tap-tapping his fingers against them.

"Off," he said.

"He tried to escape. Did you see what he did to Ro?"

A shoe smacked Lucie's shoulder and ricocheted, hitting Bill on the head. It landed on the floor, broken spiked heel hanging precariously.

"Rat-bastard. You broke my heel. Do you know what those shoes cost?"

Lucie looked back, spotted her BFF charging—if one could charge while hobbling on one stiletto. Joey intervened, stepping between Ro and her prey, grabbing her around the waist and hauling her backward as she kicked and waved her fists. "I'll kill him. I'll squeeze his balls until they burst!"

"Wow." The cop whistled. "That's hot."

"Hey," Tim said, his voice sharp and carrying. "Everyone shut. The hell. Up!" He pointed at Lucie. "You. Get off of him. Right now." He pointed at Bill. "You move, and I swear to God I'll shoot you." He pointed at Joey and Ro. "Get her out of here. What a flipping cluster!"

Talk about hot.

Ewww-weeee a churned-up Tim O'Brien was a sight.

Lucie gave Bill one last smack and climbed off him, more than ready to hop back on if he tried anything funny.

"Dude," he said to Tim, "she's crazy." He rubbed the back of his head. "I want to press charges. Assault. Am I bleeding?"

Tim grabbed hold of him, got him to his feet, checked his pupils and apparently satisfied they were in working order, shoved him the direction he'd just come from. "Shut up and get moving."

In front of the room, the Maxmillian model and Mr. Dukane stood side by side in a long-faced sort of stunned shock.

"Inside," Tim said to them. "I want answers."

TIM AND HIS COP BUDDY ESCORTED LUCIE, BILL AND MR.

Dukane back to the hotel room, which turned out to be an oversized suite complete with a conference table that seated ten.

Once everyone was seated, Tim gave the cop instructions to stand guard and ducked back into the hall to make a phone call.

Ten minutes passed while Lucie, Bill and Mr. Dukane sat quietly, but took turns staring each other down. The model stood by the window, staring out over the Chicago skyline.

All that poor thing wanted was a modeling gig, and she wound up in the middle of a Cock Head fight.

Tim entered the room, jaw set, big shoulders back and ready for battle. He swung the safety latch so the door wouldn't close all the way and headed toward the table. His suit jacket flapped open as he moved and Lucie's breath caught. Tim was one of those alluring men that pulled off playful one minute, commanding the next.

If his stony cheeks were an indicator, the occupants of this room had better behave. Lucie, seated at the far end of the table, scooted back in her chair. She wouldn't be the one to cause trouble.

No way. At least not any more trouble.

Two seats down, Mr. Dukane leaned in and jabbed his index finger into the table. "I want to know the meaning of this. I'm a businessman conducting private meetings. I've paid for this room."

Idiot.

Tim propped one hand on his hip, revealing his service weapon and badge. "Mr. Dukane, I'm aware of that. We have one small problem."

"What's that?"

He pointed to the model. "That dress she's wearing. It looks like the original."

"It's a copy."

Such a liar. A dirty, rotten, rat-bastard liar. "Ha!" Lucie smacked her hand on the table. "Look at the feathers. They aren't uniform. If those were dyed feathers, the eyes would all have the same shape."

Mr. Dukane made a *pffting* noise. "They would not. What do you know?"

"I know the real thing when I see it. And I also know a swindler when I see one."

For effect, she narrowed her eyes and pinched her lips. Mean Lucie. Spine-melting Lucie.

"Lucie," Tim said, "please be quiet."

Whoopsie. She sat back, shoulders hunched, arms crossed. "Sorry. I got carried away."

He flashed his wide smile, and a million little explosions blasted inside her. Even angry, he found a way to let her know they'd be okay.

Hopefully.

The hotel room door swung open. Detective Bickel. Terrific. Her favorite person. And the one Tim must have called from the hallway.

Bickel nodded at her, and Lucie returned the nod. If Ro were here, she'd call this a hot-ass mess.

"Whatcha got?" Bickel asked Tim.

"Nothing yet. I waited on you. Your case. But what I think is she's wearing the missing Maxmillian dress." Tim gestured to the model. "And one or both of these guys has something to do with it."

Mr. Dukane sat forward again. "It's him. He's been black-mailing me."

A stream of obscenities flew from Bill's mouth, and Tim and Bickel both raised their hands to shut him up.

"He's lying." Bill jabbed a finger at Dukane. "You greedy son of a bitch. I'm not going down for this."

Dukane sniffed and turned away. "I don't know what you're talking about."

"Huh," Detective Bickel said. "Mr. Dukane, you sure you don't know what he's talking about?"

"He knows," Bill said. "He knows he paid me and my buddy to steal that dress. That's what he knows."

Whoa! Lucie shot her gaze straight to Tim, who slid his eyes toward her, but then away again. She took the hint and, as much as it killed her—absolutely destroyed her—sat quietly.

"That's absurd," Mr. Dukane said. "I'm a collector. Why would I want the dress stolen?" He rose from his seat. "This is ridiculous. I'm calling my lawyer."

"Sure," Bickel said. "Tell him to come on down. While you're doing that, we'll talk to Bill here. Get his side of the story."

The uniformed cop slid in front of the door. Did he expect someone to run for it? With three armed officers in the room?

Not to mention a psychotic Rizzo.

"Bill," Tim said, "when you contacted Ms. Rizzo about buying the dress, did Mr. Dukane know?"

Bickel gave Tim a hard look. Either he didn't like Tim butting in, or he'd just been made aware of Lucie possibly buying stolen merchandise.

Oh, the tangled web.

Bill winced. "No. Well, yes, he knew I had a possible buyer. He didn't know who it was. He planned the whole scam around this stupid convention. Figured he'd have a ton of buyers. Then he sent me to that fan club meeting."

"The Cock Heads," Tim said.

"Yeah. I came back from the meeting and told him I had someone hooked. When all that heat came down and I realized she—" he pointed at Lucie "—was the witness, I bolted."

Tim pursed his lips. "Un-huh."

"He's lying," Dukane shouted from his spot near the bathroom where he held the phone to his ear.

"You be quiet," Tim said.

Bickel circled one finger. "Take me back to the beginning."

"Dukane wanted the dress stolen, so he could collect the insurance payout."

"Preposterous!"

"That's it." Tim pointed to the door where the cop stood. "Take him outside. Cuff him if you have to."

Wow.

Tim, Tim, Tim. So hot.

Wait until she got him alone tonight.

The hotel room door banged shut, and Bickel waved at Bill to continue.

Bill nodded. "He figured if the dress was robbed from the auction place, the insurance company wouldn't clue in on him arranging it. Then he told me to try and sell it, and that he'd split whatever we got for it. Greedy."

"So," Tim said, "he had you steal the dress, intending to collect the insurance money *and* then he'd get a black-market buyer."

"Yeah. Double the cash."

Bickel let out a long, low whistle just as the hotel-room door opened again and Mr. Dukane reentered.

"Have a seat, Mr. Dukane. I can't wait to hear your side of this."

Dukane straightened his tie, hitched his pants and sat. "I have no idea what you are talking about."

Oh, so smug. Pompous and smug and . . . hateful. He'd come to her that day and begged—*begged*—her to go to the authorities. He'd insulted not only her but her family name, and, all along, he'd been behind the entire thing.

Lucie leaned halfway across the table. A few inches more and she'd be able to wrap her skinny fingers around Dukane's throat, watch his lying eyes pop right from his head. "You jerk."

"Lucie—"

"No, Tim." She poked a finger at Dukane. "He came to me, begging me to tell the police what I knew. Then he insulted me when all the while he knew what he'd done."

"I didn't do anything."

"Yes, you did," she said. "You set this whole thing up. You couldn't be satisfied with just the insurance money. You needed more. Well, guess what, mister? I—or as you put it—*the likes of me* just took you down." She slammed her open hand on the table. "Don't mess with a Rizzo, buddy."

Bickel frowned hard enough that his bottom lip rolled out. After a few seconds, he turned to Tim. "What the hell is she talking about?"

"I'll explain later. You done with her? I can get her out of here."

Yes. Please do. She'd calmed down from the bitch-slapping she'd given Bill in the hallway, but sitting there, across from that pompous ass, Mr. Dukane, wound her up again. If she wasn't careful, she'd launch herself over the table at him and that would really be embarrassing.

"Just so you know," she said to Dukane. "I think you're a jerk."

"Okay." Tim waved her up from her chair. "Let's go. You're done here."

He led her from the room and closed the door, holding his finger to his lips and then pointing to the elevator. Apparently, he didn't want them to be overheard.

Lucie turned the corner and spotted Ro sitting in one of the club chairs that were probably more for ambience than sitting. She had one shoe off and the broken one in her lap. Joey stood beside her, his thumbs going hyperspeed on his phone.

"Hey," Lucie said.

Ro threw her hands up. "Thank God! I saw that detective come off the elevator and nearly peed myself."

"Luce, you okay?"

"I'm fine, Joey. Thanks. For everything. I'm sorry I almost got you arrested."

"You didn't. It was those lunatic Cock Heads." He tucked his phone in his back pocket and faced Tim. "What's going on with her? Do we need a lawyer?"

"I doubt it. Those idiots are in there hanging themselves."

Lucie nodded. "Get this. That Bill guy," she turned to Ro, "the one who destroyed your shoe—"

"That rat-bastard. He better not go to sleep tonight."

"Right. Well, Bill started spewing about how Mr. Dukane wanted the insurance money for the dress, so he had it stolen."

A low groan came from Ro. "He stole his own dress?"

"Can you believe it?"

"Please, honey. Lately I believe everything."

"Anyway," Tim said, "it all has to shake out. And I really

can't talk about this with you. I'm gonna head back in there, and you three can rip it apart." He turned to Lucie. "Please go home or back to your office. I'm begging you, stay out of it. Let us work through it."

This poor guy. She'd driven him to begging. She'd have to make it up to him. Somehow. Maybe naked.

"I'll go back to the office. I promise. No interfering. I know you'll take care of it from here."

He tugged on a loose hair that had slipped from her ponytail. "Thank you. I'll call you in a while. Give you the update."

Ro stood and hobbled toward the elevator. Joey laughed. If Lucie knew her brother at all, some sick, demented comment would soon fly from his mouth.

"Listen," he said to Ro's back, "you're a mess right now, but you've still got the best ass ever."

Lucie drew a long breath, then exhaled. "Poetry, Joey. Truly."

"Yep." Tim bent closer, right next to her ear. "I'll call you later. And be ready for a replay of last night."

Go. Lucie.

"Oh, I'll be ready."

* * *

AT FIVE FIFTEEN, THE DOGGIE BELLS ON COCO BARKNELL'S front door jangled. Lucie looked up from the array of feathers Ro had dumped on her desk to find Tim stepping into the shop.

A wave of something—relief? Happiness? All of the above?—swished around inside her.

If that man wasn't a sight for sore eyes she didn't know who was. As usual, he'd ditched his suit jacket somewhere, stripped off his tie and popped the top button of his shirt. She loved this relaxed look on him.

And with his big shoulders, he wore it well.

Plus, he'd come to see her. That alone might be worth celebrating, since she'd spent all afternoon wondering if he'd decide life with Lucie Rizzo might be a tad too eccentric.

Among other things.

Yes, he'd given every indication that he'd gotten over being mad—that more-than-subtle hint about wanting a replay attested to that—but that had been hours ago. Plenty of time for a man like him, a catch among catches, to change his mind.

She dropped the feather she'd been studying. "Hey, handsome."

"Hey, yourself. What's with the feathers? Or should I even ask?"

Lucie laughed. "It's nothing criminal. Believe me. After all this craziness, Ro wants to create doggie coats with feathers. Couture coats."

"Wow."

"I know. It sounds nuts, but she's been spot-on since we started this accessory gig so I'm rolling with it. What's new with our other feather problem?"

Tim came around her desk, sat on the edge and the faded scent of his cologne reached her.

He ran his hand over his face and yawned. "Dukane's lawyer showed up and knocked some sense into him. He copped to the whole thing."

"Really?"

"Yep. He's got a ton of debt. Figured the dress would make him even."

"I can't believe he paraded the actual dress through that lobby."

Tim shrugged. "The model is his son's girlfriend. I guess they figured the dress would blend in with the rest of the fakes. And, by the way, the feather Bickel took from you that first morning?"

"The one I found?"

"Yep. It's from the dress. No surprise there. It must have fallen off when those idiots left the gallery. The lab couldn't get any of your prints off of it. Even if they had, you admitted to picking it up."

"Just crazy. What about the other thief?"

"We're working on it. He's running, but won't get far. All three of them will probably take a plea. Armed robbery, conspiracy, insurance fraud. It'll be a nice, long jail sentence. The other good news is you've been cleared." He grinned. "And I don't have to slog through thousands of tips from your reward offer."

Cleared. *Thank God.* She dropped back in her chair, her torso collapsing in on itself. "Thank you."

"I did my job, Luce."

"You did more. I know you did. So, just, thank you. And I'm sorry if I made you crazy."

The side of his mouth quirked. "You may not believe this, but I get it. I watched Bickel doubt you because of your last name, and then the cop from this morning did it with Joey. That's gotta suck." He shifted a little and faced her. "But here's the thing."

Oh, no. *Here it comes.* The breakup. The "I can't do this" speech she'd given to Frankie thousands of times.

"It's okay, Tim. You don't have to say it."

"I think I do. I think you need to hear it."

So cruel! "Well, okay, then. Let me have it."

He snorted. "So damned cute. Luce, if something like this happens again—God help me—you've got to give me a break. If I ask you to stay out of it, it's for your own good. I'm not gonna hurt you."

Huh. Was he dumping her? Didn't sound like it. She took a chance on grabbing his hand and squeezing it. To her immense relief, he squeezed back.

She nodded. "Ro gave me a good talking-to. I don't want to feel crappy about who I am anymore. As my dad likes to say, 'it is what it is.'"

"Yeah, and look at you. Look what you've done with a tiny dog-walking and accessory business. You're building something here. Be proud of that."

"Fortune 500, baby. That's the goal."

"It's a good one. Just please, when I tell you to stay out of police business, trust me. Okay?"

"Deal."

"Good. Now, can I buy you dinner?"

"You betcha." She scooped the feathers into the plastic container Ro had left for her and set them on the side of her desk. "I have no idea what she plans on doing with all these, but it'll be a hoot to watch."

The doggie bells jangled again. Dad. *Oh, boy.* She knew Joey had filled him in on the morning's activities.

"Hi, Dad."

"Hiya."

So far so good. And he didn't look too enraged. None of that squished face and hard eyes that usually preceded one of Dad's tirades.

As he approached, Tim held his hand out. "Mr. Rizzo."

The two men—the Irish cop and the mob boss—shook hands. "Tim, I hope you got something good to tell me."

"The case against Lucie has been cleared, sir. All set."

"Good. And thank you for getting my son out of that jam."

"All I did was move things along. He tried to break up a fight. No need for him to get locked up."

"Yeah, well, a lot of people don't see it that way."

Tim looked down at Lucie. "I'm learning that, sir. And I'm sorry."

The two men exchanged some look that Lucie didn't understand. Acceptance maybe. Who knew with men? Plus, after today, she'd figured out that Tim had a bit of caveman in him.

"Awright," Dad said. "Lucie, your mother called. Dinner at six. She made that meatloaf you like. With the bacon."

Oh, she loved that meatloaf, but . . .

Wild, orgasmic sex with Tim or meatloaf? Hmmm . . .

They could save her a piece. She waggled her hand between her and Tim. "We have dinner plans."

Dad shrugged. "So, he'll come, too. You know your mother. She makes enough for twelve."

"But . . ."

Tim set his hand on her arm. "That sounds great, Mr. Rizzo. Thank you."

What the heck was he doing? Tim was so not ready for a Rizzo family dinner.

"Sure. Don't be late. We eat at six sharp."

Dad left the shop, and Lucie whirled on Tim. "Are you insane? You're not ready. Believe me, you're not."

He laughed. "Uh, Luce, have I mentioned I'm a Chicago cop? I mean, I don't want to presume anything, but I see some ugliness on the job."

He wanted to draw that ridiculous comparison? The streets of Chicago would never compete.

"It's different. Apples to oranges. The conversations that happen at the dinner table will make your ears bleed."

"Kinda sounds like fun."

"And, you know, you're a cop, going to Joe Rizzo's house for dinner. Have you thought about that?"

"Every night for the last three months. People are going to talk." He tweaked her nose then dropped a kiss there. "Let 'em. You're the only thing I care about. I'm on your side, and that means interacting with your family. Even if it makes my ears bleed."

Team Lucie. The thing she'd always wanted. Someone by her side who, no matter what, backed her up, stood with her, *defended* her. Right or wrong, she wanted that unconditional promise.

And the Irish cop had just given it to her.

"Well, I don't want your mother mad at me when you're hospitalized for mental health issues."

Tim snorted. "You're cute, Luce."

She tugged on the front of his shirt and snuggled into him. "So are you, Detective. I just hope your health insurance is up-to-date because after tonight, you'll never be the same."

Book four in The Lucie Rizzo Mystery series:

Some animals were just not built for bathing suit modeling.

Lucie watched her favorite client, an Olde English Bulldogge named Otis, lumber down the runway toward her. His big body moved with the speed of a snail, while the attractive blonde holding his leash did a slow-mo version of the strut only experienced models could pull off.

Otis stopped to lick his parts, the ones squeezed into a too-tight swimsuit, and the blonde looked over at Lucie, her pretty face twisting into a mass of panic and confusion.

"What should I do? He just *stopped*. What happens if he does that in the actual show? This dog could ruin my career."

"Luce," Ro said, "I know you love Otis, but those fitted swim trunks aren't working for him. He's too fat. And, hello, she's right. Is he going to stop and lick his privates in the middle of the show?"

Lucie sighed. Already two hours into this ordeal, she sat on a director's chair in the middle of a hotel ballroom for the latest round of doggie auditions. They'd been at it since eight a.m., and Lucie's mid-morning sugar craving kicked in. Or maybe she simply needed chocolate to get her through this nightmare.

Beside her, Roseanne, Lucie's BFF and Coco Barknell's vice president of sales, furiously jotted notes about each of the prospective models. Stubby legs. Long neck. Big head— all of it on paper for future deliberations. Deliberations that would surely force Lucie to poke her eyes out.

With a screwdriver.

Who knew finding canine models for a charity fashion show could be so difficult?

"He's not fat," she said. "He needs a bigger size."

Ro pointed one well-manicured finger. "That's the XXL."

"Your designs run small."

Ro laughed. Of course she did. They both knew Ro's designs didn't run small. Otis was simply a big boy.

Day four of auditions wasn't going so hot. The biggest issue was fitting the dogs for Ro's unforgiving designs. An extra pound here or there would throw the whole ensemble off.

Fifteen doggie outfits needed models. They'd already gotten lucky and managed to fit two dogs with multiple outfits—thank God for V-necks and belts. But they were still short six dogs.

A yip, followed by an "ouch" came from behind a rolling screen that doubled as a curtain. A round of barking and growls followed, and Lucie clawed her fingers into her scalp.

"Is everything all right?" she called.

"Ow." A hand appeared from the side of the screen. "Fine. We're fine. Ow! This little one is an ankle biter. Shit. Ooh, sorry."

The screen fell over and five dogs leaped on top of it, two of them tugging free from the models holding their leashes.

"Here we go," Ro said. "Ladies, you need to hold those leashes."

The two dogs shot by Lucie and Ro, and Lucie swiveled around to track them. A few volunteers stood behind them waiting for assignments. One of them sidestepped, blocking the dogs' path. Both animals skidded to a stop. Just like that, bam. A spurt of jealousy rose inside Lucie. One day, she'd have that obvious command over these animals. Now? Not so much. When they saw Lucie, they saw fun and playtime and love.

Not a pack leader.

"Wow," Lucie said. "She's good."

"Sure is. We should hire her."

The volunteer walked the dogs back to the once-again-erect screen, and handed the leashes off.

Buzzy Sneider, Lucie and Ro's much more famous partner in this charity gig, and her assistant slipped into the ballroom via a side entrance. The pet product mogul had more damned assistants than the president, but Reece seemed to be the most senior of the bunch.

Please don't let Ro see them.

"Ooh," Ro said, "there's Buzzy. We need to talk to her."

Thanks, universe, for the help. "Uh, no we don't. You promised to let me handle it."

"And I have."

Ha. Good one.

Buzzy's claim to fame came from designing custom dog houses for celebrities and the filthy rich. In the animal world, she carried a lot of weight. If she endorsed a product, it immediately broke sales records.

The problem was, Buzzy had decided to expand her empire to dog accessories and clothing, acting as if she'd created the industry Lucie and Ro had been operating in for nearly a year.

In short, Ro wasn't happy about Buzzy's expansion. Neither was Lucie, but, as the levelheaded half of the dynamic duo, she'd taken the high road and approached Buzzy to partner with Coco Barknell for the fashion show.

Buzzy's mass appeal could only help spread the word about an exceptional non-profit that provided service dogs to people in need. And, oh, right, Coco Barknell.

A win-win.

Except...

Want more? Don't miss the next Lucie Rizzo mystery.

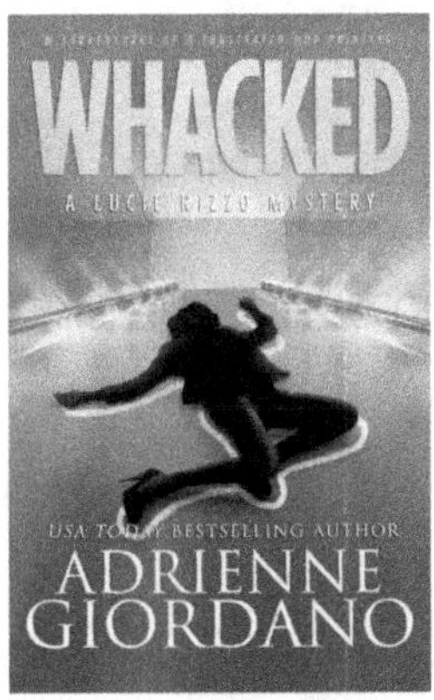

A NOTE TO READERS

Dear reader,

Thank you for reading *Boosted*. I hope you enjoyed it. If you did, please help others find it by sharing it with friends on social media and writing a review.

Sharing the book with your friends and leaving a review helps other readers decide to take the plunge into the nutty world of Lucie Rizzo. So please consider taking a moment to tell your friends how much you enjoyed the story. Even a few words expressing what you enjoyed most about the story is a huge help. Thank you!

Happy reading!
Adrienne

ACKNOWLEDGMENTS

First, thank you to all the readers out there who help me chase my dream. From the time I was in high school I dreamed of seeing my name on a book cover, and, without the tremendous support of my readers, I wouldn't be writing. So, thank you!

Jay and Marge Briscione, thank you for bringing the maniac known as Fin into the family. He always makes me smile. Thank you to my usual suspects, Tracey Devlyn, Kelsey Browning, Theresa Stevens and Misty Evans for the amazing plotting help. Special thanks to Kelsey for that wacky conversation about the right name for the fan group. Just wicked fun! Milton Grasle, you always welcome my questions and help me find solutions when I've written myself into a corner. Thank you!

Cynthia Magno, I can't thank you enough for sharing your expertise. You helped me take this book in a new direction, and I'm so grateful for your insight. Thanks also to Anthony Iacullo and Dana Diorio for helping me get "unstuck" on insurance and legal questions.

To John Leach and Scott Silverii, you rock! No matter

what I throw out there, you indulge my nutty questions. To Liliana Hart, thank you for always generously sharing your knowledge. I'm so grateful.

To the fabulous Gina Bernal, you teach me something new with each book. You're awesome!

And, as always, a big thanks to "my guys" for always supporting me and encouraging me to do more. I love you.

ABOUT THE AUTHOR

 **Adrienne Giordano** is a *USA Today* bestselling author of over twenty romantic suspense and mystery novels. She is a Jersey girl at heart, but now lives in the Midwest with her workaholic husband, sports-obsessed son and Buddy the Wheaten Terrorist (Terrier). She is a cofounder of Romance University blog and Lady Jane's Salon-Naperville, a reading series dedicated to romantic fiction.

For more information on Adrienne, including her Internet haunts, contest updates, and details on her upcoming novels, please visit her at:

www.AdrienneGiordano.com

agiordano@adriennegiordano.com